olYMpIα
InVEStIgatIonS
The First Four Cases

ShERRY δ. RαMSEY

Ramsey, Sherry D., 1963-, author
Olympia Investigations: The First Four Cases / Sherry D. Ramsey
Email: sherrydramsey@gmail.com
Web: www.sherrydramsey.com
Cape Breton, Nova Scotia, Canada

Olympia Investigations: The First Four Cases
Print ISBN: 978-1-9995756-7-0
Ebook ISBN: 978-1-9995756-6-3

δεδιcατιοη

*For Huttser and Reilly, who have spent more time
in my office with me while I wrote than any other
members of the family.*

OTHER BOOKS BY
Sherry D. Ramsey

The Nearspace Series
One's Aspect to the Sun
Dark Beneath the Moon
Beyond the Sentinel Stars

The Murder Prophet

The Seventh Crow

Planet Fleep: A Science Twins Adventure

To Unimagined Shores

The Cache and Other Stories

Beacon and Other Stories

ταβlε οϐ cοnτεnτς

addicted to love

An Olympia Investigations Story

The first time Frank Garret sat down in the blue leather chair on the opposite side of my desk, I didn't know he was dead. My cousin Oliver didn't seem to pick up on it either, when he showed Frank in from reception. My new client wasn't looking great, mind you; he was obviously a man who'd been through some stuff. But he seemed as solid and well, *alive* as any other client I'd ever had.

Hell, more alive than some. And I didn't notice anything strange when we shook hands, except that his grip was cool and firm.

Oliver left us reluctantly, as usual—he hadn't quite grasped the concept of "assistant" as opposed to "partner" yet—and the client didn't waste any time.

"I need you to find my wife," he said, leaning forward with his elbows on his knees, hands twisting a battered Jays ball cap nervously.

I thought, *another divorce case, here we come*, but I didn't say it. Before I could say anything, in fact, he held up a hand.

"I know what you're thinking, Miss Sheridan, but it's not like that. She doesn't even know I'm looking for her. And I promise you that she hasn't run away from me." He paused and glanced out the window, although there was not much to see on the other side but a dingy back alley. "Not deliberately, anyway."

The guy wasn't making a whole lot of sense, but I decided to hear him out. I didn't have much on the go, and these days I could track down a "missing" person in twenty-four hours or less if they'd used a credit card or checked into social media.

"Would you like a cup of coffee, Mr. Garret? Tea? Oliver will be happy to bring it." Oliver would fume to me afterwards that he wasn't the maid, but the clients don't need to know that.

He shook his head. "Call me Frank. I'd love one, but it's not possible. And I don't have much time."

"All right, we'll get to business, then. And please, call me Acacia." I pulled my notebook out of the drawer and wrote his name at the top of a blank page. "Your wife's name?"

"Ellie Garret. E.P. Wyse-Garret," he added. "The writer."

I felt my eyebrows lift slightly in surprise. E.P. Wyse-Garret was the acclaimed author of the Frankie and Ellie mysteries, featuring a wise-cracking and lovable pair of middle-aged sleuths based loosely on herself and her husband. Something tickled the back of my brain. She'd been in the news a few weeks ago, but I couldn't remember why. I'd been in the middle of the Medstrom case without a lot of attention to spare for local celebrity news.

"How long has she been missing?" Funny there'd been nothing on the newsfeeds about her disappearance.

"A month now," he said, misery twisting his features as he continued to mash the hat. "But look, you gotta understand, no-one else thinks she's missing. It's only me who can't find her."

I squinted. "So, she's on vacation? Or a writer's retreat or something?" I cudgeled my brain. What *had* that news item been?

He shook his head. "I don't know. She's not home, hasn't been there since just after—well, about a month. I don't have any way to contact her, but I need to. *She* needs me to. She just doesn't know it. And I don't have much time!"

His voice rose to a despairing wail and I stared at him, trying to get that news story back from my recalcitrant memory. And then the right mental file drawer opened. Weeks ago, Ellie Garret's husband Frank, inspiration for the beloved sleuth Frankie Pasquale, had been killed in a car accident.

He must have seen the penny drop behind my eyes, because his shoulders slumped even further. He seemed to...shimmer...a little, and for a second the chair back wavered into view behind him. "Yeah," he said, "I'm

3

dead. And the Frankie and Ellie series will be dead, too, if I can't find Ellie. And you're my only hope."

I don't take on many ghosts for clients. Most of them are too caught up in the whole clanking chains and walking through walls schtick, even the ones who'd like you to find out who murdered them or whatever. It gets tiresome, and my job should never be tiresome. Olympia Investigations offers somewhat niche services to non-humans, along with our more mundane clients. I'd named my detective agency after my (100% mortal, as far as I knew) maternal grandmother, since the family quirk was generally acknowledged to have started with her. Whatever the provenance, my mother and her siblings, and now their children, are able to see, communicate, and interact with all manner of beings, many of whom slide under or past the radar of most humans. Ghosts, vampires, werewolves, demons, fae...these make up a lot of my clientele.

Which is why my cousin Oliver was a decent choice when I decided I needed an assistant. He's arrogant, bossy, and wants to be a full partner even though he doesn't even have a PI license, but he has the requisite sense—sixth, seventh, who knows?—to deal with any client without freaking out.

But ghosts are rare, and ghosts who can appear normal enough to fool me into thinking they aren't dead are really rare. I was intrigued. First things first, though.

"All right, Frank, I do have to get this out of the way first. If you're a ghost, how do you propose to pay me?"

He nodded. "Thought about that. I feel certain Ellie will take care of it, but if she doesn't, I can direct you to a couple of places where you'll find items of sufficient value to cover the fees."

I frowned. "Items?"

"I lost a gold ring at the back of our garden once, digging flower beds for Ellie. Never could find the thing, and was Ellie upset—she'd given it to me. Now—I can see it plain as day. You could retrieve that and sell it." He shrugged diffidently. "There are a few things like that."

The possibilities of ghosts as lost item finders had never come up before. Interesting, but I shelved it for now. "All right, we can work with that. Tell me about your wife's disappearance."

He closed his eyes and wavered for a moment. "After—the funeral, she announced that she wouldn't write any more Frankie and Ellie books. I thought that was a terrible shame—and worse, those books are her livelihood! If she keeps writing them, I'm sure she can live comfortably off the royalties for the rest of her life. I could go in peace if I knew she'd be okay."

I nodded to encourage him.

Frank drew a deep breath. Or appeared to. Maybe it was just a habit. "I wanted to tell her not to be so foolish, to go on writing them. At first, I didn't know why any part of me was still hanging around. Why I couldn't just go on

5

to whatever's next. Then I thought it must be to give her that message. And--I couldn't bear to leave her. When I stayed close to her, I felt better. Stronger. Like maybe if I stayed close enough, long enough, I'd be able to, well, manifest. Talk to her." He got up from the blue leather chair and paced my small office. Looking closely, I could tell that his feet didn't really touch the worn brown carpet but hovered an inch above it.

He stopped behind the chair and put his hands on the back, one still clutching the Jays cap. "It was like...like a physical hit, when I was near her. Like I was addicted to my wife." Frank chuckled nervously. "Sounds weird, I know."

I shook my head and smiled. "Not weird. Sweet. So did you do it? Appear to her?"

His face sagged. "I did, finally. A couple weeks after the funeral I felt like I was strong enough. I didn't want to be some see-through horror and frighten her. I wanted this." He gestured to his surprisingly solid-looking body. "I waited until she was alone, and I put all my effort into manifesting."

I could guess what was coming next. "It didn't go well?"

He shook his head. "She thought she was hallucinating, going crazy—I don't know what. I tried to calm her down, tell her why I was there, but she wouldn't listen. Ran out of the house crying and drove off somewhere. I didn't have the strength to follow her, didn't know where she'd gone." He circled to the front of the chair and sat down again. "Then three days later, she came back with her sister. Ellie packed some stuff, they left, and I haven't felt strong enough to go hunting for her." Tears seemed to glisten in his eyes, and I wondered what would happen if they spilled over. Would they leave little ectoplasmic droplets on the carpet?

Frank sighed. "All my energy went into that meeting, and when it went south, it drained me. I've been hanging around our house, getting as close as I can to her things since then, building up the energy to appear to someone else. It takes a lot longer when she's not there physically. The energy for me to...er, feed on, is weaker. I didn't go to her sister, or her agent, or her editor, because I'm afraid it'll go down the same and I won't be able to come back from it again. If I could even build up enough energy to do all that. I need someone who can do it for me." He looked at me very steadily from blue eyes that, at the moment, didn't look ghostly at all. Just sad. "Will you do it for me? Will you find my Ellie?"

The dust in my office must have been particularly bad that morning. I had to blink my own eyes a couple of times to clear them. "Frank," I said sincerely, "I'll give it a try."

"Just let me come along. I can help! I haven't been out in the field in weeks!"

Oliver stood blocking my exit from the office, arms

crossed over his chest and a delicate frown darkening his brow. Frank had...left, not by the front door but by unceremoniously dissipating to—somewhere. I'd told Oliver that I was going out to check out the house where Frank and Ellie had lived, and that's when he'd leapt elegantly in front of the door and made his demands.

I protested automatically. Oliver and I have always had a prickly relationship, even when we were kids, and it's followed us into adulthood. My mother says we're too much alike, at which observation I usually roll my eyes and abandon the conversation. "Who's going to watch the office, answer the phone, if we both leave? I hate to break it to you, but that's sort of your job, you know?"

Oliver closed his eyes momentarily, as if to ask some higher power for strength. "You said I'd have a chance to learn the job from an investigator's point of view," he reminded me. "That it wouldn't be all office work. We're supposed to be a team. And we can forward the office phone to my cell."

I sighed. "Oh, all right." I suppose I *had* said the team thing when I hired him. And a second pair of eyes might come in handy at the house.

Oliver grabbed his windbreaker from the hook behind the door and slipped it on with a grin. "Excellent. I'll even spring for coffee on the way."

Frank had told me where I could find the spare key to the house he and Ellie had shared, and on the way I filled Oliver in on the parameters of the case. The neighborhood was middle-class tidy, with well-groomed yards fronting homes that ranged from new to fifty or sixty years old, but well-maintained. I parked on the street a few houses away from the address Frank had given me, and Oliver and I walked casually up the drive and around to the back of the two-story saltbox, sipping our takeout coffees and chatting as we walked. I found the key just where Frankie had said, taped inside one of the hollow tubes of a set of wind chimes by the back door. We slipped in, and I felt pretty sure no-one had taken particular notice of us.

The porch featured windows covered with rattan blinds, lush greenery, a couple of wicker chairs, and a small closet. It led into a kitchen with clean, white-painted cupboard doors and red brick accents; homey, cozy, and cared-for, but chill now with the extended absence of its inhabitants. Ellie and her sister must have tidied up before she'd left—it didn't have the air of a hasty exit. I opened the fridge and found it empty of pretty much anything but long-lasting condiments. Oliver stood in the middle of the room, sipping coffee and observing. A wall phone hung nearby, but the notepad on the counter beneath it was blank. I pulled a pencil from my bag and rubbed the side of the lead lightly over the surface of the top page, revealing a jumble of marks from notes written on previous sheets. Nothing particularly legible or seemed important. I hit the phone's redial button, but the number that appeared on the screen matched the one Frank had given me for Ellie's sister.

In the dining room, the light from the large windows tinted slightly green as it passed through the plants lining the windowsill and suspended from plant hangars. They looked healthy enough, so someone must be watering them. The sister? In the living room, a book lay on the sofa. A paper protruded slightly from near the back cover, so I crossed the room and picked it up. The book was a mystery by another well-known author. The paper turned out to be a brochure from a local real estate agent. I raised an eyebrow and showed it to Oliver.

"You think she wants to sell?"

I shrugged. "Could be. Maybe too many memories here." I pocketed the paper and returned the book to the sofa. Dust lay thick on the coffee table, another testament to the house's deserted state.

As I turned to leave, a shimmer distorted the air near the doorway, and Frank appeared between me and Oliver. A little less solid-looking than he'd been in my office, but he smiled thinly.

"You found your way in."

I returned the smile. "No problems. I hope you don't mind that I brought Oliver along to help me out."

"Not at all." Frank gave Oliver a nod and a smile.

"Nice house," Oliver said.

Frank nodded and the smile faded. "Sure is," he agreed. "I miss it already, and I'm still here, sort of."

"Well, I haven't found much yet," I told him, hoping to distract him from that line of thought. "There was a real estate brochure in a book in the living room. Think Ellie's planning to move?"

Frank shook his head. "We were looking at cottage properties before..."

"Ah, okay." So that was a dead end, so to speak. "I'm just heading down the hall."

"I'll walk with you," he said. "Just along here is Ellie's office."

I stood for a moment, studying the room. This one might warrant a more careful search. It was a bright, cheery space, with plants crowding the windowsills and a hand-hooked rug covering most of the laminate floor. Two of the walls held floor-to-ceiling bookshelves. Oliver ran his finger along the spines on one shelf, while I inspected her desk. A stack of colorful sticky notes contained jottings and scribbles that I assumed related to story ideas—at any rate, nothing looked like travel plans.

"Can I check the computer?" I asked Frank.

He shrugged. "Sure, I guess."

I sat down in the padded leather desk chair and booted up the machine, looking the question at Frank when the screen paused, asking for a password.

"FridayNightCoffee," he said with a sad smile. "It was a little joke between us. We never went to bed early on weekends, so we could drink coffee as late as we wanted on Friday nights."

I typed in the phrase and the machine completed its startup routine. By the time it finished, Oliver had come to look over my shoulder. I clicked open the files list and groaned. It would take a month to look though this many files, hoping to stumble upon something useful. I glanced over some recent documents, but they seemed to also pertain to her writing, or research she'd been doing for the current book. Nothing helpfully labelled "travel plans" or "itinerary," so that was a dead end. A laptop desk leaned against the wall, but I didn't see a laptop— presumably she'd taken it with her, wherever she was. Eventually I shook my head.

"Nothing I can see here."

"Were you upstairs yet?" Frank didn't sound too hopeful, but he looked a little more solid now. Maybe talking about Ellie, and being in her space, helped him, too.

I shook my head and shut the computer down. We climbed the stairs to the second floor, Oliver trailing behind us, unusually quiet.

Frank led me into the master bedroom. On one side of the bed, a pile of books had been haphazardly stacked in a basket that was too small for the task it had been set. I checked the closet and drawers. All of Frank's clothes still seemed to be in the closet. Ellie must not have had the heart to deal with them yet.

The second bedroom had been used for storage. I

popped the lid on a large storage container marked "summer clothes" and found it full to the top with women's wear.

"I guess it's safe to assume she hasn't taken off for warmer climates to the south," I said, snapping the lid closed again.

"That doesn't narrow things down much," Frank observed in a glum tone.

"No, but it's something."

I glanced around the bathroom, but nothing seemed out of the ordinary or appeared to be a clue.

"That's it for the house, with the exception of the basement," he said, leaning against the bathroom door jamb and crossing his arms over his chest. "You want to go down there?"

"Think there's any use?"

He shook his head. "I doubt it. Ellie never really liked to go down there anyway."

"Okay then. Best to make our escape before any nosy neighbors come to investigate." We went back down the stairs, the silence of the house pressing around us. In the back porch I turned to him. "You want to come with me?" I don't know why I asked, but it seemed like the polite thing to do.

Frank shook his head. "I'm feeling pretty...thin," he said. He looked it, too. "Think I'll hang around here, try to build up a little more energy."

"All right. Check in with me when you can."

Five minutes later Oliver and I were back in my car and driving out of the neighbourhood. I drummed my fingers on the steering wheel as I pondered my next move. I was going to have to look further to find out where Ellie had gone to ground.

"Well, that was depressing," Oliver observed, looking out the side window.

"I know."

"I hate that Frank's dead. It doesn't seem fair."

I sighed but didn't argue the point. "I'm going to try Ellie's sister next," I said. "I'll drop you back at the office. I want you to try and get appointments for me with Ellie's agent, and her editor."

"You think they'll see you? What will I say it's about?"

I pondered. "Just tell them I'm trying to locate her in relation to a case I'm working on," I said finally. "That's all you know. If they'll see me, I'll figure out what to tell them."

"All right." Oliver tipped his coffee cup up to catch the last dregs, although they'd be cold and unpleasant by now. "I'll actually be glad to get back to the office."

A little shiver prickled goosebumps down my arms, thinking of the lonely house and its sole ghostly occupant. "I hear you," I said. "Let's get back to the land of the living for a while."

Ellie's sister, Charlotte MacLaren, lived in a small

white bungalow perched in a yard given over almost entirely to flower beds. One narrow walkway led from the sidewalk to the front porch, edged by lush borders of delphiniums and lavender. Three shallow steps led up to the porch, which had been invitingly decorated with wicker chairs and a comfortable-looking swing seat suspended from the sloping roof overhead. I climbed up, resisting the urge to try out the swing, and knocked politely on the cheery yellow door.

I heard footsteps inside. Then came a pause during which I was probably surveyed through the peephole, and then the door opened. A diminutive woman with grey-streaked hair and a clutch of laugh lines bracketing her brown eyes regarded me with a slightly puzzled air. She was perhaps in her fifties and wore trendy jeans and a flower-print t-shirt.

"Can I help you?"

I showed her my PI's license, giving her a chance to get a good look. "I'm looking for Ellie," I said, and quickly put up a hand to forestall any protest as a frown began to shadow her face. "I know, it's a terrible time for her, but I'm not looking to intrude. I have a very important message that I'm trying to get to her, that's all."

The frown softened a little. "I can give her any message you have."

"So you do know where she is?"

She ran a hand down the side of her jeans and quirked a half-smile at me. "I'm her sister, of course I know where she is. That doesn't mean I'm going to tell you."

I smiled as engagingly as I could. "No matter how important I tell you it is? I really have to deliver it in person."

Charlotte shook her head a little and sighed. "She doesn't want to see anyone—not even me, truth be told. I have to respect that." She motioned me to take a seat in the swing and came out onto the porch, closing the door behind her. She didn't sit, but leaned back against the porch railing, crossing her arms. "Can you tell me what it's about?"

I sat on the swing and it swayed under my weight. It would have been lovely to curl up on the cushions and let the breeze push it into gentle motion. I wondered how many times Ellie and Frank had sat here when visiting.

I pulled a deep breath. "The message is from Frank, Charlotte."

Her face pinked and the frown came back. "Frank's dead. He left something before he died?"

"I can't really go into the details," I said carefully. "But please believe me, Ellie would want to get this message. I wouldn't be involved in anything I thought would make things worse for her."

She shook her head. "Things can't get any worse. But it's not like Frank knew he was...knew that anything was going to happen. How could he leave a message?"

"I'm sure Ellie will explain it to you after I've talked

to her," I said.

Charlotte looked past me. I wasn't sure if she was trying to see inside the window of her house or just didn't want to meet my eyes while she thought it over. Finally, she shook her head again.

"I can't tell you." She held up a hand just as I'd done to her, to stop my protest. "But I'll ask Ellie if I can tell you," she said. "That's the best I can do."

I could tell from the hint of steel in her voice that I wasn't going to get any further with her. Charlotte reminded me a little of a teacher I'd had once, and with her, no amount of wheedling would budge a decision. I stood up and offered her one of my cards, then held out my hand. "I appreciate that," I said, "and Ellie will, too. Please speak to her as soon as you can, all right? There's a certain amount of urgency."

She took my hand, and her clasp was firm and warm. "I'll talk to her. That's all I can promise you."

Back at the office, Oliver reported that the editor had agreed to see me, but not until next week. He hadn't caught up with the agent yet. Next week might be too late to do Frankie any good, but maybe Charlotte would come through for me before that.

Frankie showed up briefly at my office before I headed home for the day. He wasn't looking so good. I mean, yes, he was dead, but aside from that. This time, there was no way I would have been fooled into thinking he was a normal human.

"You're not drawing as much energy from the house anymore," I guessed, eyeing him speculatively.

He shook his semi-transparent head. "Ellie's been away too long. Her power is fading," he said. "I'm worried. I don't know what will happen to me if I just evaporate without getting to talk to her. It feels so important."

"Well," I said, "I talked to Charlotte today, and she's going to talk to Ellie. So things are looking up!" Frank looked so dejected I had to stay positive.

He stood from the blue leather chair and walked to the window, peering out. Could anyone outside see the ghostly apparition in my window? Not likely.

"I just don't know if I can last much longer," he said. "I might only have one more chance, and what if she reacts the same way she did before? What if I just scare her?"

I drew a deep breath and sighed. "I'll try my best to prepare her," I said. *Mrs. Garret—Ellie. Your husband's a ghost, but he has an important last message for you.* She'd probably just think I was crazy, and insensitive into the bargain.

He turned from the window and looked at me with soft, ghostly eyes. There was only the barest hint of the blue they'd been in life. "I appreciate everything you're doing. You should go and get that ring from the garden soon, in case this doesn't work out and I disappear.

You've earned it. And if Ellie comes back to the house it'll make that more difficult for you."

I waved a hand. "The job's not finished yet. Let me worry about that end of it, all right? And you're still going to be here a while. I'm sure of it."

The ghost of a smile lifted the corners of his mouth. "Don't wait too long, Acacia. See you soon—I hope."

And with a touch of one transparent hand to the brim of his hat, he was gone.

I spent a fretful night, worrying that I wouldn't hear from Charlotte soon enough, or that I would hear from her and the news would be bad. In the morning, I was just unlocking my office door, balancing takeout coffees in a tray for myself and Oliver, when my office phone started to ring. I answered it breathlessly. It was Charlotte.

"Miss Sheridan?" she asked. "I've spoken with Ellie, but I'm afraid it's no go. She simply doesn't want to be disturbed, and she doesn't see how you could possibly have a message from Frank for her."

I dropped into my chair, feeling leaden. "Did you try to persuade her?"

Charlotte was quiet for a moment. "I told her that you seemed very sincere to me, but I didn't push her, no. This is a terrible time for my sister. I want to be very careful with her. Surely you understand that?"

"I do," I said with a sigh. "But this message would

certainly bring her more peace...maybe some closure. Would you ask her again?"

"I'm sorry," she said firmly. "I took you at your word, and I did what I promised, but without knowing more, I'm not willing to push Ellie on this."

I floundered wildly for an idea. I couldn't tell her about Frank—she'd write me off as a nutcase. But I needed to prove to her that I was serious, that I really had something. "Could I drop by again later today, then?" I asked her, desperate. "I'll tell you more about what's going on."

There was a longer hesitation this time. I might have piqued her curiosity.

"I'll be home after three o'clock," she said finally. "But I'm not making any promises beyond that."

"Thank you. You won't regret it. See you at three."

I hung up and wondered what I was going to come up with, in the next six hours, to make Charlotte believe me.

After pacing my office for an hour and hashing the problem over with Oliver, we'd thought of only one possibility.

I drove out to Frank and Ellie's house again and let myself in at the back door. After carefully closing and locking it behind me, I called, "Frank! Frank, are you here?"

I moved into the kitchen and Frank came into the

room from the other side, gliding silently. He looked about the same as he had yesterday.

"You look better!" I told him, but he only gave me a skeptical half-smile.

"Any news?"

"Let's sit down," I said, pulling out one of the kitchen chairs. Frank sat in it, and I pulled out another for myself. "So far, no luck," I told him. "Charlotte talked to Ellie, but she wouldn't agree to see me."

The ghost hung his head. "That's it, then," he murmured. "It's over."

I put out a hand to pat his arm, but of course it went right through. I pulled my hand back, feeling awkward. "Look, don't give up yet," I told him. "I have an idea."

He raised his head, a faint glimmer of hope in his eyes.

"I know you don't have the strength to manifest anywhere but here," I said. "But what if I could take something to Charlotte that would convince her that I've seen you, talked to you, and this is important. I might be able to convince her to tell me where Ellie is."

He shrugged his shoulders. "Sure, it might work. But how are you going to prove anything to Charlotte?"

I dug in my bag and pulled out my notebook. "What if you wrote her a note? Would she recognize your handwriting?"

Frank seemed to sag in on himself a little more, although he looked at me kindly. "Sure," he said, "But

21

Acacia, how am I going to hold a pen? I'm not as substantial as I was the day we met. I've—thinned out a lot since then."

I bit my lip. "I know, but it's the only thing I can come up with. What if we go to the part of the house where Ellie's energy is strongest, and see what you can do?"

"I've been spending most of my time in our bedroom," Frank said. "I figure, we spent the most time together in that one spot, a third of our lives sleeping, right? But it's just not working anymore."

I thought for a moment. "That's one way to think about it," I said slowly, "but you're looking for *Ellie's* energy. Wouldn't it make more sense to look in the place where she probably expended more than anywhere else?"

Frank perked up. "Her office! Why didn't I think of that?"

I nodded. "Worth a try. You know, I noticed when we were here before that you perked up a bit in there."

When I followed Frank into Ellie's office, he went straight over and sat in the chair at her computer. He closed his eyes and I waited. Then he opened them and nodded. "I think I feel a difference. Let me hang out here for a while and we'll see what happens."

"Great!" Now to work on the other part of my plan. "I was thinking about what you said. Can you tell me where that ring is? I might as well try to find it while I'm waiting."

Frank nodded, his eyes sad again. He must think I didn't believe our plan was going to work, but all he said was, "Good thinking," and then proceeded to tell me precisely where to dig in the garden at the bottom of the hedge-rimmed yard. "There's a trowel in a basket in the back porch," he told me. "You shouldn't need anything else."

I'm not one for yard work, but fifteen minutes later I was back in the house, rinsing the ring under warm water at the kitchen sink. In the cupboard underneath I found some cleaning supplies and an old toothbrush, and in no time the ring gleamed gold in the noonday light, apparently no worse for the years it had lain in the earth. The cleaning revealed an inscription: *My two addictions – words and you.*

Frankie turned brighter eyes to me when I entered the office. The chair he sat on was barely visible through him, just the hint of an outline, and the colours in his clothes and skin were intensified. "It's working!" I exclaimed. "And I found it!" I held the ring out for his inspection.

He smiled and put out a hand, and I held my breath as I gently placed the ring on his palm. If it fell right through, it would be devastating for both of us.

But it sat, steadily aloft, on his palm, winking in a shaft of light from the window.

"If I can hold this," Frank said on an intake of breath,

"let's try that pen."

It took a painstaking half-hour as Frank figured out what he wanted to say, and he laboriously wrote it in my notebook. By the end, though, he held the pen with ease and seemed as solid as when I first met him.

"You should probably come with me now," I said as I tucked the notebook back into my bag. "You're back to full strength, and if Charlotte tells me where Ellie is, we could go there right away."

Frank's brow furrowed under his Jays' cap. "But if I move away from here, I'll start to fade. What if I can't come back again?"

"I think we have to take a chance." My eyes lit on the shelf beside Ellie's desk, where copies of her books proudly lined a shelf. "Okay, wait. I have an idea. Stay put for half an hour, and I'll be back, okay?"

He looked puzzled, but nodded. I patted him on the shoulder—successfully, this time—and hurried out to my car. I called Oliver and said, "I have a mission for you."

"Thank the gods. I'm sitting here bored out of my mind. Did Frank write the note?"

"Yes, but he needs a boost. Close the office for half an hour. Here's what I need you to do."

It actually took me forty-five minutes to run my own part of the errand and meet up briefly with Oliver before returning for Frank.

I pulled up in front of Frank and Ellie's house this

time and simply called into the air, "Frank? Can you hear me? Can you come out to the car?"

He materialized in the front seat beside me. "What are you—hey," he said, turning to me in surprise. "I still—feel it. Ellie's energy. How can that be?"

I nodded toward the back seat, and Frank turned to look. Bookstore bags filled the seat, each of them holding copies of Ellie's books. Oliver and I had hit every store in the city between us. Frank turned to look at me again, understanding dawning on his face.

I nodded. "Ellie's energy. It's all there, in her books. And now it's portable." I shifted the car into gear and checked the rearview mirror. "Let's go talk to Charlotte."

Back at Charlotte's house, I parked on the street and walked through the profusion of flowers again to the front porch. The door opened as I put my foot on the first step, and she came outside. I climbed the steps and smiled.

"Thanks for agreeing to talk to me again."

She sighed. "It's foolish of me, really. I guess I just wish you really did have a message from Frank, and that it might help Ellie a little."

"Let's sit on the swing," I told her, and settled into the cushion at one end. Charlotte took the space beside me. I reached into my bag and pulled out the notebook in which Frank had written his note.

"I know you went to Ellie's house with her and

helped her pack for this trip," I said gently. "Did Ellie tell you anything about why she wanted to get out of the house just then?"

Charlotte glanced at me, then away. She shrugged. "It makes sense. The house is full of...reminders. She and Frank lived there together for thirty years. I don't think it's all that odd—"

"But did she say anything...happened? In particular? Anything that frightened her or made her even more upset?"

This time when Charlotte looked at me, she held my gaze. Finally, she sighed. "She thought she saw... something. She was afraid she was losing her mind from the grief. She didn't know how else to handle it."

"She thought she saw Frank," I said firmly. "She thought she saw his ghost."

Charlotte went pale. "How could you—? You couldn't know that."

I opened the page to Frank's note and held it out to her. "I know it, because it's what happened."

Hesitantly, she let her eyes fall to the page and run over the words. I heard her sharply indrawn breath, but she kept her eyes on the page, apparently reading it again.

Dear Lottie,

I know Ellie and I were the only ones who ever called you that, so I hope between that and the handwriting you'll believe this is from me. Please help

Ellie understand that I need to see her—I need to tell her some things before I...move on. I frightened her before, and that is killing me; well, you know, it would be killing me if—anyway. Please tell Miss Sheridan where Ellie is; she'll get me to her. And tell Ellie not to be afraid. This is real, and it's important. This is the last favor I'll ever ask of you, Lottie. Promise.

Your loving brother-in-law,

Frank

Charlotte finally looked up at me with eyes glistening with tears, and I knew she would help.

Frank still sat in the car, looking as solid as he had when I'd left him.

"Come on," I told him, holding the door. I suppose it wasn't technically necessary, but it seemed like the right thing to do.

"Don't tell me Charlotte's still not on board? I have to show myself to her? I can't leave the books!"

"We won't need the books. Charlotte just told me what I'd already suspected," I told him. "Ellie's here."

He stared at me. "I thought Charlotte said she didn't know where Ellie was?"

I shrugged. "She lied. She was protecting her sister, and I'm sure it seemed like the right thing to do at the time. But your note convinced her. She's gone inside to try and convince Ellie. But that will be a lot easier if you're standing there too, don't you think? Just give me five minutes first to help Charlotte prepare her."

He smiled. "I'll see you inside," he said, and disappeared.

I shut the car door, hoped no-one had seen me talking to an empty car, and hurried back up the walk. I knocked once on the front door and let myself in.

"We're here," came Charlotte's voice. I followed it.

Ellie Garret stood in a bright sitting room, near wide windows facing out into Charlotte's considerable garden, arms crossed over her chest and a defiant look on her face. Charlotte stood next to her, one hand on Ellie's arm. Charlotte turned to me.

"She's not buying my story, or yours," she said with a smile that bordered on tears.

"This is nonsense. I don't know what your game is, but it's a horrid thing to do—" she broke off, as close to tears as Charlotte was. She wasn't going to be easily convinced, and I had to make her more receptive to the notion before Frank actually joined us. I reached into my bag and pulled out the ring.

I stepped toward her, holding it in my open palm. The sunlight caught it and the ring gleamed. "You don't have to believe me, Mrs. Garrett," I said. "I'll admit it's a crazy story. But maybe you'll believe this. Frank told me where to find it."

She looked at the ring with puzzlement.

"It's Frank's," I told her. "The one you gave him, that he lost in the garden. Read the inscription."

She reached out slowly and took the ring. She turned it and peered inside, letting the light illuminate the tiny, flowing letters.

My two addictions – words and you.

Ellie's hand trembled and she almost dropped the ring, then clutched her fingers around it. She looked up at me, eyes wet. "Frank's really here?"

"I am," Frank said from the doorway behind me, and it was a lucky thing there was a well-stuffed wing chair right behind Ellie. She sank into it, eyes fixed on the apparition of Frank. I turned to look. He was as solid as I'd ever seen him, if a bit shaky. He crossed to Ellie, though, and sat in a matching wing chair opposite her. Leaning forward, elbows on knees, he pulled off his Blue Jays cap and twisted it in his hands just like he'd done in my office.

"Ellie," he said in a hushed voice, almost as if he were afraid to frighten her away again, "I might not have long. Can we talk?"

She swallowed hard and nodded. Charlotte and I tiptoed out and she closed the door behind us. We went to the kitchen, where Charlotte made us tea.

Later, the door to the living room was still closed when I left, but I thought I heard laughter behind it when I passed.

A week later I got a lovely card and an even lovelier cheque in the mail from Ellie Garrett. No, of course I didn't keep the ring—I didn't even tell her Frank said I could take it as payment. Even if they'd replaced the lost one years ago, there was no way I was taking it back. But the cheque more than covered the time I'd spent on the case. She told me in her card that there's a new Frankie and Ellie novel in the works, and I'll have my very own autographed copy when it comes out, so Frank got his message across.

But I knew that already. Frank made one last visit to the office, the day after he and Ellie spoke.

He materialized without warning, standing beside the blue leather chair. Oliver was sitting in the chair as we went over some case notes, and he almost fell out of it when Frank appeared. Frank grinned rakishly and tipped his Jays cap to us when we both jumped.

"You're feeling better," I observed.

He heaved a deep sigh. "I came to thank you," he said. "Both of you. I don't know what's next. I'm feeling strong as a horse after spending time with Ellie. She's like a tonic. I always joked that I couldn't live without her," he added with a smile.

"Love is the drug, as they say," Oliver observed with a grin.

"But I don't know how long that will last, so I came by to give you this." Frank reached forward and placed a folded piece of paper on my desk.

I raised my eyebrows. "What's this?"

Frank tucked his hands into his pockets.

"Remember I told you I knew where to find a few...items that you might recover as payment?"

"Like the ring. Yes, you did say that."

"Well, I know you didn't take the ring back from Ellie," he said. "And she's going to send you payment in full for what you did. But that," he nodded to the paper, "is a little something extra from me. You can do what you want with it--nothing at all, or, comes a time when you need a little help...let's just say something there might come in handy."

I took the paper and opened it up. There were five items listed in Frank's distinctive handwriting, each with a brief description of where each could be found. "Seriously? Some of these things—"

He shrugged and put a hand up. "It's up to you. They've all been lost so long, no-one else is going to find them or claim them. Just think of it as a little bit of...insurance," he said with a wink. "And thanks again."

And then he was gone, as quickly and without ceremony as he'd appeared.

"What's on the list?" Oliver asked, leaning forward with wide eyes.

Slowly I smiled, opened my desk drawer, dropped the slip of paper inside, and closed and locked it. "I'll tell you later," I said, "maybe. Let's just say that a little insurance is never a bad thing."

"You're not serious," Oliver said, collapsing back into the chair with a groan. "You are the Worst. Boss.

Ever."

"Why don't you get us both some coffee, and we'll finish up these notes," I suggested sweetly. Maybe my mother's right, and we are too much alike.

Oh, I'll share it with him eventually. After all, we're a team.

THE END

THE GODDESS PROBLEM

An Olympia Investigations Novelette

The moment she walked into my office, limned in a faint silver sheen, with that grinning, lupine dog at her heel, I knew she was no ordinary client. She didn't proffer a hand, just sat down in the blue leather chair opposite my desk, and said, "Hello, Ms. Sheridan. My name is Selene. Do you find missing persons?" Her eyes were very serious, very blue, and very fixed on mine. They shimmered a little with unshed tears.

She'd made it past the reception desk and Oliver, my often-annoying assistant and cousin, so he must think I should hear her story. Despite our frequent personality clashes, Oliver had developed a keen proficiency at weeding out the cases I'd absolutely hate. I gave Selene my most professional and sympathetic smile, and met those unnerving, if lovely, blue eyes. They were hard as sapphires, old as the sky.

"I do my best for every client, but I won't make any promises beyond that," I told her. "I've had some success with missing persons cases in the past."

The dog, rangy and shaggy as a wolf—maybe it *was*

a wolf?—settled on its haunches beside her and panted lightly, tongue lolling. Selene stroked the creature's head with gentle fingers, never breaking our eye contact. "This will be a difficult case, Ms. Sheridan, and I may prove to be a difficult client. I will tell you some things that you may find challenging to accept."

I leaned back in my chair, which protested with a squeak. I was suddenly intensely aware of the dust in the corners of the room, the scratched and scabbed surface of my desk, the faint layer of windswept grime on the window behind me, and the lingering scent of tuna sandwich from my lunch. Oliver had been pestering me to repaint the place and freshen it up, but I'd resisted. Maybe he had a point.

"I'll try to keep an open mind," I said. "Challenging clients are a bit of a specialty here at Olympia Investigations, which is probably why you chose me."

She smiled a little, and didn't deny it. I'm the person to see when a non-human client needs help, and I rely on a lot of supernatural word-of-mouth.

"So, will you be explaining why your skin seems to glow? And I don't mean the kind of glow they promise in tv commercials."

She lowered her head in a slow nod. "I will. What you make of that explanation will be up to you."

I was intrigued, and business had been—let's face it, boring—the past two weeks. Too many mundane insurance investigations and spousal surveillances, and I start to wonder why I wanted to be a private investigator in the first place. A faintly glowing woman with a half-wolf for a pet promised to be, at the very least, *not boring*.

"Fair enough," I told her. "Two hundred a day plus expenses, I report to you at least twice a week, stop when you're satisfied with the results or don't want to pursue it any further. If that's agreeable?"

She shrugged elegantly, nodded, and held out a hand. I shook it, her skin pale and cool and luminescent against mine.

And that's how I first met Selene, Greek goddess of the moon.

The missing person in question, she told me, was her...hmmm. Not *husband*, because they'd never married, although according to legend he had fathered some fifty daughters for her. Consort, perhaps? I put him down on my information sheet as "significant other." Endymion, the man who, either at Selene's request or his own (reports varied), and by the acquiescence of Zeus himself, slept eternally in order to avoid growing old and dying.

I didn't know that it was much of a trade-off, but there were those fifty daughters to consider.

We'd made it only that far when Oliver knocked on the door and bustled in without waiting for me to answer, even though he knows I hate it when he does that. He was the picture of the efficient assistant—ebony hair slicked to one side, not a strand out of place, lint-free black turtleneck with the sleeves pushed up just so, and charcoal grey trousers pressed with a crease sharp enough to cut paper. And a mild, disinterested smile, camouflaging his raging curiosity.

Oliver carried a tray bearing two steaming mugs: sweet black coffee for me, and something pale and floral-smelling for Selene. She accepted it with a smile, so I assumed he'd asked her in the waiting room what she'd like. He looked a question at me with raised eyebrows—*anything else? want me to stay?*—and when I shook my head minutely, he left us again. To listen at the door, I had no doubt. Oliver could play the detached professional, but it was all an act.

Anyway, Selene's story went something like this: after hundreds of years of peaceful slumber in a secret cavern, where Selene joined him every night, Endymion had somehow disappeared. A week ago, Selene arrived at the cave on a Tuesday night and found it inexplicably empty. Although she'd searched for him herself and questioned her fellow divine and semi-divine colleagues, she'd found no sign of him and uncovered no clues to his whereabouts. That's when she decided to hire me.

As I said, Olympia Investigations is rather singularly placed to handle cases for non-humans. I have no superpowers or special abilities save one: thanks to some ancestral quirk or covert dalliance, my mother and her siblings, and now their children, are able to see, communicate, and interact with all manner of beings. Ghosts, vampires, werewolves, demons, fae...the list goes on. I hadn't even realized until I was about seven that not everyone could see these beings. And now I could add "displaced deities" to that list. Anyway, having grown up with the ability to see the non-standard, it doesn't faze us. Which is why my cousin Oliver was practically my only choice when I decided I needed an assistant. I'd named my detective agency after my (100% mortal, as far as I knew) maternal grandmother Olympia, since the family quirk was generally acknowledged to have started with her. I kept a low profile so that my "special" clients knew they could count on my discretion.

Initially, of course, I had no proof beyond my own intuition that Selene was who she claimed to be. She might be completely human, if slightly delusional and operating in a self-defined alternate reality; the faint glow of her skin could have been some kind of paint or dye she bought over the Internet. But she paid me cash up front for the first week and I was willing to play along.

After all, the Greek pantheon boasted a considerable history of interacting with we mere mortals.

She'd left the blue leather chair and paced the room slowly while she detailed the background of the case. Her pale blue silk blouse fell open at the throat and tucked neatly into a charcoal broomstick skirt that swirled around her ankles as she walked. I caught the flash of

37

tiny silver crescent earrings peeking out from her masses of night-black hair. The wolf-dog, whom she'd called Kyon, lay belly-down on the braided rug, head resting on massive paws, and watched her progress back and forth across the room as if she were the only thing in the room. Perhaps, for him, she was. She moved with grace and precision, as if movement helped marshal her thoughts and words. Her summary of the facts was concise and unemotional.

"Okay, I think I get it," I said finally, putting down my pen. "Now, I have a question for you."

She stopped moving and turned to face me, her head tilted to one side in anticipation.

"What do you think happened?" I asked.

She frowned, delicate creases tracing her pale brow, and shifted her gaze to stare at Kyon, or perhaps past him. The tears, resolutely denied, glistened in her eyes again and she swallowed a few times before she answered. "I think someone has taken him away," she said finally.

"Why? I mean, for what purpose?"

Selene pursed her lips. "I don't know."

"I can think of a few possibilities," I told her, and ticked them off on my fingers. "One, financial gain. Someone found him, realized who he was, and figured there was money to be made selling him or his story to the news media—or selling him back to you for ransom. Two, personal gain. Someone wanted to disrupt your relationship with him for their own reasons, which could be legion—lust, spite, revenge, who knows what else. Three, curiosity. Again, someone found him, and then had questions they wanted answered. Four—" I broke off. The last possibility could trigger the goddess' tears—or anger.

"Go on," she urged.

I licked my lips. "Four, he left on his own, for his own reasons. I'm sorry, Selene, but it is a possibility."

She pressed her lips together in a thin line, made her way back to the blue leather armchair and lowered herself into it. One tear escaped and trickled down a cheek, but she didn't raise a hand to dash it away, refusing to acknowledge its existence.

"I doubt it's number one or number three," she said finally in a controlled voice. "The chances of a human stumbling into the cave and thinking they could turn a profit from it are remote—it's sealed off entirely. And while curiosity is a great motivator, I think a person would be more inclined to bring someone else there, instead of trying to remove Endymion from the cave." She paused. "Which leaves numbers two and four. Either of which is entirely possible, if they found some way to get inside the cave. But even one of the other gods should have trouble doing that."

"Would someone have had to wake him first, before he could leave of his own volition?" I asked her, acutely aware that we were discussing the possibility that she'd been effectively dumped.

She nodded. "I believe so. But I don't know who could do either—get into the cave or wake Endymion—apart from Zeus."

"So no human could wake him, even if they'd found him?" I pressed.

She thought for a moment and then shook her head. "No. Zeus himself put Endymion to sleep, so it would take at least a modicum of magic to wake him."

"You suspect anyone in particular?"

"Not really," she said. "It's been so long...it's hard to imagine why anyone would bother with us now."

"Well," I said with a grin, "if it can't be a human, that eliminates a few billion suspects. I'll want to talk with Zeus for a start, and have a look at the cave, too."

"Whenever you're ready," she agreed.

"Meet me here in the morning, and we'll get underway," I told her. I wanted at least a few hours to do my homework. Before I met any other gods—or supposed gods.

Selene nodded. "Thank you, Ms. Sheridan."

"Please, call me Acacia. If I can call a goddess by her first name..." I said with a grin.

She smiled. "See you tomorrow, Acacia." Now that she'd revealed her true identity, Selene didn't bother using the door to leave. Instead, she and Kyon simply shimmered out of my office.

The intercom had been broken for three weeks now,

and Oliver and I had defaulted to texting each other between the offices. It seemed to work just fine, so I'd shelved the idea of even fixing the thing.

Could you come in here? I sent.

I could, but do you want me to? he responded. That's Oliver.

However, he did knock once and then open the door. He looked momentarily surprised that my client wasn't there any longer.

"Yeah, I guess she's the real thing," I said. "Just disappeared when we were done talking."

"I knew it!" he said, grinning. "Missing persons case, she said. I want details." He dropped into the blue leather chair and rubbed his hands together in anticipation, propping his loafer-clad feet on my desk. I'm not entirely sure Oliver understands the difference between the words 'assistant' and 'partner,' but we're working on it. I glared silently at his feet and he put them back on the floor with a sigh.

I briefly told him Selene's story. "Can you help me research the Greek gods before we finish up for the day?" I asked. "I might have to tread carefully on this one."

His dark eyes brightened and he raised an eyebrow. "True. I think they had a penchant for dealing with humans who got in their way in very inventive ways. Flaying them alive, turning them into plants or animals— or monsters—and boy, could they hold a grudge—"

I held up a hand. "Enough. That's why I want to do

41

the research, right?"

"And I don't want to be out of a job, dear cousin, if you get transformed into a spider or a pig or something. I'll get my laptop," Oliver assured me with another grin.

It was going to be a long afternoon.

By the time Selene showed up punctually in the morning, Kyon by her side, I'd had a crash course in Greek mythology. I now knew, for instance, that Kyon was named for a dog who had guarded Zeus in his infancy, and later been placed among the stars as *Canis Major*. I knew that Selene's love, Endymion, had likely been a shepherd, and that only Selene, among several moon-goddesses, was thought to be the personification of the moon itself. Today the moon looked a little less contemporary urbanite and a little more Greek-goddess, in a white, belted tunic dress and metallic gold sandals. A silver crescent clasp tamed her fall of dark hair. I felt underdressed in denim capris, Skechers, and a pale green blouse, but I wasn't going to a fashion show.

"How about you show me the cave first?" I asked her. "Then I can get a feel for the possibilities."

Okay, I might have been putting off the audience with Zeus. Despite his supposed paternal interest and fondness for mortals, I wasn't quite ready to tackle him.

"Certainly." There was no trace of the tears this morning. She must have given herself a little goddess pep-talk the night before, and today would be all stiff upper lip and head held high.

"So, how far is it? I can get my car out of the parking garage," I offered, but she raised a hand. A faint smile quirked one corner of her mouth.

"We'll need something more efficient," she told me. "Will your assistant be coming with us?"

I knew Oliver wasn't listening right outside the door, because he would have flung himself into the room with a breathless "yes" if he'd heard that.

"No, thanks, he'll be staying here to watch the office," I told her.

"All right then, are you ready?"

I nodded, slung my bag over my shoulder and stepped out from behind my desk. She surprised me by taking my hand.

And then the world folded. I shut my eyes involuntarily, dizziness buzzing my brain and threatening to buckle my knees. Selene's hand stayed tightly clasped around mine, though, and only an instant later I smelled cool, earth-scented air and a tang of fish and seawater. I shivered. *Should have brought a sweater.*

Cautiously I opened my eyes as I felt Selene release my hand. I blinked in the half-light to adjust my vision, but she whispered an unfamiliar word and torches flared to life atop elegant, polished brass standards. The temperature rose a couple of degrees, too. I looked around.

It was a cave, but that word doesn't accurately describe the chamber where Endymion enjoyed his endless—at least until recently—slumber. Walls of pale-veined, rough-cut stone rose on all sides, swathed and partially masked by swags of soft fabric. Six fluted Ionic columns supported the ceiling. A polished marble floor, inlaid with Greek keys around the border of each tile, held richly woven scatter rugs. Kyon ambled over to one of the columns and sniffed around its base, then lay down and put his head on his paws. He was obviously comfortable here.

The bedstead was the centerpiece of the room. Larger than king-sized, it looked invitingly soft, with richly adorned carvings at each corner and gold tracery skimming the curves of the headboard. Hammered silver shod the foot of each post. Drifts of vividly-embroidered linens trailed off the sides, and thick pillows crowded against the head. As I stepped closer to it, faint scents of laurel and something I didn't recognize tickled my nose.

Grandeur aside, however, the most striking attribute of the bed was—it was empty.

I turned in a circle, taking in the chamber. It measured perhaps thirty feet by twenty. A chair, matching the bed in design and decoration, and a small table piled with books, occupied one corner. Since Endymion spent no waking time in the room, I assumed that sometimes Selene passed time here in pursuits other than assignations with her slumbering lover.

"I don't see an entrance."

Selene shook her head. "There is none. Some natural vents in the rock reach the surface, but I asked Zeus to close off the original opening decades ago, when humans began to get more...exploratory. It used to be open to the sea."

"Why even stay here?" I asked her. "I'm assuming you could have moved him anywhere, even up to Olympus."

She sighed. "I suppose. But this has been my—our—sanctuary for so long..." Her voice trailed off. Apparently, even goddesses could be sentimental.

I nodded. "So that's why you're ruling out human involvement in this. Humans couldn't get in here on their own unless they blasted the rock, and obviously, that hasn't happened."

Selene nodded.

"So, besides Endymion, anything else missing or changed?"

Slowly she turned a full circle, casting her gaze around the room. When she finished, she crossed to the chair and the books, inspecting the stack.

"Huh," she said in a surprised tone. "A book is missing."

"You didn't notice it before?"

"I didn't look before."

"What's missing?"

She frowned. "A volume of poetry. *The Complete*

45

Poetical Works of Wordsworth."

I made a note. "Anything significant about that particular volume?"

"No, I like the poetry, that's all. In some ways Wordsworth could have been Greek."

I like Wordsworth myself. Slowly I paced the perimeter of the room, observing it from all angles. Kyon got up and joined me, his nose to the floor. He broke away from my path as we neared the bed and followed his nose until it pushed beneath the edge of the counterpane trailing the floor.

I crossed to him and lifted the fabric. A small white feather lay against the base of the bed. I picked it up, and it seemed to radiate its own warmth against my hand. A shimmer rippled across the soft vane in the torchlight. I showed it to Selene. "Does this look familiar?"

She blanched, although it was barely noticeable beneath the luminescence of her skin. "No, it isn't mine."

I tilted my head and gave her a hard stare. "But you know whose it might be? Come on, Selene, you're the one who hired me."

She swallowed. "I can't be sure, and I don't want to influence you. It could belong to any number of people. Wings and feathers aren't rare in my circles. Or it could have come from one of the pillows."

I tucked it into a pocket. "Have it your way. But you might have to tell me at some point, if you want this case solved."

She nodded.

As I stepped away from the bed, something crunched underfoot. I knelt to examine a small patch of crystals on the marble floor, and when I swept some up on one finger I caught the distinct scent of ammonia, and something else—cough drops? I scraped the crystals carefully into a small plastic bag and added it to my pocket. Then I called the wolf-dog and he padded over to me. "Sniff around, Kyon, there's a good boy. See if you can find anything else that doesn't belong."

As if he understood me, he put his nose to the floor again and worked his way around the room in an amazingly methodical manner. I suppose I shouldn't have been surprised: he was a goddess' companion. Not likely a "normal" animal on any level.

However, a few minutes later he returned to me and sat, tail sweeping a slow, elegant swath across the floor behind him. The look in his intelligent golden eyes said, *nothing, sorry*.

I patted his head awkwardly, hoping it wasn't an insult.

"All right, I'd better question some of your colleagues, Selene."

"Where do you want to start?" she asked, as she crossed to me and took my hand again. I steeled myself for the uncomfortable transport I knew would follow.

I took a breath. "Might as well start at the top. Take me to Zeus."

She nodded, and the cave folded, flattened, and vanished.

When the world stopped doing uncomfortable things around me, I stood in a courtyard so painfully bright, especially by comparison to the cave, that I squinted through tear-brimmed eyes and tried to focus.

"Knock it back a bit, would you, Father Zeus?" Selene asked. "I've brought a mortal with me, and you know they're extra-sensitive."

"Very well," a booming voice drawled, and the light dimmed to bearable. I managed to open my eyes and take in the area.

The classical Greek architecture got another workout here, with dazzling white columns ringing the plaza and apparently holding up nothing but bright blue sky. Everything seemed to be covered with gold leaf, intricate carvings, and delicate bas-relief. And that was just the throne. Something that looked like a lightning bolt leaned crookedly against one arm.

The owner of the booming voice sat on the throne, looking half-bored and half-peeved. He sported the iconic white beard and long white hair, but wore an incongruous navy polo shirt embroidered with a tiny thunderbolt logo, and slate grey khakis. "Another mortal, Selene?" he asked in a withering tone. "Tired of the other one already?"

"In case you've lost count, it's several hundred years

48

since I brought Endymion to you," Selene said drily. "And in case you haven't noticed, this one's a girl."

Zeus shrugged. "Boy, girl, your tastes are no concern of mine," he said. "What do you want me to do with this one?"

Selene drew a breath and released it slowly. When she spoke, I thought her teeth might be clenched. "Zeus, this is Ms. Acacia Sheridan. Ms. Sheridan, meet Zeus, King of the Gods of Olympus. If you wouldn't mind, Zeus, Ms. Sheridan is conducting some investigations on my behalf and would like to ask you some questions."

He raised an extremely bushy and skeptical eyebrow. "Ms. Sheridan is going to ask me questions?" He sighed deeply, as if this were just another in a long line of trials he would have to bear.

"I won't take up much of your time, sir," I said politely.

He raised his eyes above my head and I looked up. Some skittish white clouds had appeared, scudding across the blue. In a mournful voice he said, "'*Time drops in decay, / Like a candle burnt out, / And the mountains and woods / Have their day, have their day; / What one in the rout / Of the fire-born moods, / Has fallen away?*'"

I glanced at Selene, but she only shrugged. "Riiight," I said. "Yeats?"

"From 'The Moods,'" he said with an approving nod.

"Very nice, sir. Now, what can you tell me about

49

Selene's...er...companion, Endymion of Elis?"

It was Zeus's turn to shrug. "What's to tell? She fell in love with him, he was mortal, she asked if I'd set him to sleep eternally and not age. She was a little smarter than her sister Eos, who forgot the whole 'not aging' clause with that fellow—what was his name, Selene?"

"Tithonus," she answered, tight-lipped. I made a mental note to look up that story when I got back home.

"All right, so do you know why anyone would want to tamper with your setup there? Wake Endymion, or take him away from the cave where he slept?"

Zeus closed his eyes, tilted his head to one side, and intoned, "*Celestial visitant, once more / Thy needful presence I implore. / In pity come, and ease my grief, / Bring my distempered soul relief, / Favour thy suppliant's hidden fires, / And give me all my heart desires.*"

"Sappho? Seriously, Zeus?" Selene asked in an exasperated tone.

"You don't think 'Hymn to Venus' is appropriate in the circumstances?" he asked her with a smirk.

"Just yes or no would really be great, sir," I interjected. Maybe so much time on the Olympian throne in all this heat and bright light had made the great Zeus a little loopy.

He levelled a pair of steely blue eyes at me, and I swallowed. There was nothing crazy about those eyes, unless it was the insanity born of uselessness and a longing for past glories. "No," he said in a voice that reverberated around the walls that weren't there. "I do not know why anyone, save Selene herself, would wake or move Endymion."

"Me?" Selene practically squealed. "Why would I hire a private detective if I'd done it?"

He shook his head, his long white curls swinging. "I didn't say you did it, Selene. I meant I would understand if you wanted to, if you were tired of his long slumber and wanted him awake with you. That's all." Zeus slumped back in his throne. "I swear, you youngsters are so excitable."

She glared at him and turned away. "That's probably all we'll get out of him right now," she muttered.

"I heard that."

I stammered, "Thank you for your time, sir," and followed Selene. He might not wield the power he used to anymore, but I didn't think I'd want to get on his bad side.

"What's up with you and your father?" I asked when I'd caught up to her. She strode down a column-lined path that magically sprang into being about twenty yards ahead of where she trod.

"He's not my actual father," she said witheringly. "My father is the Titan, Hyperion. Everyone calls Zeus 'Father.' If you're going to figure this out, you might have to study your pantheons and time periods a bit. Next I suppose you'll be calling me Artemis."

"Uh, sorry. I've been trying to reacquaint myself with the history, but even the sources aren't definitive about everything. So you, Artemis, Diana—although you're all goddesses of the moon—are not the same person?"

She rolled her eyes and shook her head.

"Okay, got it. You have to go easy on us mere mortals," I said, and she threw me a grudging half-smile. "Next question: What's with Zeus quoting all the poetry?"

"Most of us do that. I don't know, it must be something in our makeup. You get used to it after a time. At least some of us keep up with modern poets so we're not spouting the same thing constantly." She huffed. "*Sappho*, for goodness' sake!"

I quirked a smile at her. "So I guess I'll be hearing Wordsworth from you at some point?" Not that I considered Wordsworth exactly modern, but perhaps from an Olympian perspective, he was.

She returned my smile. "I'll try to restrain myself."

"All right, give me the abridged guide to the gods, would you, so I don't mess up again? At least the one you're close to."

The columns ceased and the path opened up into a garden, complete with a small pond and white ducks paddling serenely. A pair of black swans floated, majestic and aloof, on the far side. A white marble bench coalesced to one side of what was now a well-tended garden path. She sat and motioned me to the space beside her.

"All right. What do you want to know?"

What did I want to know? I decided to treat this like any normal case. "Tell me about your family, friends, anyone you deal with on a regular basis. For most cases, the answers lie pretty close to home."

She raised her eyebrows but nodded. "Okay. My parents are the Titans Hyperion and Theia. I have a brother, Helios, and a sister, Eos, as Zeus mentioned. I hardly ever see Helios, because he's gone all day, every day, and I'm a night person. Zeus' parents are two other Titans, so I guess that would technically make us cousins, of a sort."

"Okay." I scribbled madly in my notebook as she spoke. It seemed important to get all the relationships straight. "Friends? Enemies? People you encounter a lot."

"Friends?" She gave a bitter little laugh. "You really don't know a lot about Olympus. There's constant competition for whatever attention humans will pay us these days, and everyone sleeps around a lot. I don't know that there are many real friendships here."

"Well, since we ruled out humans when we were talking in my office, I think it must be someone close to you. Let's just focus on the people you deal with most."

"Keep your friends close, and your enemies closer?" she asked with a smile.

"Exactly."

I held my pencil poised. I had to understand the interactions between the gods if I was going to solve this case. Gods or no, they acted and interacted remarkably like we poor powerless humans did.

"Well, besides family, I get along pretty well with Leto, Hermes, and Aphrodite. I'm not sure I can trust them all, but we're not enemies. Hermes is Zeus' son, and Leto is another cousin. Aphrodite—well, her origins have never been entirely clear."

"Goddess of Love, though, right?" I asked. "She could be involved here."

Selene nodded. "Maybe. I don't think I have any actual enemies," she said, furrowing her brow. "Not obvious ones, I guess, despite what I said before."

"Okay. I'd like to talk to your sister, Eos, and those three you mentioned. Maybe one of them will give us an idea where to go next."

She looked off into the middle distance for a moment, and I had the distinct impression that she was communing with someone else. "I'll take you to see Eos first," she said. "I doubt my sister could have anything to do with this without my knowledge, but you never know."

She laid a cool hand on mine and, bench and all, we went.

Eos had created a home for herself in a clearing on a small island, ringed with sentinels of dark pine and spruce, where the dense, springy grass was sprigged with tiny white and purple flowers. Her home was completely unlike the classical Greek architecture of Zeus's abode. It was, instead, a well-appointed log cabin with tall windows and an inviting view of the nearby beach. I took in the vista while Selene knocked on the front door, but turned back when it was answered promptly.

The goddess of the dawn had unsurprisingly rosy cheeks and a warm smile. She wore a simple but elegant robe in saffron yellow, bearing intricately embroidered multicoloured flowers along the hem. Large, white-feathered wings sprouted from her back, but she carried herself as if they were weightless. Blonde hair, perfectly waved, had been pulled loosely back from her face and gathered in a low chignon. Eos had a matronly beauty that might once have been quite overpowering and supernatural, but had mellowed over the centuries. She held the door open for her sister and me and motioned us in towards a chunky but polished wooden table. The small house was cozy, decorated in a charming country-elegant style.

Selene went ahead of me into the room and her back stiffened. Glancing past her shoulder, I saw another, older woman already seated at the table. She wore what I can only describe as a rusty-looking black toga. Her hair, braided and coiled in an intricate knot atop her head, shone the golden red of autumn leaves, and she fixed ancient but bright black eyes on us as we entered.

The barest hint of a smile curved the very corners of her mouth. She sat with her hands curled around a steaming mug of dark liquid, as if to warm them. Her fingernails were long, slightly curved, and painted the colour of old blood. The word 'harpy' came to mind.

"Apate, what a surprise," Selene said. She didn't include the word pleasant.

The red-haired woman inclined her head a fraction of an inch. "Selene. So sorry to hear of your current troubles."

She didn't sound at all sorry.

The woman continued, "I'd just dropped in to say hello, but I offered to leave when I heard you were coming. Eos wouldn't hear of it until I'd finished my ambrosia."

"Smells like coffee," I observed with a smile.

Apate flashed me a smile that held no warmth. "It is coffee," she said. "Just a little joke we enjoy up here."

"What news, Selene?" Eos asked, turning to her sister, her face filled with empathy. "No word of Endymion?"

"None, but Ms. Sheridan has undertaken to try and locate him for me. She wished to speak with you, among others."

Eos raised her eyebrows in surprise. "With me? I'm afraid I know nothing of the matter, except what my sister has told me."

I nodded. "I understand. But the job of uncovering

the truth often involves much work that is merely routine."

"Well, I'll help if I can," Eos said. "Will you take a cup of coffee while we talk?"

Selene acquiesced for both of us, and I was glad she had. I was secretly dying to try the coffee of the gods, because it smelled absolutely amazing. When Eos set mugs in front of us, I took a tentative sip and thought I could die happy. It was the best coffee I'd ever tasted. I wondered briefly if it did contain ambrosia, because my research had indicated that things often went badly for mortals who partook of the heavenly substance. After another mouthful, however, I decided I didn't care.

Eos joined us at the table and looked at me expectantly. I forced my attention away from my mug and back to the topic at hand.

"Have you ever had occasion to visit the cave where Endymion slept?"

She pursed her lips in thought. "You never took me there, did you, Selene?"

There might have been a hint of accusation in the words, and it wasn't really an answer.

The skin around Selene's eyes was tight. "No, I don't think so, sister."

"Do the two of you spend much time together?"

Eos and Selene both shook their heads, half-smiling. At that moment I could see a sisterly resemblance, despite their differences.

Selene said, "My sister and I get along well, Ms. Sheridan, but rather obviously, she's a morning person and I'm a night person, so we don't see all that much of each other."

"And yet you're alike in many ways," I said. "Both beautiful, powerful—and you both fell in love with mortal men. Selene with Endymion, and Eos with Tithonus." I watched Eos to see how she would react.

She smiled a thin smile that did not reach her eyes. *"Love is a breach in the walls, a broken gate, where that comes in that shall not go again; Love sells the proud heart's citadel to Fate."*

I knew that one; "Love," by Rupert Brooke. I tried to catch Selene's eye, but she wasn't looking at me. She stared hard at her sister, who met her gaze evenly. I waited a moment, but neither goddess seemed inclined to break off first.

Apate suddenly glanced up at the ceiling and said in a faraway voice, *"What is the gift we have given thee, Sister? What is the trust we have laid in thy hand?"*

The two sister goddesses broke off their staring contest at the same moment and reached for the distraction of their drinks. I wasn't sure what had just happened, but this Apate, whoever she was, gave me the creeps.

I reached into my pocket for the white feather I'd found in the empty cavern and laid it on the table. "You wouldn't have lost this, would you, Eos?"

Even as I said it, I thought it must be hers. In close proximity to her beautiful wings, it held a minuscule echo of her magnificent plumage.

She had the grace to take it and examine it carefully, then raised her eyes to mine as she handed it back. Unlike Zeus's steely eyes, hers were violet-hued and warm, although at that moment they weren't the friendliest I'd ever seen pointed in my direction. "No, I don't believe I did," she said. "I would know in an instant if it were mine. It is not."

And despite what my eyes were telling me, I believed her. She likely wasn't the only person around here sporting a set of white-feathered wings.

Well, that was all I had for now, so I shot a glance at Selene and nodded. The goddess looked relieved.

"We won't keep you from your visit, then," Selene said, and we got up to leave, but only after I had gulped down the last of my coffee. I was not about to leave a drop behind, and I didn't care how it looked. Apate merely nodded at our departure and sipped nonchalantly from her own mug. The sister goddesses embraced briefly and Selene and I left the cabin.

We walked down to the beach, where the lapping waves hissed gently across the sand. An errant breeze lifted Selene's hair and she tilted her face up to it. The white sand felt invitingly warm and I slipped off my shoes, dangling them from one hand as we walked. Someone had built an intricate sandcastle near the water's edge and then left it for the waves to erode. Glancing back at the cottage to be sure we were out of earshot—although with gods, who knew?—I said, "The feather. You thought it might be hers."

Selene looked at the sand her perfect feet trod and shrugged. "I thought it was possible, although I didn't want to believe it." She glanced at me. "You believe Eos? That it wasn't hers?"

I sighed. "It might have made things easier if it were, but yes, I believe her."

The moon goddess nodded and we walked in silence. After a moment I asked, "What was Apate quoting, back there? I didn't recognize it."

"It's from a war poem by Frederick Scott," the moon goddess said absently. "'To France,' I think. 'Sorrow hath made thee more beautiful, Sister' and more cheery thoughts like that. An encounter with Apate is never what you need if your spirits are already low."

"She didn't exactly light up the room," I agreed. "But don't let her get you down. It's early days yet."

Her wan smile told me my advice might be a little late, but we pressed on.

We visited Leto, Hermes, and Aphrodite after that, all of whom Selene had said she got along with, but also wasn't sure she could trust. We were still stymied on a motive for whoever had tampered with Endymion, although having met several of the deities and demigods, I was of the opinion that in the end it would come down to jealousy. Either someone wanted Endymion, or someone wanted Endymion out of the way to free up Selene's affections. Maybe it was what happened to gods when they didn't matter anymore and wielded ever-diminishing power, but they seemed almost obsessively concerned with relationships. Love, friendship, alliances, enemies—little else seemed to matter.

We found Leto, a slender goddess with upswept dark hair, reading on a modern-looking chaise longue under an arch of fragrant climbing roses. She rose to wrap Selene in a quick, friendly hug, then settled herself back on the chaise. As we spoke, she smoothed the skirt of her pale sapphire dress absently with one hand, one finger of her other hand bookmarking her place. I surreptitiously noted the cover—it wasn't Wordsworth, but a recent academic title on feminism.

She answered my questions easily—had never been to the cave, didn't know who might have wanted to break up Selene and Endymion—and seemed genuinely concerned for Selene. As we wrapped up the conversation she sympathetically quoted Keats to us, from "Endymion," no less: *A thing of beauty is a joy for ever: / Its loveliness increases; it will never / Pass into nothingness; but still will keep / A bower quiet for us, and a sleep / Full of sweet dreams, and health, and quiet breathing.*"

Which was very pretty, but entirely useless.

When we caught up to Hermes not far from Zeus' throne room, he grinned at us and deftly caught a golden coin he'd been idly flipping.

"God of luck," Selene whispered to me as we approached. "Sometimes he's kind of cocky about that."

"What else?"

"Hmm...athletes, travellers, shepherds, thieves, and merchants," she said quickly. "And messengers, of course."

At my first question about Selene and Endymion, Hermes quoted Robert Frost to us:

Yet some say Love by being thrall
And simply staying possesses all
In several beauty that Thought fares far
To find fused in another star.

But I couldn't let Hermes off with a smile and a snatch of poetry. On his feet he wore the famous "winged sandals" that gave him his legendary speed. And those wings were adorned with pure, white feathers.

"You wouldn't recognize this, would you?" I asked innocently, displaying the white feather I'd found in the cave.

Unlike Eos, who'd stayed calm in the face of the feather, Hermes seemed startled by its appearance.

"No, that's not mine," he said, recovering his aplomb quickly. He didn't reach out to take it as Eos had done. Selene snatched the feather out of my hand and held it close to him, and it vibrated a little, despite the lack of any breeze. A faint hum whirred in the air around us.

"It is yours," Selene accused, frowning. "You don't think I'd be fooled, surely. Hermes, why are you lying?"

He looked uncomfortable. "All right, it's mine," he said finally. "But I don't know where you got it. I get around a lot, you know? The whole 'messenger of the gods' thing."

I reached out and retrieved the feather from Selene, sticking it back in my pocket. "Endymion's cave," I said. "Let me guess; you have no idea how it got there?"

Hermes shook his head. "No, I don't. I've never been inside that cave."

Selene looked at him as if she'd found something nasty on the bottom of her shoe. "Oh really, Hermes," she spat. "You expect us to believe that?"

Apparently even a god could look guilty as Hades, but he turned a resolute face to Selene. "I mean it, Selene. I've never been in that cave in my life."

I felt reasonably certain he was telling the truth—but maybe not the entirety of it.

Selene turned on her heel and stalked away. Hermes gave me an *I-don't-know-what-to-tell-you* look and said nothing more, so I followed the moon goddess down another seemingly interminable garden pathway.

When I caught up to her I said, "I thought you and Hermes got along well?"

She sighed and absently pulled a leaf off an exotic-looking shrub starred with tiny fuchsia flowers. "We do.

But Hermes is a bit like a teenager. He's your friend one day, but the next he's hanging out with someone 'cooler.'"

"I think he's telling the truth about not being in the cave," I said cautiously. "But maybe not the whole truth."

Selene shredded the leaf, long fingers tearing at it while her eyes stayed on the path. "Maybe Zeus could make him tell us more."

"It's a little early for drastic measures," I said. "Let's keep that as a last resort."

She tossed the remainder of the leaf away. "We're almost at Aphrodite's bower," she said. "Maybe we'll have better luck there."

But we didn't. Aphrodite, ensconced in a much-decorated, flower-garlanded gazebo of pink marble and sipping what I was sure was a margarita, gave no impression of hiding anything. She was breathtakingly beautiful and expressed her sincere sympathy that Selene was experiencing relationship difficulties. With an artful half-smile and tilt of her head, though, she managed to convey the feeling that it was Selene's own fault, and concisely quoted Wordsworth: "*She suffered, as Immortals sometimes do.*"

That, and her insouciance, gave me pause, considering the missing Wordsworth volume from Endymion's cave.

"Do you think she cared overly for Endymion, herself?" I asked Selene, as we left Aphrodite's rather overblown (in my opinion) bower. "She is the goddess of love, after all."

Selene fetched a deep breath and blew it out. "I don't truly suspect her, for that very reason. Although none of us retains the power we once did, when we had worshippers and supplicants in plenty, she still wields enough ability to take him and his heart much more directly if she wished; even, likely, to erode my own feelings, so that I wouldn't care as much."

The gentle thrum of a stringed instrument reached our ears and I turned, surveying the wide garden that surrounded Aphrodite's sanctuary. On a bench off to our left sat a man, strumming a lyre, not looking in our direction. Intuitively, I knew he was nonetheless acutely aware of our presence.

"Who's this?" I asked Selene.

She rolled her eyes. "Don't let him hear you ask that. Apollo, principally the god of music, but if you ask *him,* he'll be sure to add prophecy, colonization, medicine, archery, poetry, dance, intellectual inquiry, sun, light, plague and the care of herds and flocks. And if his personality is any indication, vanity, manicures, and bio-lift facials."

I snickered quietly, as we'd begun walking in the god's direction. He pretended to just notice us.

"Ah, Selene," he said mournfully, accompanying his words with a minor chord. "No joy in finding your lost love?"

"Not yet," she said, "But Ms. Sheridan here is assisting me now."

He stood and bowed dramatically over my hand, the folds of his robe falling equally dramatically around his muscled shoulders. The laurel crown that graced his curling brown hair stayed firmly fixed even when he bent over.

"Still putting her faith in mortals, that's our Selene," he said as he straightened, although the hint of a smile danced around the corners of his admittedly sensuous mouth. "I have no doubt she'll be better served by you than she ever was by Endymion, my dear."

"Thanks for the vote of confidence," I said drily. "Now, you wouldn't know anything about Endymion's disappearance yourself, would you, Apollo?"

"Alas, no," he said with fervour, hugging his lyre over his heart and tracing the thick strings with a finger. Faint notes floated in the air around us. "I never met the man, awake or asleep," he said. "Perhaps in light of Zeus' waning powers, he simply woke of his own accord and walked away?"

"He might have encountered a bit of difficulty leaving a sealed cave on a remote mountain," I said, "so if that weren't the case, you don't know of anyone who would want to...remove him?" I asked. I couldn't let him off easy just on account of his good looks.

He lifted his shoulders expressively. "'Tis said that some—well, that some of us have always been...

competitive...when it comes to affairs of love and lust," he said. "And it must be a god, to access the hidden boudoir, correct? Find he—or she—who desires one or the other of the pair, and you'll find your answer, Acacia."

And softly playing a beautiful, melancholy air on his lyre, he meandered off down one of Aphrodite's garden paths. Neither Selene nor I had mentioned my first name, so I knew he'd thrown it out there to put me off-balance. I narrowed my eyes at his over-confident back.

Selene wasn't watching him go. She stared off in another direction, her eyes probably not even registering the stunning blooms arrayed all around us. "If only I knew where he was," she said. "And that he was all right."

Her voice was so wistful...so human...that I knew it didn't matter that she was a goddess; she was in love, no matter how strangely that love had manifested itself across the many years, and her pain was as real as the pain of any human who has loved and lost.

Selene took me home when it was obvious I was too tired to do anything else just then. I was surprised to learn that I'd been away only a few hours by earthside reckoning, and fell into bed anyway. I was asleep almost before my head hit the pillow, Apollo's soothing music still echoing in my mind.

I slept the rest of the day and through the night, in deep, dreamless repose. In the morning, I sat at my computer and typed up my notes from the day before, adding my own impressions of the gods we'd spoken with and the things they'd said. When I got to work, I recruited Oliver again and we turned to the Internet again. Together we looked up every scrap of poetry they'd quoted to me, and did some more research into the gods' areas of influence and relationships. After a couple of hours, I closed the browser and rubbed a hand across my eyes.

"Everyone has at least two names and scores of lovers. No-one bats an eye at adultery, incest, or consorting with animals," I complained. "I can't keep it all straight."

Oliver blinked at his screen. "I could set up some kind of mega-spreadsheet for reference."

I blew out a sigh. "No. Not worth the time and effort. I'll stick with the gods and goddesses I've already encountered, for now. Maybe we're missing something. I think I'll get Selene in here again this afternoon."

Oliver brightened. "I'll pick up refreshments on my lunch break."

I mentally rolled my eyes. I could understand Oliver being smitten with the beautiful moon goddess, but I didn't think she was currently open to being impressed. But I wasn't going to crush his dreams.

"That'd be great," I told him, and went back to the computer to read over my notes. If I did that enough times, maybe something would make sense.

"Okay, we have a few things to go over," I told Selene

later that afternoon. We sat in my office, and Oliver unloaded steaming mugs of coffee and a plate of *loukoumades* onto my desk. He must have gone all the way to the Greek bakery across town. Since there were three mugs, I assumed my cousin had every intention of staying for this discussion, and I decided I'd let him. He took the other client chair, next to Selene, and popped a cinnamon-sprinkled honey puff into his mouth.

"After yesterday's interviews, Oliver and I did some research. Now I have more questions."

"All right," the moon goddess said, shifting nervously. She took a mug and sipped from it, but didn't reach for a pastry. I suppose earthly bakeries can't compete with the fare on Olympia, but it was thoughtful of Oliver to have made the effort. I took one myself to show him I appreciated it. They were delicious.

When I'd swallowed the two-bite confection, I began, "You said you usually get along well with Hermes. Why do you think he tried to lie about the feather?"

Selene's nervousness dissolved into exasperation. "I don't know. Hermes is hard to read sometimes. I often think he cares more about humans than he does about the rest of us—he's always been protective of humans and taken your part."

I nodded. I'd picked up that much in my research between last night and this morning.

"But I don't know why he'd be interested in Endymion particularly," she continued.

69

Oliver licked cinnamon from his fingers and said, "He's a bit of a trickster, right? And the second-youngest of the gods. Do you think he might get involved in something just for a bit of fun, or to flatter one of the older gods? Even if it meant someone—like you—might get hurt in the process?"

Selene pursed her lips, one hand absently stroking Kyon's fur. "It's definitely possible. You think maybe he was helping someone else?"

"I don't know. If he did," I mused, "Maybe he's feeling bad about it now. He quoted that Frost poem, and it's all about how love is, in the end, stronger than thought. Could that mean something?"

"Maybe, but what?" Selene asked.

Oliver looked at me, too. I didn't answer, because I didn't know. Yet.

"Next question." I fixed her with a steady stare. "Why didn't you tell me about your sister's extensive interest in men?" Apparently Aphrodite had, once upon a time, cursed Eos with an insatiable sexual desire, and she'd gone through—abducted, actually—a string of lovers, including the unfortunately long-lived Tithonus.

The moon goddess fidgeted in her chair. "I didn't want you to suspect her just because of that," she admitted finally. "I mean, I know it looks bad, but I really don't think she's involved."

"Well, I need to know these things when I'm questioning someone," I said. "I can't do this job if you're going to hold pertinent details back."

She looked suitably chastised, and I reminded myself silently that I was dealing with gods, here. Maybe I should take it easy with the scolding. However, I hadn't been kidding about needing to know things. "Who's Apate? She seemed to make you uncomfortable, and she certainly had the same effect on me."

Selene shuddered. "I don't know what she was doing at Eos's place. She tends to keep to herself, and just as well. I find her creepy."

"She was unnerving," I admitted. "But what's her power? You're all gods of something or other. What's her area of influence?"

"She's not a goddess *per se*," Selene said, pursing her lips. "More of a spirit, or personification. And she's a fine one to toss around words like 'trust.' She's only the spirit of deception and lies. Did you hear how she said she was sorry about my trouble? No-one has ever sounded less sorry about anything."

I frowned and drummed my fingertips on my desk. "You didn't see any problem with my questioning Eos while the spirit of deceit sat at the same table, sipping coffee? Like maybe she could help Eos lie convincingly?"

"Um." She stroked Kyon's head, where the half-wolf had rested it in her lap. I noticed that contact with the creature seemed to calm her. The wolf seemed to be eying the plate of honey puffs and I wondered if I should offer him one. "I guess I didn't think of it that way."

I sighed. "All right, is there anything else you haven't told me?" I asked, while she still felt bad.

"I don't think so. I mean, I could go on and on to you about the other gods...but things that could be important to the investigation?" She shook her head. "I really don't know."

"All right, we'll drop that for now," I said. "Let's go and see Eos again. And hope she's alone this time."

Oliver's eyes widened in hope, but I had to disappoint him.

We caught the goddess of the dawn at a late breakfast, buttery fingers shredding a croissant and eating flakes of the pastry distractedly. Her blonde hair seemed mussed, as if she hadn't brushed it yet, and she'd wrapped herself in an incongruous fuzzy purple bathrobe.

"Late start to the day?" I asked with a smile when we entered.

She gave me a withering look, even as she nodded us into the other chairs at the table. "I've already been out and brought the dawn," she said. "I like to come home and relax some mornings." She smoothed a hand over her hair and it settled obediently into the shining waves of yesterday. "It was a bit windy out there this morning. Coffee?"

Oops. Perhaps an annoyed goddess would be less inclined to be intimidated by me.

Both Selene and I accepted the offer and I was soon sipping the wonderful liquid again. Selene and Eos chatted for a moment, and then I cleared my throat.

"I wanted to go over a few things from yesterday, if you don't mind," I said.

Eos inclined her head, licking butter from her fingers. She fed the last morsel of pastry to Kyon, who accepted it gravely.

"You're sure you've never visited Endymion's cavern?" I pressed.

"I answered that question yesterday," she reminded me lightly.

"Well, you didn't exactly answer it, and you also had Apate sitting at this table with you," I said, meeting her eyes. "I know her...influences might make it easier for you to deceive us."

She turned hurt eyes to Selene. "And you, Selene? You think I was lying?"

Selene bit her lip. "I don't know. I'm letting myself be guided in this by Acacia." Then she caught her sister's hand. "But I do want you to tell us the truth. Perhaps you think you have something to hide, but I know you would not willingly hurt me."

Eos turned her eyes to me, but I met them. She might be a goddess, but she'd have to bring more to this game than a piercing stare. Zeus had unnerved me, I'll admit, but Eos seemed less daunting. We locked eyes for a long moment, Selene still holding her sister's hand.

Amazingly, Eos looked away first. "All right. I have visited the cave," she said in a soft voice, "and not so long ago."

Selene looked surprised but, to her credit, didn't pull away. "Truly, sister? I was not aware."

"How could you access the cave?" I asked sharply. "I thought only Zeus or Selene could do that."

Eos raised her eyebrows. "I'm the goddess of the dawn," she said. "When the first rays of light touch the mountaintop above the cave, I'm able to enter."

I looked at Selene. "Did you know that?"

The moon goddess shook her head and narrowed her eyes at her sister. "No, it never occurred to me. And I'm not even sure how you'd figure that out, Eos."

A shadow of guilt flickered across Eos' face. "Zeus told me. I was complaining to him about Tithonus, and he told me to go and see Endymion and then come back if I still felt like whining." She sighed. "So I went to see him. I wanted to know what it could have been like for me and Tithonus if only Zeus hadn't tricked me so cruelly."

I nodded, knowing the story.

"I knew you were busy with your moon duties," she said to Selene, clutching at her sister's other hand. "I went and watched him for a long time. I sat in your chair. I rifled through your books." She chewed her lip in a most un-goddess-like fashion. "It crossed my mind to interrupt his slumber. After so much time, the spell could be weak. Jealousy is a bitter worm when it tunnels into the heart, and what you had...well. In the end, I did nothing, and crept away, leaving him snoring in peace."

"He doesn't snore," Selene muttered.

"Did you see anyone else while you were there?" I asked. "Or evidence that anyone else had been there recently?"

Eos shook her head. "No, nothing, else I would have said so," she said. "I am sorry, sister."

I could almost feel the internal struggle Selene fought, but in the end she squeezed her sister's hands and said, "Thank you for telling us. But you could have come to me about this sooner."

Eos nodded. "Miss Sheridan, if there's any way I can help you with your investigations, please let me know. I have a debt to repay for lying to you, and to my sister. I'll assist you if I can."

"All right, let's put our heads together," I said, pulling out my notebook and looking over my notes. "What about Apollo? He was the only person we ran into yesterday who didn't quote poetry at me, although I thought he started to. And he definitely had an attitude when we spoke to him. He was trying to put me—maybe both of us—off-balance. Why?"

Selene splayed her hands. "I don't know Apollo that well. I avoid him, most of the time." She reached down and stroked Kyon's head, as if for reassurance. "I turned him down once—well, more than once, if I'm going to be honest."

"Turned him down as in, wouldn't sleep with him?" I asked bluntly.

"One of the few who've said no to him, I'd say," Eos said, then blushed a deep pink. On the goddess, it was beautiful.

Selene nodded diffidently. "It seems like everybody on Olympia sleeps with everybody else eventually, and it's no big deal. But I just never felt that way about Apollo. And I had Endymion. I didn't want anybody else." Her blue eyes sparkled with unshed tears for a moment.

"Hmm. So that does give Apollo a motive," I said. "If he still wants you, he might see Endymion as the biggest obstacle. And he strikes me as a god who usually gets what he wants."

Selene sighed. "You could be right. He does think he's god's gift to...er, the gods. And mortals too."

"I've seen him watching you, Selene," Eos said, pursing her lips in thought. "I didn't read any particular meaning in it before."

"And," I said, the wheels turning faster now, "you're the moon. He's the sun. If he believes in the old 'opposites attract' thing, he's probably miffed that you weren't open to his attentions. That would hurt his pride, which he seems to have in abundance."

"But I don't see how even he could have managed it."

"If some gods' special abilities allow them to interact with the cave, as mine did..." Eos said, then trailed off. "I can't think of anything in particular about Apollo that would apply, though."

"Maybe Zeus can tell us something about that," Selene said in a grim voice. "Come on, Acacia, we're going to go ask him."

"Remember my offer," Eos said, and hugged her sister.

"We will, and thanks," Selene told her, and we took our leave of the cottage. From outside, she, Kyon and I made the transition back to the throne plaza. It was getting a little easier to take. I didn't feel physically sick this time, at any rate.

Selene marched up to Zeus' throne and he lifted his head to watch her approach. He seemed more annoyed than apprehensive.

"Back so—"

"You told Eos how she could get into Endymion's cave." Selene cut him off. No "Father Zeus" or "King of the Gods" this time. "Who else did you tip off?"

"'Tip off'? How very 'pulp detective,' Selene," Zeus drawled.

"Don't avoid the question. You should have told us earlier who else could access the cave, and if they knew that." Selene had stopped in front of the throne, glaring up at Zeus with her hands on her hips. Kyon stood next to her, his own yellow eyes fixed on the elder god, just the hint of a low growl rumbling in his throat.

Zeus flipped a casual hand at the moon goddess.

"Almost anyone could access the cave, if they thought about applying their abilities in creative ways. That's not up to me, and despite my wide-ranging abilities, I can't yet read the minds of other gods."

"Apollo hinted that your abilities are waning," I said, keeping my voice polite. Selene might not be afraid of Zeus, but I wasn't ready to tackle him quite so head-on.

Zeus' face clouded for an instant, but then he quirked his mouth in a wry smile. "We don't wield much power in the 'real world,' as you humans like to call it, these days," he said. "We're the stuff of myths and legends. But there's a certain amount of residual power; quite enough to keep me—us—going for a while yet. Apollo can say what he likes—and look to his own eroded influence. But low-level celestial interventions still aren't difficult for most of us."

"So you didn't directly tell anyone else that they might be able to access the cave?" Selene asked doggedly.

Zeus bent forward and fixed his grey eyes on her. "No," he said, "I did not. But I can't swear that no-one overheard me talking to Eos, or followed her there, or that she didn't tell anyone else. I'm afraid I have no further clues to offer, you, Selene. As I've said before."

He leaned back and looked away, obviously signalling the end of the audience. Selene pressed her lips together in wordless rage for a moment, then turned and stalked out of the courtyard, catching my arm and dragging me with her. Kyon followed us, nails clicking softly on the polished marble.

Once outside, I tugged my arm out of Selene's grip. "Okay, okay, calm down. First rule of the detective business: not every lead turns into something useful."

"He drives me crazy!" She balled up her fists and then let them relax, blowing out a long sigh. Kyon nudged her hand with his head and she stroked one silky ear. "Okay. Where do we go from here?"

"I think we need to go back to the cave," I said after a moment's thought. "Maybe there's something we're missing."

She didn't look any more hopeful than I felt, but she nodded, took my hand, and we went.

The cave looked exactly the way it had the last time we'd been here. I knelt to speak to the shaggy half-wolf, stroking his soft head tentatively. "Sniff around some, boy, see if there's anything different, or anything we didn't find the last time." He put his wet black nose to the floor and began to snuffle around.

I walked the perimeter of the room again, looking for any signs that the walls had been physically tampered with. I tapped the wall in a couple of places and was rewarded with scuffed knuckles. Then I went to sit in the big reading chair, tapping my fingers on the arm. Selene stood motionless, staring at the empty bed.

"Do you have any regrets?" I asked her.

She turned to me and smiled. "It was an odd relationship, I know," she said. "Him asleep all the time.

But when we were together, we...communed. Communicated in a way that didn't have words or actual conversation, but felt very real."

"Telepathy?"

Selene shook her head, dark hair swishing. "Nothing so crude, or definitive. I guess I can't explain it. But he was the one who chose to sleep, and within the confines of that choice, we had something."

I'd still never asked about the fifty daughters, and the time still didn't seem right.

"You never got the feeling that he'd changed his mind, or was having second thoughts? That he might be wishing things could change?"

"I never did," she said, "and even if I had...what could he have done about it? Call on Zeus?" she quirked an eyebrow at me. "You met him—do you think he'd care much about Endymion or what he was thinking down here? I can't see him making an intervention for that, even if he knew."

I nodded. Zeus had struck me as more bored and self-absorbed than interested in the foibles of either humans or the gods and goddesses who inhabited Olympus.

"But Eos thought she might be able to wake him," I mused. "Did you ever try?"

"No. This was his choice," she said simply. Selene moved to the bed, pulling the coverlet off and shaking it out. "Well, if I can do nothing else, I'm going to straighten things up a bit."

"Eos used her special ability to get in here, and considered waking Endymion," I said. "If she could do it, then other gods probably have powers they could use, too. To get inside, and maybe to wake him up. We just have to figure out who."

Selene flung the coverlet back onto the bed. She threw a wry glance at me. "Do you have any idea how many gods and goddesses are up there, and how many powers and abilities they have?"

I almost missed it, but something fluttered to the stone floor in the flickering torchlight. Kyon saw it too, and we both moved toward the small object. When he snuffled at it, it drifted under the bed.

"Kyon, no!" I scolded him, afraid he'd eat or destroy whatever it was before I could get a good look. "Get back, boy!" I forgot that I was talking to the half-wolf of a goddess, but lucky for me, he didn't bite my head off.

Kneeling, I felt under the bed until my questing fingers found it. I pulled the tiny, smooth thing out and held it up for Selene to see. I knew immediately what it was, and where I'd seen more just like it. "Maybe we just got a lucky break," I said.

It was a laurel leaf. And only one god had been wearing a crown of them when we'd talked.

Apollo.

I made Selene take me back to my office, having

convinced her that there would be little use in going to confront Apollo just yet. He'd shrug off the leaf, correctly noting that it proved nothing, that anyone could have left it to point to him, and that they were plentiful both in Olympus and on Earth.

No, before we confronted the god of Music and Assorted Other Things, I wanted to have all the pieces of the puzzle firmly in place. I invited Selene to make herself comfortable in the blue leather chair while I asked her a question.

Oliver must have sensed our arrival because he came in without knocking and placed a steaming mug where Selene could reach it. Without catching my eye, he sat down in the other chair and crossed his arms. Message received—he wasn't leaving.

I ignored him and spoke to Selene. "I suspect that Hermes was involved somehow, as well as Apollo. And he did give us a clue."

"He did?"

I nodded. "He quoted Robert Frost's poem that pits Love and Thought against each other. And Apollo is the god of intellectual inquiry—or *thought*. I think Hermes knows more than he feels comfortable saying."

"But why would Hermes help Apollo?" Selene asked.

"I was hoping you might have some ideas about that."

The goddess got up and paced behind the blue leather chair, tapping a long, slender finger against her lips. The wolf-dog raised his head and watched her progress, but didn't rise to follow her. "He is a younger god," Selene mused. "And I think sometimes he gets weary of being ordered around by all the others. He might have welcomed a chance to do a real favor for an older god, one that might benefit him later."

"He might have thought he was helping Endymion," Oliver suggested. "He's the god of shepherds, right? And Endymion was one."

"The problem is, how to get Apollo to confess," I said. "It's still all circumstantial, unless Hermes tells us everything, which I don't think is likely."

"If we could find Endymion, he might be able to confirm that it was Apollo," Selene said, but then she slumped down in the chair again. "But if I could find him, I wouldn't have had to come to you."

"I don't think Apollo would have harmed Endymion," I mused. "He's certainly done some nasty things to people—humans and gods alike—who opposed or harmed him, but he'd have no particular grudge against Endymion. He wanted him out of the way, sure, but I don't think there was a lot of malice in it."

"That's true," Selene said, a note of hope in her voice. "Apollo's got a mean streak, and a narcissistic one, but he has no reason to hate Endymion."

I stood and paced. "So that means he sent Endymion—somewhere. Somewhere he'd be safe, but out of the way."

Selene looked skeptical. "Endymion has been asleep for centuries," she said. "The modern world is going to be a confusing bedlam for him. Where's he going to be safe on his own?"

"Let me sleep on that," I said. "The answer's got to be in Apollo's character, and Endymion's. Hermes might have had a hand in it. And Apollo might even have asked Endymion where he'd like to go."

"I'll think about it, too," Selene offered, but her voice was dubious.

"Come and get me first thing in the morning," I told her. "One way or another, we'll go and confront Apollo."

With a sad smile, she left, and I sat down at my desk, booted up my computer, and went online.

"Go get your laptop," I told Oliver. "We've got more research to do."

I'd like to say that I was waiting at the office for Selene the next morning, ready to go and pin the disappearance of her lover on Apollo, but I can't. The truth is, I was up half the night hashing over the case, our possible avenues of inquiry, and the various abilities and influences of Greek gods, with Oliver. He kept us going by uncomplainingly refilling the coffeemaker—but that meant I didn't sleep well the other half of the night. Selene actually came to my apartment to rouse me, which was more embarrassing than I can say. If you don't habitually wake up looking like a goddess yourself, you might have some inkling of what I mean. However, I was glad to see her.

"Can you get in touch with Eos and ask her to come see me?" I asked Selene as I filled the coffeemaker. "She said she'd help, right?"

She frowned. "Yes. But what can she do that I can't?"

"Your job is to get everyone together on Olympus."

"Aren't we going to confront Apollo?"

"Absolutely." I pulled a mug from the cupboard and offered her one, but she shook her head. No doubt what I called coffee—even my good, fair trade variety—was unpalatable to the gods. "But I don't want Apollo to squirm out of this. I have a job for Eos and Oliver, and I have this job for you. Can you do it?"

She looked affronted. "Of course. And what are you going to do?"

I filled my mug and added a dollop of cream. "Drink a coffee, and get a shower," I said with a grin. "I can't go to Olympus looking like this. Come back for me when you have everyone rounded up."

The moon goddess looked like she wanted to ask more, but did as I asked. She sent out some kind of wordless message to Eos and disappeared. Eos arrived in response to her sister's call and I outlined her task, giving her directions to go and collect Oliver to help. He knew the plan we'd worked out last night. If it didn't work, I had an Alternate Plan B in mind, but I hoped it wouldn't come to that.

I had time for the shower and two cups of coffee before Selene returned for me. We arrived on Mount Olympus and found an impressive array of deities awaiting us. Impressive, and intimidating. I was glad I'd taken a little extra time to shed my scruffy-detective persona, and dress in a black pantsuit with a brilliant red power-blouse. This is my sole 'impressing-people' outfit, and I hoped it was up to the task.

I'd left Selene to figure out a way to gather them all together, and she in turn had recruited Zeus to assist. From the sour and sullen looks on some of the beautiful faces gathered in Zeus' throne room, they'd been ordered to attend and weren't happy about it. I sought out one face in particular and soon spotted Apollo, lounging on a marble chaise longue, plucking softly at his lyre and looking completely unconcerned. My heart faltered. What if I was wrong? It would be quite a stunning audience to have for an utter failure.

I steeled myself and approached Zeus. "Good morning, O Father of the Gods."

He granted me the merest of nods, but I thought he looked pleased. I turned to the assemblage and said, "Thank you all, for coming. You probably know that I am here to reveal what has happened to Selene's lover, Endymion."

"Finally woke up and bolted," someone said in a stage whisper, and some snickers stuttered around the room. Selene ignored it and I did the same.

"I won't bore you all by relating every step of my investigation," I said, "But I will tell you what evidence I've relied on in reaching my conclusion. In the cave where Endymion had previously slept, we found a single white feather and a laurel leaf. From that location, in addition to Endymion, a volume of poems by William Wordsworth had also gone missing."

There was some whispering at the mention of the poems, but the gods and godlings settled down at a glare from Zeus.

"You all know that the cave was sealed, and although Selene had freedom of passage in and out, it would not have been so easy for anyone else, even an immortal. Some of you could do it, yes, but you'd have to know how to utilize your particular influences or abilities to visit the cave."

I saw Zeus turn an interested look on me, but I pretended not to notice. Let him ask me, if he wanted to know everyone I'd pegged as possibilities.

"Are we going to be here all day? Because I didn't bring enough wine for that," a rotund little god yelled from his seat next to a marble column. A lithe goddess with long auburn hair and sheaves of grain embroidered on her robe nudged him in irritation.

"Stow it, Bacchus," Apollo said, coaxing a languid chord from his lyre. "Let the mortal spin her tale. At least it's something different."

Bacchus stuck his tongue out at Apollo, but

subsided.

"All of this suggests to me that more than one perpetrator was involved," I continued. "And I've concluded that one of those was Hermes."

Hermes jumped to his feet. In fact, he jumped higher than that, and hovered a few feet above the floor, the wings on his sandals and helmet beating furiously. "Outrageous!" he cried, face flushed. "Why would I do such a thing, and why would any other god need my help?"

I waved my notebook (containing my Wikipedia notes) in his direction, "One of your spheres of influence is described as 'transitions and boundaries,'" I reminded him. "That would presumably give you the ability to gain access to the cave, or to manipulate things so that someone else could go inside. And possibly pass out again."

Hermes scowled at me, but said nothing.

"I did believe you when you said you'd never been inside it yourself," I added. "I'm willing to accept that you were tricked or coerced into helping." Hermes had helped me, however circumspectly, and I wanted him to know I wasn't throwing him to the wolves.

"I believed him, too," Selene breathed. "So are you saying maybe the feather was planted there?"

I pointed at her. "Exactly what I was thinking. The feather definitely belongs to Hermes, and it's possible that it came to be in the cave by accident. But it's also possible that whoever really took Endymion planted that feather to implicate Hermes, or at least to throw us off the track. The person may have given Hermes a perfectly understandable reason why he or she wanted access to the cave—but now Hermes is afraid to confess that he helped."

Hermes remained silent, but his wingbeats subsided and he let himself sink gently back to floor level. He didn't say anything, but he looked relieved.

"The laurel leaf," I continued, "leads me to believe that Apollo was also involved in Endymion's disappearance."

The beautiful god struck a horror-movie chord but smiled languidly. "Shocking! Of course, if Hermes' feather was planted in the cave, then a single laurel leaf could have been, too. I'm not sure your evidence adds up to anything yet, dear Acacia."

"Granted, but there is still the volume of poetry," I said. "I've noticed that all of you have a penchant for working verse into your conversations, and Selene confirms that this is true."

"*TRUTH, so far, in my book,*" someone piped up with a laugh. I thought the quote might be Browning, but I wasn't as fluent in poetry as the rest of the assembled company.

Someone else recited in a booming voice, "And truth, you say, is all divine; *'T is truth we live by; let her drench / The shuddering heart like potent wine; No matter how she wreck or wrench.*"

I held up a hand. "Lovely, and thanks for verifying that for me, but if everyone has to get a verse in, this will take all day. What actually struck me about the poetry thing was that Apollo was the only god I spoke with who *didn't* quote verse to me—especially notable since he is the god of poetry."

Apollo rolled his eyes. "I don't always quote poetry. Perhaps the mood simply didn't strike me when we were speaking. You might ask them about that," he added, nodding to a group of nine young women who seemed to move as a unit. Seven had their shining heads bent over what looked like smartphones, the eighth stared dreamily into space, and the ninth regarded Apollo with a strange mix of amusement and adoration. The Muses, I guessed. But I wasn't going to let Apollo distract me.

"You almost did," I said, shaking an admonitory finger at him. "I'm sure you thought I didn't notice, but you began to say, *'Tis said that some*—and then you changed tack, talking about the competitiveness of gods in the arena of love. It was very smooth, and I almost didn't catch it. However, there's a Wordsworth poem, "'Tis Said That Some Have Died For Love," that begins exactly that way, and I think you caught yourself just in time. If you'd simply quoted it, I might not have thought anything of it—everyone up here does that. But you changed your mind, because you didn't want to be caught quoting Wordsworth—of all poets, considering the book missing from the cave as well—to me at that moment."

Apollo raised his eyebrows. "A fascinating theory," he said, "but perhaps 'not quoting poetry' doesn't quite meet the evidentiary standard you're hoping for, either."

"There's also this." I pulled out the plastic bag containing a few white crystals. "When I found these, next to Endymion's bed, they smelled like ammonia and eucalyptus—a strange combination, I thought. Cleaner and cough drops? However, I discovered that ammonium carbonate, often in combination with another aromatic substance, is smelling salts. It occurred to me that the powers of a *god of medicine*, using a chemical compound for arousing consciousness, could have been just the ticket to wake Endymion."

Apollo strummed another lazy minor chord. "Fantastic detective work, Miss Sheridan. But pure speculation, nonetheless."

It was my turn to shrug. "I could put Hermes on the spot, and perhaps Zeus could force him to tell the truth, but I don't think I'll need to."

While I'd been laying out my evidence, Eos had discreetly joined the gathering and now sat, her ankles crossed demurely, watching the proceedings. Today she wore a fire-yellow dress with tiny flames embroidered at the hem. She'd piled her hair into a practical twist atop her head, no doubt to keep it out of the way whilst tackling the job I'd given her. When I caught her eye, she nodded once, stood, and disappeared.

A mighty whispering broke out among the gods, and Selene looked puzzled. I hadn't disclosed to the moon goddess the task I'd set Eos and Oliver, in case it didn't pan out. But that nod told me that it had.

Before the whispering could grow to full-blown speculation, Eos reappeared, holding hands with Oliver on one side and a young man I'd never seen before on the other. Oliver staggered and then caught his balance. His mouth slowly opened as he looked around the opulent throne room at the assembled deities, but no words escaped. I didn't waste too much time worrying about him—he'd recover his aplomb quickly, because he was Oliver. Instead, I studied the other young man. A mop of dark curly hair cascaded below his shoulders. He wore a somewhat vacant expression, jeans a size too big, and a Proclaimers t-shirt. In his other hand, he still held a beer mug, half-full of foamy amber ale. He looked around the assemblage of gods and saw Apollo. His face split in a somewhat goofy grin.

"Hey, Paul," he said, his words slow and thick from the ale, apparently not his first of the day. His brow furrowed into a frown and he added, "You shaid you'd come back for me. You din't."

Apollo fidgeted and wouldn't meet Endymion's eyes. "Sorry, pal, I, er...got a little tied up."

Endymion burped and quirked a half-smile. "'S'no problem. Good pub you left me in, anyway." He took a pull from his mug and surveyed the group again. This time he saw Selene. She smiled meltingly and took a step toward him, but Endymion's posture changed. He stiffened almost imperceptibly, then affected extreme casualness, glancing away. "Oh, hey, Selene."

The goddess faltered, her smile fading. I thought I should come to her rescue.

"As you can all see," I said to the assemblage, "Endymion himself is here. I think we should listen to what he has to say."

Eos led Endymion to a chair and urged him into it. He sort of fell the last few inches, but didn't slop out a drop of his beer. He took another swig and fixed his eyes on Oliver.

"Now?"

Oliver nodded. "Now, buddy. Just tell everyone what happened."

Endymion sighed, and suddenly he looked very young. "I don't 'member everything," he started, "but Paul came to see me—"

"And this is 'Paul'?" I interrupted, pointing to Apollo.

Endymion nodded. "Yup, but I think that's not his full name, you know? More like a nickname." He belched again. "So Paul came and woke me up, and I was like, whoa, what's going on? Because I haven't had anyone...much...to talk to for a long time." He didn't look at Selene when he said that.

I suddenly wished that I'd talked to Endymion in

private instead of setting up the big reveal this way. Selene looked pale, even for a goddess of the moon, and I hadn't meant to subject her to such a public embarrassment. But I'd been afraid that Apollo would need a very public unmasking for it to make any impression. It was too late now. Once he was started, Endymion plowed on.

"So we talked and Paul said the world had changed a lot while I was asleep, and wouldn't I like to get out for a bit? Just a breath of fresh air and a drink, and catch up on things. And I said sure, now that I thought about it, it was a long time since the last Harvest and by Demeter, I'd love a beer."

The harvest goddess perked up at the mention of her name. She was the redhead who'd nudged Bacchus earlier, and the god of wine snorted. "Beer! Peasant."

"So Paul said he knew a place where I could get some beer and conversation, and I've been there ever since." He took a swallow and regarded the now-empty glass with regret. "Nice people," he said. "Know a lot about sheep."

Selene looked at me in confusion and I put up a hand. "I knew that Apollo wouldn't take Endymion anywhere in Greece," I said. "Too easy. First place you'd look, right? And then I got to thinking that Endymion had been a shepherd, and that Hermes, who's got a reputation as a trickster, might have been in on the decision about what to do with him..."

Hermes wouldn't meet my eyes now, although I could see that his ducked head hid a smile.

"So where was he?" Selene asked. Her voice was admirably controlled.

"Scotland," I said succinctly. "At a pub called the Shepherd's Rest."

"You would not believe how many pubs in Scotland are named after shepherds or sheep," Oliver groused. "Took us almost all night to find him." Then he seemed to remember where he was and fell silent.

"Eos and Oliver tracked him down and brought him here," I explained. "So all that's left to talk about is—" I turned and caught Apollo's eye and held his gaze, "Why?"

The sun god pulled his face into a haughty pout. "Can't you figure that part out, too, Acacia? Since you've proven yourself to be so clever."

I tilted my head at him. "I have some ideas. You're the sun, Selene is the moon. You probably have some notion that she *should* be attracted to you. She's one of the few females up here that you haven't slept with."

Muffled giggles erupted from the cluster of Muses and elsewhere around the room, but I ignored them. "You saw it as a challenge," I said. "You took the book of Wordsworth to study up on what might appeal to her— or simply because you could."

I turned to Hermes. "And you helped, maybe because you're a younger god and wanted to ingratiate yourself with Big Brother, or maybe just because it appealed to your mischievous nature. Maybe Apollo wasn't completely truthful about why he wanted access to the cave. Or maybe," I added, "you did it because you've always had a soft spot for humans, and you thought Endymion might enjoy a bit of freedom. I have no doubt Scotland and shepherds was your idea, a place where he'd fit in."

Hermes looked abashed.

I turned to Selene and continued, "At any rate, there's your answer. Endymion himself has identified Apollo—nicknames notwithstanding—as the person who woke him and took him from the cave. And he's no longer missing. I think my job is done." I didn't add, *although he may not want to go back to that cave.* He and Selene would have to figure out that part on their own. I'd had my fill of gods for a while.

The crowd dispersed fairly quickly after that, and, after thanking me distractedly, Selene went off with Endymion to talk. I thought she'd have to get him sobered up quite a bit before they could have any meaningful conversation, but I expected she might be able to bring some divine ability to bear on that front. Eos kindly offered to take me and Oliver home, to which I agreed. Oliver whispered that he would have liked a chance to look around a little more, but I deemed it wiser to get out of Apollo's sight as quickly as possible. I don't think Selene ever would have given him the dalliance he wanted, Endymion or no, but to all appearances I was the one who'd spoiled his plans.

Eos took us to my office and looked around with a puzzled air. "This is where you work?" was all she said, but I was acutely aware of the shabby surroundings. Maybe Oliver was right, and I should invest a little money in sprucing the place up.

"Well, thank you for helping my sister," she said, beaming a sunny smile at me. "We're not always the best of friends, but I do love her."

"Thanks for your help," I returned. "I don't think we would have gotten anywhere with Apollo if you and Oliver hadn't found Endymion. And that was really what Selene wanted, anyway."

The goddess' smile faltered a little. "I don't know how that's going to work out for her."

I nodded. "It'll be better than not knowing, anyway. Maybe you and she will end up with something to commiserate over."

"Well, thanks again," she said. "If I ever need an investigator, I'll come to you, Acacia."

I rather hoped she wouldn't. Dealing with gods was exhausting. But I smiled and shook her hand. She tipped Oliver a wink and disappeared.

I raised an eyebrow. "I saw that. Did it really take you two that entire time to find Endymion?"

"Of course! It was completely business. Although," he mused, looking at the spot where she'd been. "We did get along. Maybe there was a little bit of chemistry there."

"Don't read too much into it," I told Oliver. "You know what we learned about how she goes through men."

"Yeah, I know," Oliver said speculatively. "Still, she's very attractive."

I let it go. If Oliver got involved with Eos, it would be his goddess problem, not mine.

THE END

δεαδ hunGRy

An Olympia Investigations Novelette

Oliver's texts from the outer office told me he was getting frustrated about the broken intercom.

The M.E.'s office is on the phone. The client waiting in front of my desk thinks I'm texting my girlfriend. So unprofessional.

I hadn't realized anyone was waiting, so I didn't bother to text him back and merely picked up the phone to get the call out of the way. "This is Acacia Sheridan."

"Acacia? It's Caro. I have something—someone—you might want to see."

Caroline Lewis is the local medical examiner, and my friend since high school. Possessing a deep spiritual life—and a very open mind—she's one of the few people I can talk easily to about my inborn ability to detect and interact with supernatural creatures. Caro never gets freaked out, accepting my dealings with ghosts, faery, paranormals and anything else with stolid equanimity.

"Hey, Caro. I've got someone in the waiting room, but I can swing by after that."

"No problem. This guy's in no hurry. And I have other...clients, myself. I'll keep busy." The smile in her rich voice came through loud and clear.

I don't know if all medical examiners think they're comedians, but Caro does.

After promising to be there soon, I hung up and texted Oliver. *You can bring the client in now. New intercom this week, I promise!*

The door to my office opened almost immediately, and Oliver stood there—alone. He leaned against the door frame and crossed his arms. Oliver is my cousin, and although we both inherited the supernatural-communication thing, only he inherited whatever style genes the family possessed. Today the sleeves of his plum-colored silk shirt were rolled casually to just below his elbows, but his dove-grey khakis were still impeccably pressed at two in the afternoon. I don't know how he manages that, sitting at a desk all day, but I'll be damned if I'll ask him.

"There's actually no-one here," he said, quirking his mouth in a half-smile. "But if there were, it wouldn't look good for me to be texting from the front desk. Why don't you let me investigate intercoms? I can take care of that."

I stood, brushing at the wrinkles in my jeans with little success. "Because we don't need some high-tech system that'll cost me thousands of dollars, and that's what you'll bring back."

"But we *do* need something more high-tech than two tin cans with a piece of string between them," he countered, "and that's what *you'll* bring back."

"Texting is more high-tech than that."

He pulled a theatrically deep sigh and blew it out with his eyes closed. "One more week, Acacia. This is an ultimatum."

I rolled my eyes after he turned away. Oliver needs this job to pay for things like silk shirts—although what Olympia Investigations can pay for a PI's admin assistant isn't great. But I'd promised to fix the problem, and I would.

Right after I found out what Caroline Lewis had to show me.

Caro Lewis' office huddled in the basement of Healing Sisters Hospital, fully on the other side of the city from my office. Morgues always seem to be in basements. It seems to be in line with the nature of such places to be cold, but I always wondered how Caro, a Mi'kmaw woman with an abiding love of the outdoors, could stand the long days with so little natural light.

"I make up for it on my days off," she'd told me once, and we were regular hiking partners. Still, I rarely clattered down the stairwell to the basement at Healing Sisters without a shiver.

I waited ten minutes in Caro's outer office while she finished a phone call, and then she came to collect me with a smile. "*Kwe*, Acacia. Let's see what you think of this."

She led me back into the coldest room in the suite,

the one lined with typical stainless-steel drawer-type storage units. As she put her hand on one of the pulls, I blurted, "How bad is it?"

I've seen a number of dead bodies, but some of them, well, they're worse than others. Being prepared is good.

Caro flashed another smile and winked at me. "Not too bad, I promise. He's all cleaned up now."

I took a deep breath as the drawer slid silently open and the white-sheeted figure came into view. Caro began to explain the case, as she pulled back the sheet to expose the face of a white male. He looked to be in his late sixties, with sallow skin and a grizzled, shaggy beard. Longish hair had been carefully combed back from his face. I swallowed, trying to focus on what Caro was telling me.

"Up until this morning he was a John Doe," she said, "No ID. It was pretty obvious he was living rough, so the police took a photo around to the parks and my friend's house."

"Your friend's house?"

"The Garland Street homeless shelter—My Friend's House?"

"Oh, right. Sorry." Most people I knew just called it "the shelter," and I'd forgotten for a moment that it had an actual name.

"They came back with the name Peter, last name possibly Hardogan, although that's not confirmed."

"What happened to him?" Caro hadn't drawn the

sheet lower than his shoulders, sparing me the sight of his stitched-up torso.

"Knifed," she said succinctly. "Twice in the kidneys, from behind. Attacker knocked him over the head first, so he was likely unconscious until he died."

"Thoughtful of them," I said around dry lips.

"That's not why I got you down here, though," Caro said. "What do you think of this?"

She gently eased the man's head to one side and touched a gloved finger to his neck, just at the carotid artery. I bent hesitantly to look closer, and saw the two round marks, about an inch apart. They looked like partially healed punctures. I glanced up and met Caro's eyes. She half-smiled at me.

"What's your diagnosis, doctor?"

She shook a finger at me. "This is your area of specialization, detective."

"I asked you first."

She drew the sheet back up over Peter maybe-Hardogan's face and rolled the stainless-steel drawer closed. "It's not what killed him," she said as the metal clicked home. "Those marks are at least a few days old. So for my task here, they're not relevant."

"You think he encountered a vampire?"

Caro shrugged. "There are no vampires in Native lore. Maybe someone tried to make it look that way. Maybe something else made those marks. I don't know." She crooked a finger for me to follow her back out to her desk, and we left the cold room behind.

"If you don't think it was a vampire, why'd you call me?" I asked as we got to her office.

She leaned against her paperwork-cluttered desk. "Let's face it, the police are too busy to put in a lot of hours looking for who killed a homeless guy," she said, crossing her arms. "But if there's an element of—something else—going on here, I thought you should know."

I chewed my lip. "I don't have a client. I don't know what you want me to do."

Caro shrugged again. "You don't have to do anything. There might be no connection between this and the murder. But if something comes up…"

I nodded. "Thanks for thinking of me. I haven't heard of any vampires in the city lately, but there have been in the past. I'll keep my ears open. Good to know when it's a possibility."

"I'm working this weekend, but I might drive out past Brenner's Hill next Saturday for a hike," Caro said. "You want to come along?"

I smiled. "If I'm not working a case, I'd love to. I'll let you know."

Caro smiled back. "See you then. And if I get anyone else with holes in their necks, I'll call you."

Caro might have had a touch of prescience. I'd see her again before our hiking date rolled around.

Three days later on a rainy morning, I was in Office n' More with Oliver, looking at intercoms. I stood in front of a fifty-dollar set of two phone handsets, while he drooled over a five-hundred-dollar unit with multiple-line capability, touchscreens, and VOIP. Here's how this would go: after a long tug-of-war session, we'd end up compromising on something in the middle, cheaper than he wanted and more expensive than I did. Neither of us would give in without first arguing for every model along the way, and neither of us would end up happy.

My phone buzzed in my jacket pocket and I glanced at it. The screen glowed with a text from Caro, just three words.

Got another puncture.

I sighed. Might as well take the path of least resistance. I moved halfway along the aisle to Oliver and plucked a hundred-dollar unit off the shelf. "This one," I called to him, holding up the box. He came down the aisle, frowning. Not only had I strayed from our usual routine, I also hadn't given him the chance to look at this one and tell me all the ways it fell short of his expectations.

I held up a hand to forestall the tirade.

"I got a text from Caro. I have to head over to her office."

Oliver narrowed his eyes, realizing immediately that this would be non-negotiable with a potential case waiting. He cut his losses.

"All right, as long as you take me with you."

Oliver was always anxious to get out into the field more, considering his usual administrative duties to be well beneath his capabilities. Never mind that I'd hired him to *do* admin. I also suspect he has a bit of a thing for Caroline Lewis's dark brown eyes and mischievous smile. Nothing else could entice him to go near the morgue.

Giving in would be faster and easier than arguing about it, driving him back to the office, and then backtracking to the hospital. "Sure," I said. "I might need someone to take notes."

He gave me a patented Oliver eye-roll but followed me to the checkout. Traffic was mid-afternoon light, and less than ten minutes later we descended to the basement at the Healing Sisters. Caroline waited for us in her office. Her smile increased in wattage when she saw Oliver, and I wondered for the first time if his unspoken feelings might be reciprocated.

She led us through to the cold room immediately, forestalling my musings on that possibility.

"The same, only different," she said as she pulled open a drawer opposite the one where Peter maybe-Hardogan had reposed. She twitched back the sheet to reveal a heavily-lined woman's face this time. "Meet Late Kate."

I glanced at Caro. She liked to joke, but not usually about the unfortunates who turned up on her stainless-steel tables.

She shook her head. "Her nickname on the streets," Caro clarified. "She tended to show up just before My Friend's House stopped serving every day, and someone thought it was clever. Street names stick. Kate Marzik. She had ID, so the police didn't have to hunt so hard this time. They brought the shelter manager in to make the identification."

Kate Marzik looked older than Peter, with more grey in her ragged, short-cropped hair. An indigo and violet bruise blossomed around one eye, livid against her pale skin.

"You can't see it, but her skull is cracked," Caro said in a matter-of-fact voice. "Cause of death was blunt force trauma to the back of the head."

Oliver swallowed audibly. "Where was she killed?" he asked in a wobbly voice.

"The park on Holly Street."

I peered at the woman's neck. Sure enough, two puncture marks marred the skin, looking fresher than Peter's had been.

Caro followed my gaze. "Still not the cause of death," she said. "Healing was already underway before someone cracked her over the head."

Oliver drew in his breath. "Vampire bites heal faster than natural wounds," he said after a moment.

Caro pulled the sheet back up. "I've heard that," she said dryly. "But I'm sure they don't heal *after* the body has died."

"Unless the victim has been turned," Oliver said.

"No sign of anything weird going on," Caro said. "She's dead, Jim."

She and Oliver shared an appreciative Star-Trek-reference smile. There was definitely a chemistry happening there, but I had to get us back on track.

"Have the police asked about them?"

Caro shook her head, her dark, shoulder-length hair swinging. "Both Peter and Kate were bundled up in layers of clothes, and I was the only one to examine either body closely on the scene."

"But they're investigating her death, too."

"Supposedly," Caro said.

Something unspoken hung in the air between us. It was obvious Caro thought that, with a possible vampire in the mix, I should be looking into these deaths. But there was no client, and Olympia Investigations doesn't run on such large margins that I can afford to do pro bono work. Caro wasn't offering to hire me. She was just quietly expecting me to do the right thing.

And she was right.

I sighed. "I'll swing by the shelter this afternoon and ask a few questions."

Caro's face lit up. She gently covered Late Kate Marzik again and rolled the drawer into place. "I'll let you know if I get any more," she said.

"I really hope you don't."

She nodded. "Me, too."

But I didn't have to go looking for the vampire, because she found me first.

Oliver clutched his new intercom system in relieved anticipation of setting it up as I stopped in front of the office to drop him off. A twenty-something woman with short blond curls stood staring into the window of the used clothing store next door. She wore dark jeans with low-heeled boots and a stylish moss-green jacket. I wanted to call out to her to tell her to go on inside and take a look around, because they carried really *good* used clothing, and it was where most of my wardrobe came from. Decent, cheap, and conveniently located. But Oliver was blissfully unaware of my patronage and wouldn't have been caught dead shopping there himself. What he didn't know wouldn't hurt him. It also wouldn't expose me to his disapproval on yet another of my life choices. Oliver jumped out and I went looking for a parking space.

When I returned, the woman had gone, but not far— she sat waiting in the reception room, browsing a magazine while Oliver tinkered with his new tech. She looked up as I entered but did not smile. Her grey eyes were serious and her pale face sketched with worry.

At this proximity, my sense for the supernatural kicked in. She was no normal human. The coppery tang of blood whispered at the back of my throat and I sensed a dark shadow hovering over her like a pair of great wings. Excitement warmed my gut. Two murder victims with bite marks and now a vampire in my office? They had to be connected.

"Acacia, this is Valia Northern," Oliver said, catching my eye pointedly. He'd obviously picked up on her true nature, too. "She doesn't have an appointment, but..."

He let the sentence hang, because obviously there was no excuse not to see her. I had to walk right past her to reach my office. I smiled graciously and said, "Come on in, Ms. Northern."

She set down the magazine and followed me in to my office, and I gestured her into one of the blue leather chairs. "Thank you for seeing me without an appointment, Ms. Sheridan," she said in a husky voice as she settled herself in the chair and crossed her legs. She clasped her hands in her lap. "And please call me Valia. I hope you'll be able to help me out."

"What's the nature of your problem?"

She hesitated. "I was told that you...that I should see you. I don't know if you can tell—"

"You're a vampire," I said easily, nodding. "No need to explain that part of it."

Valia Northern relaxed visibly. "And you've obviously dealt with my kind before, since you're not surprised to see me out in the daylight," she said with a wry smile.

I nodded. "Nothing sunscreen and being careful can't handle. Legends take on a life of their own sometimes."

"And everything gets exaggerated in the retelling." She sighed. "I'm here because someone is killing my friends," she said simply.

I tried to keep the surprise from my face. I thought she'd come about the homeless murders. "Other vampires?" To my knowledge, there were few vampires in the city at the moment, and I certainly hadn't heard of any possible vampire slayings.

She shook her head. "I volunteer at My Friend's House on Garland Street. In the past week, two of our regulars have been killed. I don't get the impression that it's high on the police radar."

I stared at her. "Peter Hardogan and Kate Marzik?"

Her grey eyes opened wider. "You know about them? Are you already investigating?"

Leaning back in my chair, I studied her, the image of those bite marks on Peter and Kate rising in my mind. Bile rose too, and I swallowed reflexively. "You volunteer at the homeless shelter, and feed on the people you meet there?" An edge of horror strayed into my voice.

She looked stricken, going even paler. Then a very human-like flush mounted her cheeks. "Well, yes. But it's not what you think."

Valia rose from the chair and paced my small office, clasping and unclasping her hands. She wore low, charcoal-colored suede boots that whispered across my threadbare carpet as she walked. The wing-like shadow followed her, pulsing faintly.

"I'm trying to give back, Ms. Sheridan. Atone for some of my past misdeeds." She threw a half-smile at me. "It sounds trite when I say it like that, but I am sincere."

I nodded, encouraging her to keep talking.

"I've been volunteering at My Friend's House for over a year. I really care about the people we serve there. Most of them have just gotten a raw deal from life, and fallen through the cracks of various systems." Her voice had grown passionate. "What happened to Peter and Kate—that's not bad luck. It's inexcusable."

"But—you do feed on the homeless you meet at the shelter?"

She sighed. "I do. Like anyone else, I have to stay alive. I never take enough to cause anyone real harm." She stopped pacing and stood behind the chair, hands braced against the high back. "Never. It's no more than they'd lose at a blood donation clinic. And there are— rejuvenating properties, that I can infuse when I drink."

"Really?"

Valia nodded, seeming eager to explain. "When vampires take bonded companions, they take more blood at each feeding, and infuse the companion to keep the humans alive, strong, and ready for the next time." She swallowed, as if the words left an unpleasant taste in her mouth. "What I'm doing—it's a twist on that. I don't gorge, I just...sip. But I still infuse them. The people from the shelter end up stronger and healthier. It makes up, a little, for their general lack of good food and medical care."

"Do they know what's going on? That you're doing this?"

The vampire licked her lips. "Well...no. They have no memory of it. And they're unlikely to notice the marks, or have anyone else notice them either. But I promise you, I do them no harm."

It might be argued that feeding from someone without their express consent was *de facto* harming them, but we didn't have to go there. Murder was a lot more serious. "But now someone is killing off your food source."

She pursed her lips and frowned. "You could put it like that, I suppose. But they're my *friends*. Understand, Ms. Sheridan, that I'm not faced with any lack of food, should every homeless person in the city be murdered." She looked pointedly at me, the shadow of fangs slipping over her lower lip. I got it. She chose to feed from the homeless, but she wasn't going to go hungry without them.

"All right, point taken."

She sat down again. "I've been trying to watch over the folks from the shelter, but even I can't be everywhere, every night, and they all go their own ways when they leave. We don't have enough beds for everyone, and some choose the streets or elsewhere for their own reasons. I know if this keeps up, someone's going to notice the bite marks. They might put two and two together and come up with six, if someone who believed in vampires looked at me the wrong way." She pointed to her face; pale, tapering to a narrow chin, defined by dark-rimmed eyes and intense red lips. Not just a girl dressing up "goth," when you looked closely. Something... different.

I tapped my fingers lightly on the scarred surface of my desk. "Someone already did. The medical examiner happens to be a friend of mine and very open-minded. She called me about Peter and Kate. That's how I knew who you were talking about."

Valia Northern shook her head. "But I didn't kill them, Ms. Sheridan. I wouldn't. So who did, and why?"

I studied her. I didn't trust her completely, but if she were the killer, it seemed unlikely she'd be in my office at this moment. No, even if this was meant as misdirection, she'd be far better off to go to ground and stay far away from me and Oliver, who could identify her for what she was.

"I assume you can pay me," I said, my last effort to find an excuse not to work for this vaguely discomfiting client.

She smiled, just a normal, human, friendly smile. "I've been around almost five hundred years, Ms. Sheridan. I have a few nest eggs squirrelled away."

"All right then, I'll meet you tomorrow morning at My Friend's House. And call me Acacia," I said, letting go of my resistance against taking another vampire client. The last time hadn't worked out so well, but maybe this time would be different.

Unsurprisingly, Oliver did not pester me about coming to the homeless shelter. It wasn't snobbery or shallowness of character, although my cousin has his fair share of those. What Oliver's confident and careless exterior hides is a soft heart that few would suspect. But we grew up together, so I know him pretty well. I'm sure he understands what makes me tick just as thoroughly, which is why we manage to work together despite knocking heads all the time.

So I left him happily in charge of the office and set off for My Friend's House. The morning air held a chill, and I wished I'd thrown on more than a long hoodie this morning. Guilt twinged in my gut at that thought, as I remembered my destination. I should be grateful for all the options hanging in my closet.

Garland Street was in the older part of town, still boasting a couple of brick buildings dating to the turn of the century. Their crenellated rooflines looked down over a street that had seen prosperity come and go, leaving mostly despair in its wake.

Stretches of temporary wire fencing suggested that times might be changing again on Garland Street, however. It looked like some of the new development construction that continually popped up here and there in the city had found a foothold here as well. The grinding of a bulldozer echoed along the street, demolishing a building a few doors away. Parts of the frame still stood defiantly, but it was obvious they'd soon fall to the machine's onslaught.

An older man watched my approach. Long, greying hair spilled out from under a knitted watch cap pulled low on his forehead. When it became apparent I was headed for the shelter, he offered a nod. "Noisy bastard," he observed, twitching his head toward the destruction down the street.

I smiled. "Probably quieter inside."

Valia opened the door and offered me a tentative smile. "Acacia, it's good to see you. Thanks for coming. Come on in." She spoke to the man on the step. "Jacob, there's coffee on whenever you want some."

Welcome warmth and the delicious scent of frying eggs and bacon met me inside the shelter. Though not as old as some of the buildings on the street, this one was at least post-World War I vintage, and the wooden floor sagged perceptibly to the left. The wide front windows—now striped with security bars—and the high ceiling of the main room, attested to the fact that this had once been a storefront; maybe a grocery or general store. Now long trestle tables lined with benches stretched the width of the room, and colourful notices for community and social organizations offering help and support dotted the walls.

Men and women took up spots on the benches, some clustered in conversational knots, a few aloof and alone, concentrating on their food. Despite the warmth in the room, many remained bundled in mismatched layers of clothing. Maybe too many nights on the street left a chill in the bones that never went away. No traces of the supernatural lingered among the gathered patrons, for which I was grateful. That might only complicate matters.

Farther into the room, an open serving window offered a glimpse into the kitchen beyond, where a tall black man in a flour-dusted apron flipped pancakes on an industrial griddle. He glanced our way and flashed a tired but genuine smile.

"That's Wade," Valia said. "We'll have to talk to him while he works." Valia carried a large coffee pot, and she refilled mugs here and there as we moved toward the kitchen. None of the patrons seemed to sense Valia's true nature. I got more suspicious glances than she did.

We passed into the kitchen, almost colliding with a thin woman bearing a heaping tray of pancakes. She took them to the serving window and began to dole them out to patrons lined up waiting.

"Wade, this is Acacia Sheridan. She's agreed to look into what happened to Peter and Kate."

Wade shook my hand in a firm grip, but a shadow had fallen across his face. "It's terrible," he said simply. "The streets can be dangerous, but we see a surprisingly small amount of violence. To have two of our people murdered, so close together—" He shook his head.

"Did they know each other? Apart from both coming here, I mean?

Wade shrugged. "I don't know for sure, but I don't think so." He nodded to one of the small knots of patrons. "Now those folks, they spend a lot of time together, here and out there. Nights, too. Almost like a family group. Peter and Kate weren't like that, though."

"Anything else they might have had in common?"

"Besides this place?" Wade stared at the floor, obviously thinking, then shook his head. "A lot of folks just move in their own orbits, you know? They intersect here for part of the day, but then move off again."

Valia offered me a mug of coffee and I took it, wondering what else to ask. Many of the usual lines of investigation were dead ends—home, family, job, leisure activities. The victims in this case had been fully occupied with the task of day-to-day survival. Wade's words—'almost like a family group'—sprang to mind, though. "Did either of them hang out with particular friends here? Anyone they always sat with?"

Valia surveyed the room through the serving window. "See the woman by the front window, on the left? That's Lavender. She and Peter used to talk a lot. But she's a bit—"

I sipped my coffee, waiting for her to finish the sentence.

Valia sighed. "She tends to ramble. It's not always easy to get her to stay on track in a conversation. Peter was very patient with her," she added with a smile. "They were definitely friends."

"Do you think she'll talk to me?"

"One way to find out."

We crossed the room to the big front window, where Lavender sat staring out the barred panes, her hands wrapped around a cup of coffee. A large-brimmed navy felt hat perched on her head, short tufts of brown hair peeking out beneath it. She wore a dark pea coat that had probably started life in the window of an expensive store. Purple fingerless gloves covered her hands. She didn't turn to look at us.

Valia said, "Lavender, this is Acacia. She's trying to find out what happened to Peter and Kate. Would you talk to her?"

She snorted, eyes still gazing out beyond the window. "Someone killed them, that's what happened to them."

I slid into the chair across from her. "I'd like to find out who did that," I said. "They shouldn't get away with it."

Finally, Lavender turned to look at me. Her red-rimmed, watery grey eyes held a startling depth of pain. "No, they shouldn't. What do you want to know?"

"Can you think of anyone who might want to hurt Peter?"

119

She pursed her lips. "We're not the most popular people in the city, but no. Peter didn't do anything to make himself extra unpopular, if you know what I mean."

"Did he have family in the area? Any other connections from the past?"

Lavender quirked her mouth to the side, thinking. "They wouldn't hurt him. His son came out from the coast once. Wanted Peter to go back with him."

That didn't sound like a promising lead. "Do you know—"

The hollow thrum of a jackhammer sounded, startlingly loud through the window.

"Bastards," Lavender said, echoing the words of the man outside. "I'll have a headache again tonight with that racket."

"Hopefully they won't keep it up all day."

Lavender looked at me. "Honey, they've been at it for weeks. They won't be happy until every last one of these buildings is gone."

I frowned. "They're not really going to tear the shelter down, are they?"

"Not if Mr. Wade has anything to say about it," Lavender said, raising her chin proudly. "That man looks out for us, he really does. We matter to him. Not to too many others, but to him."

She turned to look out the window again, and I sensed that she'd had enough of me. "Thanks for talking to me, Lavender," I said, and took my empty coffee cup back to where Valia loaded dishes into the gaping maw of a dishwasher.

"Is this building in danger of being torn down?" I set my own mug inside.

She frowned. "I don't think so. Wade said there was an offer to buy it a few months back, but it didn't go anywhere."

"Who owns it now?"

"A non-profit called RoofOver. They maintain buildings like these for community programs, all over the region. Wade manages the property, and he gets funding for building costs from them. We get grants and do fund-raising to pay for utilities, food, and everything else."

"What's the project down the street?"

Wade came over with a tray full of utensils for the dishwasher. "Townhouses and boutique shops, I hear," he said. "There's always someone who thinks they can make something 'better.' For their own definition of 'better,' that is."

I wondered how the presence of My Friend's House would sit with potential home buyers and shop owners. "All right, I guess that's it for now. If you think of anything else about Peter or Kate, or someone connected to either of them I should talk to, just give me a call, all right?"

"Sure thing," Wade said.

Valia nodded. Her eyes were very dark in her pale face, and the shadowy wings flexed and curled slightly over her shoulders. "Thanks for doing what you can, Acacia."

I smiled in return and left, feeling like it wasn't going to be nearly enough.

I try not to rub elbows with the local police force, and for the most part our paths don't cross. Since most of my cases have a supernatural connection, I'm often moving in investigative realms the strictly mundane simply can't access. But every once in a while, my world bumps up against theirs, and when that happens, I put on my best smile and go talk to Crombie and Crux.

Detectives Sasha Crombie and Dmitri Crux are not privy to my "special" abilities. Okay, a few things in the past have made them raise an eyebrow, but on the whole I think they're happier not knowing.

I found them at their desks in the big squad room. Crombie and Crux, contrary to every portrayal of partners in police dramas, had arranged their desks with space between so they sat back-to-back, their computer screens facing each other. That way, they told me, it was easy to share information from each others' screens, and they only had to swivel their chairs to talk face-to-face. It seemed like a lot of trust, to know your partner could see your screen any time they wanted, but maybe I have a naturally suspicious mind. At any rate, they both turned their chairs to face me when I dropped by to see them.

"Just wanted to check in with you on the murders of

Peter Hardogan and Kate Marzik," I said, handing Crombie a tall latte and Crux a green-tinted vitamin water. They took the offerings with the demeanour of royalty accepting their due.

"You have a client?" Crux asked, skepticism obvious in his voice.

"I do. Let's say, a friend of the shelter, and the folks who hang out there."

Crombie sipped her latte and shook her head. "Not much to go on. We talked to the staff and some of the patrons at My Friend's House, but no-one had too much to say to us."

"Not very trusting of cops," Crux added.

"Understandable," I suggested. "Most of them have probably been rousted a time or two."

Crombie shrugged. "You're not wrong." She pulled two file folders out of a pile on her desk and thumbed the first one open. "Hardogan—we did get confirmation on the last name, by the way—he has a son, Philip, on the west coast. Hasn't been this way in a couple of years. We checked—he's there, hasn't travelled recently. No other family, no known associates except a few friends at the shelter. Worked as a building inspector, showed up drunk a few times, lost his job and it was all downhill from there."

Crux took the second folder from her. "Even less on Kate Marzik. They called her 'Late Kate' at the shelter because she almost always showed up at the end of the mealtime. She'd eat, then leave, so that didn't leave much time for socializing with the staff or the other patrons."

"Nothing about family, other friends, anything like that? Where she slept at night?" So far there wasn't much new here. I might have wasted money on the latte and fancy water.

"She crashed with a friend over on Satler Street sometimes, a Lettie Williston. But we spoke to her, and Marzik hadn't been there for at least a week before she was killed."

"Can I have her address? I might check in with her anyway."

Crux read it off and Crombie scribbled it on a note for me. "Works as a cleaner on overnight shifts, so don't go looking for her until the afternoon," she advised.

I pocketed the note. "Thanks. There's really nothing else?"

Crux dropped the folder on his desk and shook his head. "Sorry. We're not keeping anything back. There just aren't many threads to pick up."

"Marzik was over on Holly Street, where was Peter Hardogan found?"

"Alley on Cooke Street," Crombie said. "Not even close to Marzik."

I sighed. "You haven't found anything else linking the two cases? Still seems like a big coincidence."

Crombie shrugged and took a long, appreciative sip of her latte. "Different kinds of attacks, although both messy; obviously nothing seems to have been stolen—what would they have that would make them a target? The only connection seems to be the shelter, but that comes up empty. So no, no other links."

Except vampire bites on their necks. Crombie's words struck me: *both messy.* So in theory, a lot of blood that came out of wounds other than punctures...but a vampire could still drink it, right? Maybe I had to go talk to Valia Northern again. Or Caro. She'd know if the bodies had notably less blood than they should have...

"Sheridan? You okay?" Crux stared at me, frowning.

"Uh, yeah, fine." Neither detective had mentioned the bites, so either they didn't know about them, or they wanted to pretend they didn't. I'd leave it at that. I pushed off Crux's desk, where I'd been leaning.

"Well, thanks, guys. I assume we'll keep the lines of communication open?"

Crux threw me a mock salute. "We hear anything, we'll share. You do the same."

I returned the salute and went back out into the sunshine. I punched Caro's number into my phone.

"Hey, Acacia. What's up?"

"Peter and Kate—they both lost a lot of blood at the scene, right?"

"Yes. They both had injuries that would lead to that."

"Unusual amounts of blood loss? More than one might expect for the injuries? Did you check for that?"

She was quiet a moment. "Not unusual, I think. But

let me look at the reports again. I'll get back to you."

Was I really suspicious of my own client? Well, maybe. It could be an attempt at cleverness, accounting for the non-lethal puncture wounds she'd know would be noticed, professing her concern for Peter and Kate, while having killed them all along and harvested their blood in a less obvious way. I shivered. It was a dreadful thought, but with vampires, you just never knew.

I'd wait to see what Caro said, anyway. By the time I grabbed some lunch, it would be afternoon, and maybe Lettie Williston would be home.

Satler Street had seen better days. The squat, one-storey row houses had once belonged to coal miners and factory workers, but now they housed the working poor, many who were a step up from homelessness, but just a narrow step. Some of the minuscule front yards were littered with broken toys and discarded auto parts, but others were almost aggressively neat, as if the inhabitants were making a last stand against not giving a damn. Lettie lived in one of the neat and tidy ones. A carefully-tended planter with three colorful hyacinths bloomed next to the front door. I climbed the four steps over peeling white paint and knocked.

Lettie Williston answered quickly, but opened the door only enough to speak to me. Her face was a roadmap of wrinkles leading nowhere very happy. Short, steel-grey curls peeked out from under a faded kerchief that might once have been bright red.

"Can I help you?" She sounded as if she didn't expect to.

I showed her my license. "I'm trying to find out what happened to your friend, Kate," I said gently. "Detectives Crombie and Crux thought you might be willing to speak to me about her."

Lettie leaned forward to inspect my license, lips moving slightly as she read it. Then she heaved a great sigh that seemed to come from the depths of her heart and stepped back, opening the door wider. "Come on in, maid," she said. "I doubt I can tell you anything useful, but come in. Tea's on."

The interior of the house showed the same aggressive cleanliness as the exterior. Lettie might clean for a living, but she didn't shirk her own house to do it. The fading scent of lemony dusting spray hung in the air, but beyond that the warm aroma of baking lent the house a cozy feel. Lettie led me through a narrow, shadowy hallway to the back of the house, and the kitchen.

Here, at least, light spilled in through two large windows, hung with cafe-style curtains. On the immaculate, if dingy, countertop, a golden-crusted loaf cooled on a rack. Lettie deftly sliced off two generous helpings and set them on plates, poured tea, and nodded me into a seat at the tiny table.

The loaf was banana, and smelled delectable, which impression was confirmed by the first bite. No wonder

Kate Marzik liked to stay here sometimes.

"I'm sorry about Kate," I said. "You were good friends?"

Lettie sipped her tea and nodded mournfully. "Tried to help her as I could, but Kate was proud. Too proud to move in here if she couldn't contribute, though I asked her many's the time."

"The police told me she hadn't been staying with you right around the time she was killed."

"Hadn't seen her for about a week," Lettie said, breaking off a piece of the loaf and chewing it delicately. "Maybe if she had—"

Her eyes glistened, so I hastily said, "The last time you saw her, was she worried about anything? Having trouble with anyone?"

Lettie snorted. "Mad, she was, mad about that shelter."

"My Friend's House? I thought she liked it there."

"She did. She was worried they were going to tear it down, like the other buildings on Garland. Mad at 'the Developers,' whoever they were. The ones doing the tearing down. She never said a name."

"A lot of the shelter's patrons seem to think there's a real risk of that, but the people who run the shelter don't seem to think so."

Lettie narrowed her eyes. "People on the streets— sometimes they know more than what others think they do. When Kate called me—" She broke off abruptly and took a long gulp of tea.

"Kate called you?"

She pressed her lips together and looked down at her plate, breaking off another bite of banana loaf. She dabbed at the crumbs with it, lifting them from the plate, not looking at me.

"Lettie," I said carefully, "You didn't tell the police Kate called you, did you?"

Silently, she shook her head.

"Because you were scared?"

This time she nodded.

I leaned a little, trying to catch her eye. "But I'm not the police. Whatever you tell me, I'm not going to tell anyone where I heard it."

She kept her eyes averted for another long moment, then pulled a deep breath and blew it out. "She called me after Pete was killed. Said she thought she knew who did it."

"And then *she* got killed, and you got scared," I said. "I understand why you didn't tell the police. But we don't want whoever did this to get away with it, do we? Or kill anybody else?"

Finally she looked at me. "No," she said. "We don't. And I don't even know if Kate was right, because it don't make a whole lot of sense."

"Who did she suspect?" I asked, feeling a tingle on the back of my neck. I was finally going to learn something new.

Lettie leaned in over her teacup to whisper, "The Developers."

I headed back to Garland Street, wondering if I'd catch Valia still at My Friend's House. It wasn't the best setting for me to question her further about vampire feeding habits, but we could set up a meeting for later.

The street was quieter now, although not exactly quiet. A crew of men in hard hats and high-visibility vests behind the construction fence threw armloads of this morning's destruction debris into a dumpster. I stood outside the chain-link fence for a few moments and surveyed the muddied mess beyond. Like so many of the buildings in this neighborhood, the old walls had obviously been plaster at their core, and clumps of dirty white spilled here and there among the dark puddles. Splinters of ancient hardwood floor, polished by long-gone hands, were now trampled into the mud by construction-booted feet. Progress? The whole scene made me sad, but I pushed the gate open and stepped inside the fence. A portable trailer made a temporary office. A couple of the workers saw me and paused to watch as I picked my way toward it across the mud, but none of them said anything.

A couple of discarded pallets served as makeshift steps, so I climbed up and knocked on the door, then pushed it open. A beefy man in a stained lumberjack shirt sat behind a tiny, paper-strewn desk. A hard hat lay off to one side, and his hair showed the indented ring where the hat usually sat. He hadn't looked up at my entrance, staring intently down at a cell phone held in sausage-like fingers. A plaque on the desk read *T. Fowler, Site Mgr.*

"Mr. Fowler?" I asked, taking a couple of steps into the trailer. It smelled of burnt coffee and old grease, with an overtone of diesel fume. Dirt smudged every surface.

He looked up at my voice. "Who are you? You're not authorized to be here!"

I held up a placating hand and pulled out my license. "I won't take much of your time. My name is—"

"Don't care. This is a hard-hat zone and you could get me in trouble just by being here." He stood up as if to emphasize his point. He was my height, but his wide shoulders made him fill the tiny space very effectively.

"Hey, I understand," I said, "but it seems pretty safe in here. I just want to ask you a couple of questions about the people from the homeless shelter—"

He cut me off again. I hate when people do that.

"They're nothing to do with me," he said. "Long as they stay outside the gate, I got no problem with them."

I pulled a deep sigh and blew it out. "A couple of them have been murdered in the area," I said. "I just wondered if you or your men might have seen—"

"Nope. Can't tell you anything about that."

"So you can speak for your men as well?" I snapped. "Have the police been around here yet? I imagine they could really slow down the work if they had to question all your men individually. If I told them I thought maybe someone here knew something they weren't telling."

He glowered at me, but I stood my ground. I don't like bullies or being interrupted.

"What do you want?" he finally snarled.

"Give me a hard hat and let me talk to your guys for five minutes. Then I'll be out of here."

Fowler swallowed as if he were pushing down some choice words that wanted to escape his throat. "Five minutes," he said, pulling a white hard hat off a shelf and tossing it to me. "I'm timing you."

I caught the hat deftly and settled it on my head. "Thanks for your cooperation," I said sweetly.

Fowler showed me his teeth, but it wasn't a smile.

I picked my way over to the knot of men, but it was impossible to avoid the general mud and muck. They watched my progress expressionlessly.

"Hey guys," I said. "Mr. Fowler said I could talk to you for a minute. Just have some questions about the folks from the homeless shelter."

"They're nothing to do with us," one of the men said. "One of them asked me for change one day, but Fowler put the run on him."

Nice guy, that Mr. Fowler. "So they don't hang around the site at all?"

Another man shook his head. "See them walking by on their way to the shelter sometimes, but that's it."

"A couple of people who go to the shelter were

murdered recently. You hear about that?"

There were general nods. "It was on the tv," one of them volunteered. *Gee, thanks for that newsflash.*

"You ever see anyone suspicious hanging around the shelter? Or the site here?"

"They're all suspicious," someone in the back offered, and the others snickered.

A couple of the men hadn't said anything at all, but there was no subtle way to single them out or any other questions to ask. I pulled off the hard hat and handed it to one of the men, along with my business card. "Well, thanks, guys. You think of anything that might help, here's my number."

The man took the card, but I was pretty sure it was in the mud before I made it back to the gate.

Lamenting the mess of my shoes, I crossed to my car and opened the trunk to grab my running shoes. Okay, I don't do that much running in them, but I'm all for being prepared. As I changed out of the muddied ones, though, I had a thought. I sat in the car for a few minutes ruminating on it. Peter Hardogan had been killed on Cooke, and Kate Marzik blocks away. Was there anything else besides the shelter that could connect them? Crombie and Crux hadn't thought so, but maybe they hadn't looked as closely as they could. I pulled out my phone and called Caroline Lewis.

"Caro, it's Acacia," I said when she picked up.

"*Kwe*, Acacia," she answered. "Geez, I said I'd call you when I'd checked the reports—"

"No, this is something else. Did you run full DNA tests for trace evidence in the Hardogan and Marzik murders?"

Her sigh was so deep it came clearly over the phone. "I did, but it didn't do much good. There was no lack of material—the problem was too much material. Second- or third-hand clothing that sadly doesn't get washed often, living rough outdoors, coming into contact with a lot of organic material, animals, vermin, the inside of holding cells—"

I held up a hand, although she couldn't see it. "Okay, okay, I get it. I hadn't thought about that angle. I'm just looking for something else that might tie the murders together."

"Something other than those so-interesting marks on the neck?"

"Yeah, about those. *Did* you have time to check those blood amounts yet?"

Silence greeted that. "I do have other cases, Acacia." But I could almost hear the wheels turning as she thought about why I might want to know about the blood.

"Okay, okay. Whenever you have time. Back to why I called. Do you still have Peter and Kate's effects?"

"Yes, their effects are still here," Caro said. "No-one to come and claim them."

"So you can still do tests?"

"In theory, yes…"

"I'll be right over." I hung up and popped my muddy shoes into one of the evidence bags I keep in the glove box. Then I drove straight to the hospital.

Caro raised an eyebrow when I handed her the bag. "And this is?"

"Mud and old plaster and who-knows-what-else from a demolition site. I'm wondering if there might be traces of material from here on Pete or Kate's effects. Like anything that could have been tracked in the killer's shoes."

"Interesting." Caro smiled. "Leave these with me, and when I have time, I'll run some tests. We'll see if there are any commonalities. But no promises."

"Understood. And you'll check the other reports?"

"I'll check the other reports! Now get out of here before I put you to work on your own cases," she said in mock exasperation. At least I think it was mock.

"Thanks, Caro. Talk to you soon."

I still hadn't talked to Valia again, so I made the loop back to Garland Street and parked in front of My Friend's House. The man I'd seen this morning—Jacob, Valia had called him—still sat on the step, now sipping from a styrofoam cup. Steam curled up from the cup and dissipated into the air.

"Still keeping watch?" I asked with a smile as I approached.

He shrugged. "Someone's got to keep an eye on them," he said. "They want to bulldoze this place, they'll have to go through me."

"I think it's safe," I told him, and then felt bad for discounting his obvious worry. With few places he could call "home," the shelter would be very important to him.

"Someone has to," he said with a sniff. "We have enough wolves at the door without those guys adding more trouble."

I sat on the step beside him and he shifted to accommodate me. "You're really worried they're after the shelter? Wade doesn't think it's a problem."

Jacob surveyed me for a moment with rheumy grey eyes. Then he pointed a wrinkled finger at the building next to the shelter. A sign over the door proclaimed it as "Thrifty Theo's New & Used Goods," and the two structures shared a common wall. The front windows of Thrifty Theo's held two mannequins, one in a faded blue winter coat and the other wearing work overalls and a dented hard hat. Dishes, books, knickknacks and a single wooden chair had been arrayed around the mannequins.

"They threatened Theo," Jacob said in a whisper. "His father passed that building down to him. It's not much of a business, but it keeps him from landing here with the likes of us. They told him if he didn't agree to sell, he should make sure he had insurance, because the place looked like a fire waiting to happen."

"What? Did he go to the police? Tell anyone else?"

The man looked at me pityingly. "And have it burned down around his ears sooner rather than later? No way. They gave him a week to think about it, and he's almost done thinking. Reckons he'd better sell up and get out safe. If he did change his insurance right before a fire—"

"It would look suspicious," I finished for him. "But why won't he go to the police? They could protect him, protect his business."

Jacob patted my hand in a grandfatherly way. "Not forever, girl."

I sighed. He was probably right. But my blood was boiling now, and I realized the patrons' worries about the shelter were probably well-founded. The buildings shared a wall. A fire would take out both of them. And the developers, if they really were behind it, wouldn't stop at the thrift store property. They'd want the shelter land, too.

I sat in silence beside Jacob, my thoughts swirling. I still wanted to talk to Valia, but she was no longer the only possibility I had to consider.

Wade was almost alone when I went inside. The supper serving hadn't started yet, although the scent of soup or stew simmering in the kitchen filled the air. A knot of men sat at a round table in one corner, playing cards. They pointed me in the direction of a small office at the back, next to the stairs leading up to the sleeping quarters, and I found the big man inside, bent over some forms. He looked up with a smile at my knock.

"Back so soon? Is my coffee that good?"

I smiled. "Just a couple more questions. Is Valia still around?"

"She left about half an hour ago. I'm not sure where she was off to, though."

I sat in one of the two hard plastic chairs facing his desk. "Has she been helping out here long?"

Wade pursed his lips. "About two years now, I'd say. She's a great volunteer. Always here when she's supposed to be, and everyone likes her."

I supposed it wouldn't take much vampire glamour to make these folks, vilified and ignored by much of society, respond to a helpful, friendly face and ignore any psychic frisson of unease the presence of a vampire might ignite.

"She's pretty broken up about Kate and Peter."

"We all are." Wade rubbed a hand over his face. "The people who come here have had enough misfortune in their lives. To be murdered at the end is just adding insult to injury."

"Well, they seem pretty happy and healthy, more than others in the same situation," I said. "You're doing a good job." Did he know what Valia was? Did he realize she was purportedly "helping" them stay healthy, and how? I watched his face for any clue, but saw none.

Wade beamed. "Thanks, Acacia. That means a lot to me. It's a lot of work, but it's worth it."

I thought of what Jacob had just told me. "Some of

the patrons seem really worried about that construction work down the road. Lavender mentioned it, and so did the fellow outside."

"Jacob," Wade said, shaking his head. "He's a conspiracy theorist at heart. Always seeing things lurking in the shadows. I've told them, the Foundation has assured me they're not going to sell the building out from under us. We're a busy, viable shelter. There's nothing to worry about."

I bit my lip, not wanting to put Jacob, or Theo, into danger. "Well, that's good to hear. I'll try to track Valia down at her place," I said, and stood to go.

"Thanks again for trying to help," Wade said, offering me his hand. "Everyone's a little rattled about it all."

"Do my best," I told him. But I didn't know yet what that might mean.

As I left the shelter, my phone buzzed with a text from Oliver.

Are you coming back to the office today? We should test the new system.

Since the afternoon had almost run its course, I decided to wait until the next day to go and see Valia again. I couldn't do much else until I got some results back from Caro, anyway. As I climbed into my car, I felt eyes on my back from the direction of the construction site. A glance in my rearview mirror showed no-one obvious, though. I shook myself a little. Maybe working for a vampire had my nerves on edge. In all honesty, though, she wasn't the one who bothered me. Fowler's hostility was harder to take than Valia and her shadowy presence. But did it mean anything?

Back at the office, Oliver said, "I hope this intercom isn't going to be too complicated for you."

"Har, har," I said. "Listen, Caro Lewis hasn't called, has she?"

Oliver shook his head. "What's she calling about?" he asked, his interest obviously piqued.

"Just running some tests for me. She'll probably call my cell, but I want to know right away if she phones here."

"Got a lead in the case?"

I blew out a sigh and sat in one of the client chairs. "Maybe. Maybe two. It occurred to me today that a vampire could have inflicted wounds that would bleed, and drink that blood, to avoid leaving obvious bite marks on a victim."

Oliver leaned back and crossed his arms."Wow. It's bad form to suspect a client, you know."

"I'm more worried about murder than etiquette. What do you think?"

He pursed his lips. "Seems like a lot of trouble to go to, when they already have bite marks on their necks."

"But coming to me gives her a chance to explain those away, and put her in a good light. Anyway, I have

Caro checking the blood levels left in the victims."

"Good idea. What's the other lead?"

"I have a hunch the developers working on Garland Street could be trying to shut down the shelter so they can buy the land."

Oliver's eyebrows went up. "By killing homeless people?"

I shrugged. "The manager said RoofOver wouldn't sell it off because the shelter is 'busy and viable.' Kill off enough of the patrons, maybe set a fire next door—they'll scare the others off. An empty building becomes a liability, then."

"You really think they'd kill for that?"

"Sadly, I do. They probably see the shelter patrons as disposable, just obstacles in their way. You know how some people look at the homeless."

"That's horrible."

"I agree, but as a theory in the case, it makes sense. So I took mud and stuff from the construction site so Caro can compare it with samples from the crime scenes. If we get a match--"

Oliver nodded. "So it's all coming down to our intrepid medical examiner. Well, whatever's there, she'll find it."

I hid a smile as he continued with studied casualness, "Listen, are you two going hiking anytime soon? I thought I might tag along. I really don't get out in the fresh air enough, the way you keep me cooped up in this office all day."

It was true Oliver often complained that I didn't let him come along with me on enough cases, but this wasn't about that.

"We're supposed to go next weekend," I said. "But since when do you go hiking?"

He looked affronted. "I love the outdoors! Aren't I always saying I'd like to get out of the office more?"

"Mmm-hmm," I said, inspecting the new intercom system. "I didn't think it had anything to do with nature communing, though."

"Well, that just goes to show you don't know me as well as you think you do," he huffed. "Of course, if I'm not welcome—"

"Calm down, you can come along," I said. "Now, just show me how this thing works. I'm ready to go home and take a little break from vampires, murders, and cranky people. I've had enough of all of those for one day."

Late the next morning, I called the shelter looking for Valia. Wade told me she'd already left and wasn't expected back until the suppertime serving, so I told Oliver where I was headed and drove over to her apartment. Valia's address was only a couple of blocks away from my own. I pondered my feelings about that as I drove. I was used to the notion that the world was full of supernatural creatures most "normal" people couldn't perceive. But I rarely gave much thought to the possibility they were my neighbours. And I still hadn't heard from Caro, so Valia could be a vampire, my neighbor, *and* a murderer. The thought was not comforting.

Valia's apartment building was quite a bit nicer than mine. An extended lifespan apparently did afford opportunities to amass a significant nest egg. The four-storey townhouse on Marshall Street had large balconies, a clean-swept front walk, and an attached, fenced side garden where a rose trellis promised blooms once the weather warmed.

Inside the tiny foyer, I pressed the call button next to Valia's name. She answered after a moment, and buzzed me in. Her apartment was on the third floor, but I bypassed the minuscule elevator and took the stairs.

I was struck immediately by the normality of Valia's apartment. If I'd been imagining gothic elements like black lace curtains, dark rose bouquets and an altar decorated with pentagrams, I could hardly have been more wrong. White-painted walls reflected light from mullioned windows at the far end of the living room, and brightly-coloured pillows and accents popped against pale furniture. An open paperback murder mystery, steaming mug and hastily thrown-aside woven blanket gave me clues about what I'd interrupted.

"It's good to see you, Acacia" Valia said as she led me into the room and gestured to a comfortable-looking armchair. "Can I get you some coffee?"

"You drink coffee, too?" I asked, a little surprised.

She chuckled. "So your previous exposure to vampires didn't include menu items."

I shook my head. "Strictly business."

The vampire shrugged. "Traditional vampire lore turns us into real monsters, making us almost entirely different from our human selves. The truth is a lot less dramatic than that, as with the whole sunlight thing. So, coffee?"

"Sure."

She crossed to the open galley kitchen to pour a mug for me. "Any progress?"

Sitting in her comfortable living room, it felt awkward to accuse her of misleading me by becoming my client. "There's a possibility Peter and Kate's murders are linked to the development on Garland Street."

Valia raised an eyebrow as she returned with my coffee. "Some of the shelter patrons wouldn't be surprised to hear that," she said. "Wade thinks we're safe, but Jacob and some of the others are pretty worried."

I nodded. "Did Jacob tell you that Theo, next door, received threats from them?"

Her eyes narrowed, and I had the sense of those shadowy wings extending menacingly. "No, he didn't. Theo is a sweet man, barely scraping by. Partly because he'll give his stock away to someone who really needs something. So they want his building, too?"

"Probably not the building, but the land. They

intimated the place might be in danger of burning down if he didn't sell it to them."

"We share a wall with Theo's!"

"I know." I sipped coffee. "I've also heard that Kate might have seen or heard something that made her suspect the developers were behind Peter's death. And when I talked to the site boss today, a guy named Fowler, I got a really bad feeling from him."

The wings definitely extended now, and two gleaming white points slid out from behind Valia's upper lip. I concentrated on my coffee. This was definitely not the time to bring up theory number two.

"So what do we do about it?" Valia asked, in a voice I could only describe as dangerous.

I fetched a deep breath. "I don't have enough evidence to be sure, yet. I'm waiting on a report from the medical examiner. Depending on what she tells me, I might have the beginnings of a plan." *Or I might have to accuse you of the murders. But I really hope not.*

My phone buzzed before she could ask me more, and I took the call with a mix of relief and trepidation. "Caro?"

"You're a smart cookie," she said, the smile evident in her voice. "I've got two matches for that old plaster and the composition of the mud. One good footprint on Kate Marzik's coat, and a sample scraped up by an enterprising detective from Pete Hardogan's murder scene. We just had nothing to match it with before."

"And the other thing?"

"The amounts of blood left in the bodies were consistent with their injuries," she said. "Nothing suspicious there. You want me to call the police about the construction site?"

"Not yet," I told her, "if you can ethically hold off on it for a bit. I might be able to get further evidence with a bit more time."

"Hey, the police didn't bring me anything to match, that was you," she said. "But I'd say this definitely points to a correlation between that site and the murders."

"That's all I needed to know. Thanks, Caro. I'll tell you when I know more."

"*Atiu*, Acacia. Call me later!"

The vampire leaned toward me, cupping her mug between her hands, grey eyes alight with interest. "I get the feeling you heard what you wanted to hear. So what's this plan?"

I outlined what I was thinking and we talked it over.

"We'd have to bring Theo into the picture, and he'd have to be willing to take a risk. Do you know him well enough to come with me while I talk to him?"

Valia nodded. "I know him pretty well. And I'll offer to reimburse him if he ends up losing anything." She grinned suddenly, and I was relieved to see that her teeth had reverted to normal. "I'm happy to help. So. We go and see Theo?"

I nodded. "Time to catch some killers."

Theo Hirano was a soft-spoken man with a lot of worry tucked behind his dark eyes. He greeted Valia like an old friend, though, and shook my hand with a wary openness. I explained our suspicions and said, "So I want you to tell them you won't sell. We want to see what they'll do."

"They pretty much told me what they'll do. Burn down my store!"

I nodded. "We want them to try. But we'll be waiting for them."

"I'll cover your risk," Valia assured him. "No matter what happens, you won't lose on this, I promise."

His sallow skin paled, but he nodded slowly and set his jaw. "Save the store if you can," he said. "But most important, catch whoever did that to Pete and Late Kate. They were good people."

So that's how I ended up on the rooftop of Thrifty Theo's New and Used Goods at half-past midnight on a cool late spring night, waiting to see if one of the developer's thugs was going to come and try to burn it down. Valia had assured me we'd be able to get down in plenty of time if worse came to worst, and I decided to put my faith in her.

Oliver wasn't as trusting. I'd invited him along on the stakeout (a term I didn't use when talking to Valia) and he'd taken up a position in a shadowy, awning-covered doorway on the other side of Garland Street. We were communicating via text, but with the brightness on our phones dimmed to near nothing so we could stay hidden, it was something of a struggle.

Noffing yer, Oliver sent, which I interpreted as *Nothing yet.*

"I see someone moving around at the trailer," Valia whispered, peering over at the work site.

Mobememt at yhe traolwr, I texted to Oliver, who replied with *what??*

I squinted at my screen and phoned him. We'd already agreed to set the phones to vibrate-only.

He answered with a whispered "What?"

I muttered, "The texting isn't working, just forget it. Valia sees movement at the work site trailer, so keep your eyes open. If they're coming, I'll bet it will be soon."

"Okay," Oliver answered. "Just remember, I'm mainly here to dial 911, right?"

"Yes. Do it as soon as anything happens. But not too soon. We need to catch them at something."

Even through his whisper I heard Oliver's exasperation. "Soon, but not too soon. Got it."

Garland Street lay quiet, with not a moving vehicle in sight. The side of the street where Oliver sheltered held mostly little mom-and-pop stores on the bottom floors with apartments above. A few upstairs windows showed the flickering bluish lights of televisions or computer screens, but darkness blanketed street level. Most of the streetlights had burned out or been smashed. Peering over Valia's shoulder, I saw a light in the office trailer's window wink out. In the profound quiet of the street, the sound of the trailer door closing reached us.

Valia turned to me and nodded. We crouched and crept closer to the edge of the rooftop, able to see the sidewalk below but hopefully not noticeable from street level.

Two men moved down the street with quiet steps but heavy confidence. They didn't speak, or if they did, it was in whispers that didn't carry to us. When they reached Theo's, one of them glanced around the empty street and then turned off the sidewalk to walk along the side of the building. The second man followed. They were directly below us as we looked over the edge of the flat roof, but they didn't look up. As they walked, one pulled a long, dark object from inside his coat. It looked like a gun—but why would they need that? Theo didn't live at his shop, so surely they weren't expecting to find him or anyone else here at this time of night.

They went all the way around to the back, and Valia and I crawled along the roof, following them. The thick petrochemical smell of gasoline hit my nose, and as I peered over the roof's edge, I realized what kind of gun the man held—a soaker water gun, filled with gasoline. Now he pumped it, spraying the entire back wall of Theo's shop with the stuff. With the added accelerant, the old wood would go up like tinder.

I dodged back from the edge and clutched Valia's

sleeve. "Should I tell Oliver to call 911?"

"Not yet." In the moonlight, her pale face looked grim, and I caught an eerie flash of crimson in her eyes. The shadowy wings most people couldn't see stretched black and menacing above us. For a brief moment, real fear twisted in my gut. *What was I doing?* Valia was not just the pleasant woman who had offered me coffee in her cheery apartment. She was a *vampire.*

Then a soft *click* from below drew our attention and we looked down to see the second man extend a lit barbecue lighter toward the gas-soaked wall.

Without a word, Valia threw an arm around me and hurled us both off the rooftop. I barely had my mouth open to scream when she touched the ground, bent her knees to absorb the shock, and set me neatly down beside her. She'd managed to turn us around as well, so we faced the men's backs. They both whirled, startled. Valia hissed and leapt at the one with the lighter. I ducked my head and bull-rushed the other man, sending him staggering back. He was a big man, but surprise was on my side. He dropped the water gun he'd still been holding when his back hit the wall and his breath left him in grunt.

Unfortunately, he recovered quickly, and drew a knife from his belt. The blade glinted evilly in the moonlight and I backed up a couple of steps to get my bearings. He took a menacing step toward me just as Oliver ran around the corner of the building, phone to his ear. He stopped dead, staring past me and the guy with the knife, his eyes widening. A weird gurgle filled the air. Even knife-guy glanced in the direction of the noise and froze.

Valia crouched over the man she'd attacked. Dark liquid trickled from a wound—twin wounds—in his neck, and Valia stared into his wide eyes. The gurgling sound came from him, as he apparently tried to speak but couldn't manage it.

"Stay," Valia hissed at him, and he went visibly limp. The vampire's gaze snapped up to the other man, and she moved in a blur to pin him back against the wall. One hand circled his throat, the other pushed against the center of his chest. The knife clattered from the man's hand to the pebbled ground.

"Did you kill Pete Hardogan and Kate Marzik?" Valia hissed, her face close to the man's. He shook with terror, looking like he wished he could melt through the wall behind him. The vampire's dark shadow wings bent around them like a cloak.

"Wh—who?" he managed to gasp.

She shook him a little and he whimpered.

"The people from the homeless shelter."

The man's eyes went to his partner, eyes wide but apparently unseeing, staring up at the sky. "No, it wasn't—"

"I'll know," she ground out, "if you're lying."

"It wasn't...it wasn't our idea. I swear. It was Fowler. We were just following—"

His words cut off with a brief scream as the vampire's mouth darted in to his neck.

Oliver edged close to me and his hand gripped mine. His flesh was freezing, probably not from the cool evening. His eyes never left the vampire. "I called 911," he whispered, as sirens sounded faintly in the distance.

The man Valia held had begun to sag against the wall as the vampire drank. "Valia," I croaked, then tried again. "Valia, the police are on the way. We should get out of here."

She drew back from the man and let him fall, then turned to us. Her eyes shone with a crimson glow, although it was already fading. With a finger, she delicately wiped a droplet of blood that clung to her lip. "That felt good. I was dead hungry," she said with a smile. "And we have our murderers."

"Is he—" Oliver managed, staring at the crumpled man near the wall.

"He's alive," Valia said. "But he'll still be there when the police arrive. You two should get out of here. Go home. It'll be clear what these two were up to."

"But what about Fowler?" I protested. "He was the one behind—"

Valia put up a hand. "Leave Fowler to me," she said. "You don't need to be involved in anything more."

I glanced at the two catatonic men, heard the sirens growing closer, and was inclined to agree with her.

That's the problem with vampires in a nutshell: no

impulse control.

A few days later, I dropped in to the police station to see Detectives Crombie and Crux. Dmitri Crux eyed me with undisguised suspicion. "Looks like your homeless murders are off the books," he said. "Partially, at least."

I shook my head. "I know. What are the odds those guys would be attacked by a dog or something in the middle of an arson attempt? And what happened to their boss? Just creepy."

Detective Sasha Crombie tapped a pen on her desk. "A dog, yeah. A dog with just two sharp teeth. Not that we *found* a dog, or any prints that might have belonged to a dog, in that area."

"Pet control needs to step up its game," I said smoothly. "Unless it was a wandering coyote or something. I hear they come into town sometimes." I peeked inside a brown paper bag on Crux's desk. Looked like chocolate chip cookies from the nearby bakery. "Maybe it could have been an escaped snake, like a boa constrictor or something. They just have two big teeth, right?"

"How'd you know what happened to Fowler?" Crux demanded, ignoring my suggestions. "We didn't release that to the newshounds."

I shrugged. "I must have heard the details somewhere."

"There's nothing really creepy about a heart attack,"

Crux continued. "Strange, though, how that same dog—"

"—or coyote," I interjected. "Or snake."

"Or *something*," Crux said with one raised eyebrow, "with just two teeth—could have been inside Fowler's apartment."

"And arranged him on his bed with his arms folded over his chest," Crombie said. "Looking very, very pale."

"The medical examiner did rule it a heart attack, though," I said, helping myself to a cookie. "And those construction workers said he was behind the murders, so I think justice has probably been served."

Crux slid the cookie bag out of my reach. "Those construction workers are still barely coherent after being attacked by that *dog*. We did a thorough search of Fowler's apartment, dusted everything for prints," he said. "I don't mind telling you, we compared yours to all the ones we found there."

"Detective, I'm wounded," I said, putting a hand over my heart. "I don't even know where that man lived."

"There were no matches." Crombie picked up from her partner. "And your alibi checked out—you and your assistant were in The Drowned Mermaid all evening the night Fowler...died."

"That was lucky," I said, brushing cookie crumbs off my lap. "I'm home alone most nights. Just happened we were out celebrating the end of a case."

Crux pressed his lips together as if he were trying to decide whether to release the words that waited in his mouth. Crombie helped herself to a cookie and took a bite. "Well, like Crux says, it's partially off the books. We're not certain Fowler acted on his own initiative, so we're taking a close look at the developers involved. But this is it for your part in the case, right?"

I held up a hand. "Absolutely. My involvement stops here. I think justice was served," I said, looking Crombie in the eye. "But I wasn't the waitress."

"And you're not going to tell us anything else, so I guess we'll see you next time, Acacia."

I grinned. "Thanks for the cookie, guys. See you later."

Outside the station, I ran into Caro Lewis. She carried a manila file folder tucked under her arm.

"Can't you just send everything digitally these days?" I asked her.

"Sure. But the detectives want me to explain a few things about this case, so I thought I might as well walk over with the file instead of spending half an hour on the phone."

"Listen, thanks for saying it was the mud on the arsonists' shoes that matched them up to the murders, and leaving me out of it."

She winked at me. "Well, it was true. The detectives brought me their shoes after the botched arson attempt. Sure, I had some of the work done already, but they didn't have to know that."

"I still appreciate it."

"Still hiking on Saturday?" she asked.

"Yeah, about that," I said. "Oliver asked if he could come along. He's not much of an outdoors guy, so..."

Caro shrugged, but her dark eyes twinkled. "Oh, bring him. If he can't keep up, we can laugh at him."

"All right, but remember, you agreed to this," I told her, and headed back to my office. I had a feeling that Caro wouldn't be laughing at Oliver, no matter how inept a hiker he turned out to be.

Valia Northern was waiting for me on the sidewalk outside my office. "I think I make your assistant nervous now," she said with a smile. "Thought I'd just wait here for you."

"Come on in."

Oliver looked up and nodded to Valia as we passed his desk, but he did look a little pale.

"I've come to pay your bill, and to say thanks," the vampire said as she took the chair across from my desk. "I think the shelter's safe now, and all the patrons, too. As safe as they can be, at any rate."

"The police don't think I had anything to do with Fowler's death," I told her as I accepted the thick envelope she laid on the desk. Guess vampires didn't do e-transfers. "They've basically marked Peter and Kate's murders as closed, but they're taking a closer look at the developers in case it wasn't all Fowler's idea."

I immediately wondered if I should have shared that, but Valia sat back and smiled, no hint of fangs showing against her pale lips. "You did good, Acacia. *We* did good. And I feel like I've made another friend in the city."

I was a little uncomfortable with the vigilante turn things had taken at the end, but I didn't mention it. With vampires—and a lot of supernatural creatures— sometimes you have to take what you can get.

I smiled back. "You have. But you'll keep being careful when you...um..."

"Feed from the patrons at the shelter?" she finished for me easily. "I will. I care about them, remember? They benefit from it. It's a symbiotic relationship, in the end. And it keeps me...satisfied."

And not feeding on anyone else in the city, she meant. Which was good, of course. I flashed back to her face as she turned away from the limp arsonist, satiated and smiling, eyes a dull red, as she delicately wiped blood from her lip.

I decided if her relationship with the homeless kept her from being dead hungry most of the time, I'd just have to be okay with it. And having a vampire as an acquaintance could conceivably come in handy in my line of work.

But *friends*? Maybe not quite. There was that whole impulse control thing to consider. For Oliver's sake, I wouldn't invite the vampire to come hiking with us anytime soon.

THE END

toil and trouble

An Olympia Investigations Novella

chapter one

Oliver knocked on my office door and pushed it open without waiting for me to answer, which he rarely does. His eyes looked wild and his usually-immaculate dark turtleneck and khakis seemed rumpled. I stared. Oliver is my cousin and my assistant, and like me, he can discern and communicate with the supernatural— which would be most of the Olympia Investigations clientele. Unlike me, Oliver is generally poised, calm, and self-assured. It takes a lot to rattle him. He closed the door behind him and leaned against it.

"A...woman to see you," he said, just above a whisper.

"Geez, is she a Medusa or something? You're white as a ghost!"

"Worse. I think she's a witch."

Well, that made some sense. Oliver had endured a bad experience with an urban witch when he was still a teenager, and apparently it was the kind of encounter that leaves an impression—and a scar. I don't know all the details, because Oliver doesn't talk about it. Most urban witches are friendly, environment-loving, generally benevolent people—but not all.

"What's she doing?" I asked in the same low voice Oliver had used. I didn't think the witch could necessarily hear through walls, but one never knew.

Oliver's lips pressed together in a thin, disapproving line. "Burning incense," he said in a clipped voice. "And using magic, because I can see the aura."

"I'll see her right away," I told him hurriedly. In the witch's mind, she was probably purifying the outer office of Olympia Investigations, but to Oliver this would be akin to an invasion.

Oliver sucked in an audible deep breath and blew it out slowly. Then he opened the door and said to the outer office in a remarkably even tone, "Ms. Sheridan can see you right away."

He stood aside to let the witch enter and I wondered if she noticed, as I did, the way he flinched back ever so slightly as she walked past him.

I stood behind my desk and offered a hand to shake, studying the witch. She looked young, no more than twenty-five or so, although with witches, you could never be sure. A wide blue headband caught her black hair back from her face, allowing tiny curls to escape around the edges. She carried a red-wine- coloured jacket over one arm and wore a knee-length t-shirt dress in tie-dyed burgundy and aqua colours. A heavy pendant shaped in an arcane symbol rested in the neckline. Black combat boots and a black suede cross-body bag with a dramatic fringe completed the ensemble. A faint glow of the magic she'd just cast floated around her, almost as if her body gave off pale blue steam. Dark eyes assessed me, and a smile twitched the corners of her mouth as she took my hand. In her other one she held a bundle of smoldering herbs, sweet grey smoke curling lazily up toward the ceiling of my office. Her handshake was cool and firm.

"I'm Acacia Sheridan," I said. "How can I help you?" I sat down again and gestured for her to do the same.

She blew a puff of air onto the smoking herbs and the fire magically extinguished. She dropped the herbs into her bag and smiled at me. The sweet aroma hung in the air and my habitually bedraggled office felt cleaner and brighter. Urban witches knew their stuff.

"Honore Martel," she offered. She glanced at the door to the outer office and the twitching smile blossomed. "Your assistant seemed a bit...nervous around me." Her speech held a slight French-Canadian accent, although she spoke English with a fluid grace.

"You'll have to excuse Oliver," I told her. "He had an encounter with a witch long ago and it left him...wary. It's nothing personal."

"Ah." Honore Martel didn't ask, wary of what? She wouldn't be here, after all, if she didn't know of my ability to deal with the supernatural. And after the burning herbs and accompanying cantrip, she probably felt it was obvious to me what she was. Witches are human (although not, of course, exclusively), so it's not something Oliver and I can automatically sense upon meeting one. But as soon as they cast a spell or perform magic, the aura of that energy use makes it abundantly clear.

"I—we—would like to hire your services," she said, letting the topic of Oliver go. "You are adept at finding things that have gone missing?"

"I have a certain amount of experience," I said cautiously. "Who is 'we'? And what have you lost?"

Honore sat back more comfortably in the big blue armchair across from my desk and crossed her arms, the fingers of one hand tapping on the other bicep.

"'We' are myself and my six sisters—coven sisters, that is," she clarified. My eyes might have gone a little wide at the idea of seven sisters in one family. Being an only child myself, that notion was far outside the realm of my own experience. But I knew urban witches often gathered in tribes or small groups and weren't averse to using the traditional word—coven—to describe themselves. I nodded for her to continue.

"We recently tried—" she halted, then sighed and began again. "We—made a mistake. We wanted to summon a benevolent spirit to cleanse and purify a former crack house over on Cooke Street."

I felt my eyebrows lift. "Okay."

"A local housing co-op for at-risk youth bought the place after the police cleaned out the dealers, and the city put it up for tax sale. Blanche—one of my sisters— knows the coordinator and offered our help to freshen up the place. We helped them clean and paint and put down new floors, and then we thought this ritual would be the finishing touch."

I have to admit, inside I was laughing at Oliver. He was afraid of an urban witch who helped create safe homes for at-risk youth? But I didn't let my amusement show on my face. It was clear from Honore's voice that the bad part of the story was still to come.

"What went wrong?"

She licked her lips. "The spirit that appeared in answer to the ritual—it wasn't benevolent. It was—" she swallowed and closed her eyes for a breath, "quite the opposite. It broke free of the summoning circle and attacked Chloe, then disappeared. She's still in the hospital." The smile from earlier was gone now, as if it had never been.

I didn't feel like laughing any more, either. "That's terrible. But can't you call it back, or banish it, or something? I don't know much about the Practice, but if you summoned it—"

The young witch shook her head. "Without Chloe, we're not strong enough. She was the ritual's keystone, and it's—well, it's complicated. It's not so easy to just stick someone in her place. I don't know how long she'll be in the hospital."

"Could you get someone else to help? Sort of— borrow a witch from another coven? You can't be the only ones in the city."

Honore's dark eyes looked tired. "We'd really like to fix this without too many other practitioners knowing. It won't be easy to convince someone to stand in the keystone position if they know what happened, either. It could be dangerous. We'd need someone very experienced, and there can be...friction, between covens."

I pulled a deep breath and sighed. "All right. But what do you want me to do? I can communicate with a lot of creatures, but I don't have any real ability beyond that. And I'm definitely not a practitioner."

The young witch nodded. "I know. We're hoping you can help track him down, because he's doing something to hide from us. I've been scrying him for two days now and all I get are glimpses, but he's gone before we can reach him."

I really didn't like the way this was going. "What do you plan to do if you find him? And by the way, you haven't told me what 'he' really is, yet."

"We think if we can find him and get close, we can put a geas on him until Chloe's better and we can send him back for good. But when we do get a read on him, we can't get there quickly enough. We thought you might do better at tracking him down, because you'll be able to identify him just by looking."

I stared at my slightly scarred and battered desk, thinking. "With enough information I might be able to," I admitted. I looked up and caught her gaze. "I mean, I have to know where to look. And you'll have to tell me everything before I agree."

Honore matched my sigh. "That's the tricky part," she said slowly. "It's—he's—we're pretty sure he's a demon. And it's only a matter of time before he starts doing what demons loose on Earth do."

I sat back in my chair as if she'd pushed me. "You mean killing people."

The young urban witch nodded, and her brown eyes reflected the fear I knew showed in my own.

After we'd arranged to meet with the rest of the coven the next day and Honore had left, I went out to reception to talk to Oliver. The lemony smell of cleanser scented the air, erasing the witch's sweet incense. That meant Oliver was scrubbing down the tiny kitchen area in the outer office, even though it was one of the few places in the office that was usually spotless. I sat in his chair behind the reception desk. He'd managed to get me to pay for a new chair a few weeks ago, and I realized now how much nicer it was than mine. I might have to do something about that with the funds from the witches' fees. I put my feet up on the desk. Usually Oliver hates that, but this time he didn't say a word. He didn't even look over at me.

"When you finish cleaning the coffee maker, you should put on another pot," I suggested as the hot water began bubbling and snorting and the sharp tang of vinegar filled the air. When Oliver cleans—especially if it's anxiety cleaning—he goes all out. He'd pushed up the sleeves of his charcoal turtleneck and everything. This was serious.

"Are you working for her?" he asked, neatly tying off a compost bag of used coffee grounds.

I noticed he said *you*, not *we*. Not a good sign.

"She seems very nice," I told him. "Her coven helps at-risk youth find safe places to live."

He eyed me silently over the coffee maker as the diluted vinegar and water perked its way through the inner workings, spiking the air. "So you *are* working for her. May I request a leave of absence?"

"Of course you may. And I'll consider it. But I think I might need your help with this one, Oliver."

He scrubbed vigorously at a spot—probably imaginary—on the tiny countertop for a moment, then turned and shook the cleaning cloth at me. "How many times have I asked to go along with you on a case?"

"Lots, and sometimes—"

"*Sometimes* you let me go. And now there's a case with a witch for a client—"

"To be precise, there are seven of them in the

coven—"

"So there's a case involving multiple witches— *witches*—and THIS is the one where you need my help?" He dropped the cloth and leaned back against the counter, crossing his arms and glaring at me.

I swallowed. "I'm sorry? Look, I know what happened to you was—"

"No." He held up a hand to stop me. "We're not talking about that."

I let my feet drop back to the floor, leaning forward in the chair and speaking quickly. "Okay. Here's the thing. They accidentally summoned a demon, and they need help to find him before he starts killing people. You and I—well, we're uniquely qualified to do that, aren't we?"

Oliver's glare turned into a disbelieving stare as his eyes went wide. "*Accidentally*? Summoned a demon?" He gave a short bark of laughter that held no real amusement. "How inept can they be?"

That made me squirm a little, because I'd had the same thought. But Honore Martel had seemed so earnest and troubled that I'd let it slide. "I know it sounds bad, but mistakes happen. Accidents happen. We don't have all the details yet. And I think the important thing here is: there's a demon loose."

Now Oliver turned away from me, deliberately staring at an empty chair in the waiting area. He opened his mouth and closed it again. "We haven't dealt with a demon before," he said finally.

I shook my head. "Closest I've ever come were those stories Nonna Pia used to tell." Our grandmother Olympia, for whom I'd named the agency, had passed on the dubious gift of communing with the supernatural, and she'd lived an interesting life herself because of it.

Oliver sighed. "And they were bad. Really bad." He met my gaze again, and I thought some of the anger had dissipated. "You really think they're 'good' witches?"

He didn't add *if such a thing really exists*, but I heard it in his tone. I shrugged. "They sound like it. I'll make you a promise, okay? They do anything, or we even hear of them doing anything, that makes you uncomfortable, you can walk away."

Oliver picked up the cleaning cloth from the counter and wordlessly wiped down the side of the coffee maker. It had stopped its muttering and sputtering, and the scent of warm vinegar filled the air. I had to admit it felt cleansing. But I was ready for it to smell like coffee again.

"Anything at all," I reiterated. "Just give it a try?"

"All right," he said finally. "I guess we're going demon hunting. I hate it when you're reasonable." And he threw the cloth at me.

I caught it and smiled. "I have my moments."

"And I have to go and get ready to talk to witches," he said in a grim voice. "I have some things to do, so you'll have to make your own coffee. I'll see you in the morning."

CHAPTER TWO

Oliver arrived for work late, which never happens. I let it slide, though, because I saw what he'd meant by "getting ready" to deal with witches. It threw me a little. He wore a light grey flight jacket I'd never seen before, with a row of colourful embroidered sigils running down the left side, over his heart to the hem. An amulet shaped like a stylized dog nestled under the collar of his turtleneck, suspended from a leather strip. And on the middle finger of his left hand a wide aluminum band glowed dully in the office lights.

I raised an eyebrow. "What's all this?"

"Protection," Oliver said briefly. "Did you bring anything for me?" "You don't think you need it."

I made a point of looking at his various "protections." "Well, I didn't, but now you're making me wonder. Are these for protection against the witches, or the demon?"

Oliver shrugged. "Both, I hope."

"I'm going after the demon, too."

He sighed. "True enough." He slipped the ring off his finger and held it out to me. "This might have been overkill, anyway. Just don't lose it."

The band was too big to fit anything but my thumb, but I slid it on. "What does it do?"

"Gives you a plus one to Constitution," he said with the first smile he'd offered all morning.

"Great, I'll make sure the DM knows I have it the next time I play Dungeons and Dragons."

"Makes you more difficult to injure with a physical attack," Oliver said, relenting. He touched the dog-shaped amulet at this throat. "But this one does the same thing. That's why I said maybe the ring was overkill."

"All right, let's put the *Back Soon* sign on the door and go talk to some witches," I said, and Oliver grimaced but followed me out of the office.

Honore Martel had given me an address over on Riverview Road, which turned out to be an older warehouse-type building with a small storefront on the street side. The sign on the facade read "Seven Sisters Health & Beauty", and the window displayed brightly-coloured creams and lotions, and pyramid stacks of soaps and bath bombs. Notes proclaimed that all the products were made on-site and used only "natural" ingredients.

I checked the address against Honore's, and it matched all right. "This must be the place," I told Oliver. "Not too sinister-looking, right?"

He gave me a look that served as an unprintable answer, and we pushed the door open and stepped inside. A tinkling chime announced our arrival.

The riot of scents hit us the moment the door opened: vanilla, lavender, coconut, patchouli, eucalyptus, and too many others to tease apart. Two women, one younger and one in her thirties, were busy creating an intricate and precariously balanced structure of tiny soaps, but looked up with smiles as we entered. Neither of them was Honore. White-painted shelves lined the shop walls, holding bottles and jars filled with colourful potions and creams. Bunches of drying herbs and flowers hung from the rafters, interspersed with sparkling crystals that caught the morning light and tossed rainbows around the room.

"Is Honore around?" I asked one of the women.

She had flawless skin the colour of my darkest-ever tan and a smile that felt like the sun coming out. She brushed soap residue on her bright yellow apron and came forward to shake my hand. Her grip was brief but friendly and confident, and a lemon-vanilla scent wafted with her.

"She's in the wardroom," she said, offering Oliver her hand in turn. "I'm Sasha, and this is Gennai. I'll take you to Honore."

Despite whatever might be happening in Oliver's mind and heart, he shook Shasha's hand with good grace and no hesitation. The other woman lifted a hand in greeting but didn't take the other off the half-finished soap stack. We followed Sasha through a narrow door at the back of the shop and I gave Oliver an encouraging smile. He offered me a glare in return and I guessed he hadn't felt quite the same warmth from Sasha as I had. But then I'm a sucker for vanilla.

The room we entered resembled an industrial kitchen, lined with oversized appliances and stainless-steel shelving. The cozy hominess of the outer shop was replaced by a feeling of brisk efficiency. This impression was helped along by the three women— presumably three more of Honore's coven—who moved around in the room. A short, thick-waisted woman with her silver-threaded hair tied back in a Hello Kitty bandanna stirred a rich-scented mixture bubbling in an enormous pot on the stove. A slim woman with blond-highlighted hair and more piercings than I could count looked up from measuring ingredients into an array of multicoloured ramekins precisely lined up on the counter. She smiled and nodded as we followed Sasha through the kitchen. The third woman, taller than Oliver and made even taller by the gloriously messy pile of auburn hair piled atop her head, left the notebook she'd been writing in and joined us.

"I'm Jo," she said in a warm, husky voice with a slight accent I couldn't quite place. "You're the detectives?"

"Yes," I told her. "I hope we'll be able to help out."

"So do I," she said, worry lines crinkling around her eyes.

Another door led out of the kitchen and we finally arrived in the wardroom. I hadn't been sure what the term meant, although as I stepped inside I realized this was where the coven did their actual magic. It permeated the room, and my supernatural sense picked up overlays of bright, multicoloured auras tracing the walls, floors, and every surface. It was so strong it manifested as a scent as well, similar to the storefront but underlaid with metallic and earthen notes. Oliver hesitated on the threshold and then stepped inside. I saw his hands clench into fists and release a couple of times, so his senses must be jangling, too.

"Just breathe," I whispered to him. "It's going to be fine."

"It may be fine, but no place like this is *safe*," Oliver hissed back.

This room was larger than the kitchen, probably taking up two-thirds of the warehouse area. Brick walls and a soaring ceiling studded with hanging light fixtures defined the space. A huge, beautifully intricate mandala mosaic filled the centre of the floor with a riot of colourful ceramic and glass shards—no clichéd pentacles for these women, apparently. The circle's bright design was marred by one long streak of black, like soot or grease, running from the centre to one side. A long credenza sat against one wall, holding two laptops and a couple of tablets with dangling charging cords. Drying herbs and flowers festooned the far wall, adding to the rich floral and spicy entanglement of aromas. Someone had pinned botanical drawings chalked in a firm but sure hand to the wall above the credenza.

My nose was just registering something amiss, a dank chemical odor that felt wrong, when Honore rose from a seat at a long, boardroom-style table to our left, and came forward with a smile. She shook my hand but didn't offer hers to Oliver, favouring him with a smile and a nod instead. She obviously remembered his reaction to her in my office.

"Thank you so much for coming," she said. She hissed a long exhale out between her teeth, opening her arms to encompass the room. "This is where it happened."

I nodded toward the mandala. "I guess that's the explanation for the mark over there?"

Her bright eyes darkened as her brows drew down. She nodded, biting her lower lip, then led us over to the circle, stopping just outside the edge.

"We were at our usual stations around the edge for the summoning. Chloe stood there." Honore pointed to the spot outside the rim of the circle where the dark streak ended in an ugly blotch, as if someone had dropped a pouch of gunpowder and it had burst on contact.

Measuring with my eyes, I thought the mandala must be about twenty feet across. The central design spiraled out to seven distinct mosaic rosettes spaced evenly around the circle's edge. I imagined the seven witches standing, each on a rosette, around the perimeter of the mandala to perform their rites. Some eight feet separated one rosette from the next. The thing was enormous. I wrenched my attention back to Honore.

"We finished the incantation, and the demon appeared in the inner circle," she said, now stepping into the mandala and walking to the centre. I followed her, cautiously avoiding the sooty streak marring the colours. Oliver didn't follow us.

I knelt to brush fingertips across the intricate surface. The main area of the floor was poured and polished concrete, and the mosaic had been inset. It felt cool to the touch. There was, indeed, an inner circle about three feet across, scribed by three concentric lines; one white, one black, and one green. Honore knelt beside me.

"It—he—shouldn't have been able to cross these three lines, let alone leave the mandala," she said. "I still don't understand what happened." "And he went straight for Chloe?"

Honore pointed to the black mar across the circle. "As you can see. As the keystone, she should have been the best-protected of all of us."

I pursed my lips, thinking. "What else can you tell us about the summoning?"

Honore stood, not meeting my eyes. "I can't disclose particulars to someone not of the Practice."

"No, of course not." I stood, too. "I meant in general. Did it go smoothly? Did anything unusual happen, during the ritual, or before it?"

"Chloe said her battery was low," Jo said in her husky voice from the other side of the room.

the credenza. This one wasn't plugged in, and I crossed to her. The tablet's screen was marred by a spiderweb crack, as if a bullet had struck it in the centre. She turned it over, so I could see its back also bore a sooty black scar.

"I'm not...you use electronic tablets in your rituals?"

Jo smiled. "We're a very modern coven, Acacia."

I felt a little off-balance. "Okay, but I'm still not sure..."

Jo shrugged. "The Practicing community is pretty strong on the Internet. We share spells, rituals, plan events. We source ingredients for the shop and our rites."

Honore joined us, and even Oliver had unbent enough—or his curiosity finally got the better of him once technology was involved—to peer over my shoulder at the ruined tablet.

"We also draw some of the energy for rituals this way," Honore said. Jo shot her a glance, but the other woman shrugged. "They have to know at least a little bit to be able to help us."

Jo sighed. "I suppose."

"Witches have always drawn most of what you

might call our 'spell energy' from our own reserves, and our connection to the world around us," Honore explained. "And, I won't deny it, some darker Practitioners have tapped into the energy of other people, willing or not."

I felt Oliver twitch behind me, and then go very, very still.

"That's the dark side of the Practice; we don't approve of it or practice in that way," Jo said, her voice solemn.

Honore smiled, breaking a tension that had formed, invisibly, around us. "But the Internet is what you might call a gold mine of excess energy."

"How so?" Oliver asked. I was surprised to hear him speak, and his voice sounded calm.

"So many people pouring their energy into so many things on the Internet," Jo said. "Sometimes more energy than is actually needed to accomplish what they want to do. So much passion, so much enthusiasm! Think about it. The energy you can tap into from cat videos alone..." She grinned.

For a heartbeat I thought she was joking, but I realized she meant it. Oliver stepped around beside me and held out a hand for the tablet. Jo passed it to him and he turned it over in his hands. He ran a thoughtful finger over the cracked screen.

"So at least some portion of your spells run on Internet energy," he mused. "That could be significant."

I turned to him with a frown. "What do you mean?"

He looked up and met my eyes. "There's a lot of dark stuff on the Internet."

"You think they tapped into—what? A virus or something?"

"Or something. Maybe." Oliver turned to Honore, addressing her directly for the first time. "You don't have to go into detail about your ritual, just describe what happened when things went wrong."

She looked down at the mandala for a moment, as if gathering her thoughts. "We finished the summoning, and the spirit began to coalesce inside the inner circle. At that point, Chloe was about to instruct him on what we wanted him to do, the parameters of the geas—"

"That basically means the boundaries the summoned spirit has to operate within," Jo interjected.

I nodded and Honore continued. "And how long we would keep him on this plane. But she didn't get that far." Sudden tears glistened in Honore's eyes. "There was a terrible smell—that's what I noticed first—the first clue that something was wrong. As he formed more fully, I realized we had the wrong kind of spirit. And then he just *looked* at Chloe. Caught her eyes when she glanced up from her tablet. She seemed sort of— frozen. And then he moved toward her so fast. It was just a streak, almost too quick to see."

"He just—collided with her." Jo took up the story.

"I heard the tablet crack—she dropped it, but I heard

the crack before it hit the floor. A flash of light so bright I closed my eyes without thinking about it. When I opened them, Chloe was unconscious on the floor, and the demon was gone."

"Can we speak to Chloe?" I asked. "How is she doing?"

Honore and Jo shared a glance, and Honore shook her head. "I don't think she should have visitors just yet. This was a really terrible experience for her."

"All right. And you're sure he's still here? Like, on this plane?" I asked. It sounded as if no-one had seen the demon leave the wardroom. "Maybe when it broke the circle, that negated the summoning. Is it possible the bright light was the demon being—I don't know, sucked back to its original plane of existence?"

Honore gave a soft, humourless chuckle. "I wish I could believe that. But remember, our scrying has located him here, in the city. He simply disappears before we can get to where we find him. No, I'm afraid he's definitely here."

"Right. Okay." I looked at Oliver, wondering if he had any more questions, but he was staring down at the tablet he still held. He'd picked another one up off the credenza and seemed to be comparing the two devices. "Well, we'll see what we can do. I don't suppose you have description of him?"

Honore and Jo looked at each other, then shook their heads. "It all happened so fast," Jo said. "He'd barely fully apparated before he moved. And after all, he's a demon. He can change his appearance every day if he wants."

"Oh, right." I nodded as if this wasn't new information to me.

"But you should be able to sense him if you get near enough, isn't that right?" Honore asked me anxiously. "I thought that was sort of your thing."

"Sure, it is," I reassured her. It was true, Oliver and I could both sense supernatural creatures in our vicinity, even those other humans couldn't see, hear, or sense. We'd know the demon when we saw him, although I didn't know precisely what would tip us off. I'd recently worked for a vampire—her tell was a coppery taste like blood in the back of my throat and a shadow over like like a great pair of wings. All supernaturals had something. But although ours was a small city, it was still a city. It definitely would have helped to have a description of who we'd be hunting.

"All right, I guess that's all we need for now. We'll let you both get back to work. We'll be in touch."

Outside the front door of Seven Sisters Health & Beauty, I took a deep lungful of fresh autumn air. Well, city air, but at least it was outdoors. The heavily scented interior of the warehouse had seemed pleasant at first, but began to cloy after a while, particularly when the scents of magic and a demonic presence had entered the mix.

I turned to Oliver. "Well, what do you think?"
"Witches," he snorted. "Find a witch, find trouble."

And he stalked off toward the car. I followed him. I sort of had to agree.

Back at the office of Olympia Investigations, I sat behind my desk and opened my laptop while Oliver set coffee brewing. The mouth-watering scent helped clear the last of the warehouse smells from my nose, including the dank aroma of the demon. "Maybe we should borrow a dog and see if we could track the demon by scent," I called to Oliver out in reception.

He came in with two steaming mugs. "I don't know how you'd get a dog to zero in on the demon smell, though," he said. "Too much competition in that warehouse."

I took my coffee and sipped it. Heaven. "I was half-joking," I told him. "I don't know anything about dogs." Oliver left my office and came back with his own laptop under his arm. He set it on the opposite side of my desk and opened it, then pulled one of the big blue armchairs closer to my desk and sat. "I actually have a friend who breeds beagles," he said. "But I'd rather not draw her into this."

I looked at him speculatively for a moment. I knew nothing of this friend. Now wasn't the time to delve into Oliver's personal life, though. "All right. How do we tackle this?"

Oliver leaned back in his chair and cradled his coffee mug in both hands. "Roaming around the city hoping to stumble across him seems ineffective. It's not like we have long-range radar to find him—we have to at least get close first. I was thinking we should look online and research the accumulated wisdom on demons. What they like, where they go, what they do when they're on this plane."

"Yeah, that doesn't sound like an Internet rabbit hole at all. Also, I'm not keen on becoming an expert on demonic pastimes."

"I think if we stick to the 'official' channels the witches use, we'll be more likely to find something useful."

"And we find those, how?"

Oliver grinned. "One of those working tablets might have turned on when I picked it up. And I might have noticed a few things on it while the witches were explaining what happened at the summoning."

My mouth dropped open a bit and I felt my eyes go wide. "You went behind our clients' backs? You snooped on their tablet?"

Oliver shrugged. "It wasn't even password protected. Witches are secretive about the Practice, but how are we supposed to help them if they keep us in the dark?" He sketched an "x" over the left side of his chest with an index finger. "I promise I won't be drawn into the dark side of witchcraft."

"But what about me? What if I succumb to the lure of Dark Practice?"

"Some might argue you're already a witch, or some word that's very similar," Oliver said with a grin. "Now, type in this URL and let's get to work."

Half an hour and a second cup of coffee later, Oliver said, "Huh."

I looked up. "What?" We'd accessed a lot of Practitioner web pages, chat rooms, and article repositories from the starting points Oliver had collected, but hadn't found a whole lot yet that I thought would help us track down the demon. I was learning a lot more about modern witchcraft than I'd previously known, however. I was seriously considering asking for a charm to keep socks from slipping and underwear from riding up as part of the payment for this case. Who knew such wonders existed?

Oliver tapped a finger against his lips. "I wonder if Chloe might have been keeping secrets from her coven sisters?"

"What do you mean?"

Oliver read from the screen. "A minimum of six months should be allowed to pass between summonings where a Practitioner stands in the keystone position. Binding entanglements between Practitioner and Summoned Spirit may persist this long, making it impossible for the Practitioner to summon any other spirit successfully. Stronger spirits may even exploit these connections and appear instead of an intended spirit, endangering the Practitioner and causing unpredictable results."

"Hmm." I mulled that over. "So you're thinking if Chloe had summoned *this* demon before, sometime in the last six months, her connection to him might have pulled him in by mistake."

"I'd say the results qualify as 'unpredictable.' And the other witches might not have known she had that connection. I wonder how long she's been a part of this coven?"

"Or," I continued to muse, "it might not have been a mistake. Chloe should have known about the six- month waiting period. I mean, if we could find this information in half an hour, she must have known."

Oliver nodded. "Yeah. Maybe she meant to summon this guy all along."

"But why would she do that? And not tell the others? And why would he attack her immediately?"

"I don't know. But maybe we need to talk to Chloe."

I pursed my lips. "And the other witches didn't seem to want us to do that."

Oliver met my eyes. There was a bit of a challenge in them, I thought. "Do we do it anyway?"

I nodded. "I think maybe we do."

chapter three

There was only one major medical centre in our small city, supported by a few walk-in clinics, so it wasn't hard to figure out where Chloe would be. I didn't want to alert Honore and the others that we planned to go talk to their coven sister, but Oliver looked up the business information listing for Seven Sisters Health & Beauty and found Chloe's full name on the list of partners. I tease Oliver a lot, but he's darn good at ferreting out information, and he knows where to look for things.

We pushed through the doors of Healing Sisters Hospital, grateful to leave the chill wind of the parking lot behind, and stopped at the front desk. Oliver carried a spray of lavender and pot marigolds, both known for their healing properties. Our thinking was that we might as well put our best foot forward with the injured witch. I asked the receptionist where we might find Chloe August, and she looked up a room number on her computer screen. We headed for the elevator to the fourth floor.

"That was easy," I said to Oliver as we glided upwards in the metal box. "Now, as long as none of the other witches are here..."

"They were all at the warehouse earlier," Oliver said. "They're probably shorthanded without her, so they won't be visiting around the clock."

We went unchallenged in the hospital hallways, since this was the middle of afternoon visiting hours and the corridors bustled with medical staff and other visitors. The door to Chloe's room stood slightly ajar as we approached, and all was quiet within. Without knocking, I pushed it open enough to see inside. A woman with tangled, sweat-dampened blonde hair lay on the single, white-sheeted bed, apparently asleep. The room appeared empty of anyone else, so Oliver and I moved quietly inside.

As I got a better look at Chloe August, I saw more of the results of the summoning-gone-wrong. Her left hand, presumably the one in which she'd been holding the tablet, was heavily bandaged. Her face looked bruised, particularly underneath her closed eyes, as if she'd been in a fistfight and emerged with two shiners. Another large, square bandage covered her forehead, held in place with transparent medical tape. Her breathing rasped in and out, catchy and uneven, not the smooth breaths of a sound sleeper. A monitor beeped softly and rhythmically in the background.

I put a tentative hand out to touch her, but before I made contact she mumbled something I couldn't hear, and jerked her head to the side. I jumped back, startled, bumping into Oliver who almost dropped the flowers.

"Geez, Acacia," he whispered. "Who's the one afraid of witches, here?" He set the flowers on the small stand next to the bed.

I ignored him and collected myself, then put a hand on Chloe's arm. Her skin felt feverish and damp. "Chloe?" I said in a quiet voice. "We'd like to ask you some questions about your...accident."

I expected Chloe's eyes to flutter open, but she didn't appear to wake. Instead, she twitched her arm away from my touch as if it burned her, and threw her head to the other side.

She muttered something, a single syllable. Almost "no," but accented somehow. When she repeated it, I realized it was "*Non.*" 'No,' but in French. She spoke again, but her words were too low and quick for me to catch. I glanced at Oliver.

"What did she say? You've still got your French from high school, right?"

Oliver raised both eyebrows at me. "Wow, you don't expect much. I can still read some French, but catching it in conversation is a lot trickier. I might pick up a word or two—"

"Then come closer and see if you can get anything

she says!"

Obediently, although with a huff of annoyance, Oliver stepped up beside me and leaned closer to Chloe. Whatever she'd said a few seconds ago, she repeated, although with more agitation. At least it sounded the same to me. I looked the question at Oliver. He grimaced.

"...*ne me contrôleras pas...*" he said. "I think. Something about 'won't control me,' or maybe 'don't control me.'"

"She might mean the demon," I whispered.

Oliver shrugged and leaned over Chloe again. Her right hand had moved to pluck lightly at the tape securing an IV tube in the back of her left. "*L'enlever,*" she whispered. "*L'enlever.*"

"I think she wants the IV out?" Oliver said doubtfully. "She might not be talking about the demon at all. Maybe she doesn't like all this medical intrusion."

I put a gentle hand on her fretful one and guided it away from the IV tape. If she was going to pull that thing out, I didn't want to be here for it. I had visions of fountaining spurts of blood, although I knew that was probably overdramatic. The beeping monitor had increased its cadence, and the insistent sound was making me feel oddly nauseated. I tried again to get through to her, raising my voice slightly.

"Chloe, I'm trying to help Honore and your sisters. Can you tell me anything about why the summoning went wrong?"

This time the reaction was swift. She stiffened, and then her right hand swung in an arc across her body, her palm catching me squarely on the cheek with a sharp slap. "*Sortez!*" she hissed. "*Sortez!* Get out!" Her eyes remained closed, but the malevolence in her words hit me like a second slap. She lifted both hands and began twisting them in arcane gestures, intoning words I couldn't parse. This was no longer French, but something older, stranger, and infused with an almost tangible power.

I was still in shock from the slap, but I felt Oliver grab my upper arms and pull me back from the bedside. "She's casting a spell! We have to get out of here."

He'd begun to propel me toward the door, but I recovered my senses and made it there without his urging. It didn't take Oliver's paranoia to know that a barely-conscious witch casting an unknown spell was not something to stick around for. I had a thought that she might not be able to cast successfully with her bandaged hand, but it wasn't worth the risk to stay and find out. We slipped back into the hall and pulled the door almost shut, trying to appear casual as we stepped away.

A crash—or maybe a small explosion—came from the room behind us. With a glance at each other we quickened our pace. Then the scream emerged from Chloe's room, a thin, high-pitched wail that soared over hallway chatter and beeping medical devices. A nurse emerged from a station further up the hall and hurried toward Chloe's room as we stopped and stared around like everyone else for camouflage. Once the nurse had passed us, we beelined for the stairwell, not willing to wait for the elevator.

I felt like I didn't start breathing again until we opened the doors and the chill wind hit my face. I turned to Oliver. His skin was so ashen I almost made him go back into the hospital. But as I looked at him, he reached up and touched the amulet around his neck, and it seemed to calm him. I rubbed a finger across the ring he'd loaned me, wishing it would make me feel better.

"What the heck just happened?" I demanded.

Oliver shook his head. "No idea. But I think I know why the witches didn't want us to come and see her." We walked briskly toward the car, which we'd had to leave at the very end of the parking lot. There never seemed to be an empty space near the doors unless you arrived at 5 a.m.

I put a hand to my cheek, where the witch's slap still burned. I could practically feel where her fingers had made long, red imprints on my skin. "We still need more information. And I have a feeling the six other sisters have been as forthcoming as they're likely to be unless we press them."

Oliver opened his mouth to say something, but the words didn't make it out. He felt it at the same time I did, and we both stopped walking despite the desire to get out of the cold. We should have kept moving, but the sensations were too strong to ignore. A strong chemical smell like smoldering plastic itched in my nose, accompanied by a ripple of ominously dark energy.

The presence of the demon.

I shot a hand out as unobtrusively as I could and caught the sleeve of Oliver's flight jacket before he could react. "Don't move," I hissed. "Don't look around. We don't want him to know he's been spotted, right? Pretend we just stopped to talk."

Oliver hitched a deep breath. "Right. In the middle of a freezing parking lot. That'll be believable."

"It'll just be for a minute while we figure out what to do."

"I assume you have the witches on speed dial?"

I twisted a rueful half-smile. "Didn't think I needed to do that just yet, since we hadn't even started searching," I said. "But I can try to call Honore. I'll do it casually. We'll have to play this by ear and see what he's up to. Try to look like we're just carrying on our conversation before we part ways."

Oliver patted my hand as if I'd been holding his arm in a comforting way. "Yes. We just came out from visiting a family member in the hospital, and we're talking about them. Okay, where do you think the demon is? Can you see him?"

The hospital was behind me, so I scanned the parking lot beyond Oliver and to both sides, as far as I could with my peripheral vision. "Nobody moving in the lot as far as I can see."

Oliver was half-turned sideways to the hospital. "There's a couple on a bench—the woman is in a hospital gown and the guy is having a cigarette. I'm pretty sure they were there when we walked out, and I didn't sense anything. There's a nurse walking toward her car, talking on a cell phone. That's all I see in this direction."

"Okay. I'm going to keep talking to you and just turn casually to see the other side..." I did so, and spotted a lone man walking toward the hospital's front doors. I glanced away quickly, looking back at Oliver's face. I smiled and nodded as if he'd just said something encouraging. "Bingo. He's headed into the hospital," I hissed between my teeth. "Dark hair, denim jacket, cowboy boots. I mean, that seems so stereotypical for a demon, somehow."

Oliver smiled but didn't laugh. "Think he's trying to get to Chloe?"

I shoved my hands in my pockets and shrugged. "I don't know why else he'd be here." I pulled out my cell phone and scrolled through numbers, tapping the one for Honore when I found it. I put the phone to my ear and the wide ring on my thumb clinked against the case. It was an oddly comforting reminder of Oliver's "precautions."

"Is it ringing?" Oliver asked. "I feel like I have a bull's-eye painted on my back. He must be looking straight at us."

"Calm down, people stand around outside and talk all the time, and I don't want to make it obvious that I'm turning to look at him again," I told him, but I was willing Honore to answer her phone quickly.

"Did he go inside yet? Just glance over."

I risked it. The man had stopped just before the entrance doors and stood staring straight at us. The burning plastic smell hadn't left the air, and now I saw that his face was limned with reddish light, as if a penlight with a coloured filter illuminated it. Scattered, shifting runnels of black traced his skin. I assumed these weren't visible to other humans, or it would have drawn some reaction from the couple near the hospital doors.

I half-smiled and looked back to Oliver. "Shit, he's looking this way. Do not look over there."

"The guy on the bench just butted out his cigarette and he and the woman are heading back inside," Oliver observed. "The nurse just got in her car."

I heard the engine turn over, and seconds later the crunch of wheels on gravel. Unless someone else appeared, we were about to be alone in the parking lot with the demon. And he seemed unusually interested in us.

"Hello?" Honore's voice on the phone was the best thing I'd ever heard.

"We're at the hospital," I said, smiling and nodding at Oliver, "outside, in the parking lot. I think your guy is here."

"*Mon Dieu*," she whispered. "Is he after Chloe?"

"Well I don't think he's here for bloodwork," I said tightly. "Can you get here fast?"

The reassuring words I was hoping for didn't come. Instead there was a silence that seemed far too long. "I'm not with the others right now," Honore said finally. "I'll come, and I'll contact them. But I don't know how long—"

Oliver suddenly grabbed my shoulders and pushed me down behind the little grey hatchback we'd been standing beside. He hit the pavement beside me with a grunt and I felt the prickle of magic pass over our heads. The hair on the back of my neck stood up. I smelled the ozone scent of a nearby lightning strike, although nothing seemed to blow up. It was followed by an oily, dark redolence that nearly made me cough. The smell of the demon's magic.

"What the hell?" I started, but Oliver cut me off.

"I glanced over and saw him lift his arm toward us like he was going to do something. I just knew it couldn't be good," he gasped. "Shit! Are they coming?" I'd dropped my phone, and I scrabbled for it on the pavement. The screen flicked to life, but the call was gone. "She's coming," I told Oliver. "Honore's coming. We just have to—"

"Hold out till she gets here?" Oliver finished. "Geez, that sounds like something out of a bad western."

"Shh." I strained to listen for footsteps, gauge where the demon was now. I got to a squat and raised my phone to the car's side window, pressing the buttons to take a quick picture. I studied the image on the screen. Although it was blurry, taken through the windows on either side of the car, I could make out the hospital doors and the figure standing in front of them. "Okay, he's not coming after us," I said. "That's good."

"Maybe he's trying to warn us off," Oliver said. "Doesn't want to draw too much attention to himself. How does he know we recognize him?"

"No idea. Maybe he doesn't. Let's move a bit, just in case." Keeping low, I scuttled to the front end of the grey car and eased around the back of a truck next to it, calculating that the demon didn't have line of sight from the hospital doors. Oliver followed me. I crossed the short distance to the next row of cars and moved another row back next to a dark blue sedan, still confident we were out of sight.

I felt another frisson of *something* in the air, although it wasn't as close this time. I ducked and hunched my shoulders involuntarily. Oliver swore.

Two rows away, the grey car exploded.

chapter four

I don't carry weapons. That might seem odd, in my line of work, but honestly, violence just doesn't happen to or around me personally all that often. I usually come into a case *after* the violence, if any is involved, has already happened. Truthfully, I like it that way. Weapons usually only serve to complicate matters.

But when the car exploded, I felt like I wouldn't have minded that little complication.

I didn't scream, although Oliver let out a yelp that turned into a whimper he quickly stifled. We both threw our arms over our heads against the rain of shrapnel peppering the cars and pavement around us. "Hey!" A man's voice sounded from the other side

of the parking lot, and I heard advancing footsteps. I chanced a look over the hood of the car and saw a tall, sandy-haired man in a brown leather jacket making his way through the parking lot toward the hospital. I almost called out to him to be careful, but I realized he was taking care to stay behind the cover of the cars as he moved. He pulled down the zipper of his coat and yanked a handgun from a chest holster.

I didn't think he'd seen me, with his eyes glued to the front of the hospital. I peered through the windows and saw the demon still standing there. This was the first chance I'd had to really study him. His black hair slicked back from a widow's peak above that pale, black-traced skin. His face was narrow, the chin almost pointed. His legs and arms seemed just slightly too long—something you might overlook unless you were really looking for it. No-one else had left the hospital, which was weird, since it was a busy place. Although I suppose an explosion in the parking lot might encourage folks to stay inside.

As I watched, the demon raised a hand toward the man.

"Watch out!" I yelled as soon as I saw the motion.

"Get down!"

Although the sudden sound of my voice might have startled him, the guy hit the ground without delay. Nothing exploded, but the ozone smell came again, stronger this time. I realized with a sinking feeling that I'd probably just given our new position away to the demon.

"You all right?" the newcomer called, and I assumed he was talking to me.

"So far, so good," I answered. "Just get down if he moves."

The wail of distant sirens reached us then, and closer, I heard the crunch of tires as a car pulled into the driveway. I risked another look and saw an older- model green hatchback edge cautiously into the lot. I could just make out Honore's face behind the wheel, and she'd brought one of the other witches with her. I sagged against the side of the sedan. "Cavalry's here," I told Oliver.

"I'm not relaxing just yet," he said. "Who's our other friend?"

"No idea, but he's got a gun," I said. "I'm assuming undercover cop. Or just off-duty, maybe."

Oliver frowned. "That's not great. Cops like explanations for things."

He had a point, but I didn't see much sense in worrying about that yet.

"Police," the tall man called to the demon, confirming my suspicion. "Stay where you are."

I half-stood so I could see what was happening. The cop had his gun trained on the hospital doors, which I'm sure wasn't the most comfortable position to be in. The demon stared at him, apparently unfazed, but his head whipped toward the witches when Honore opened her door. I saw Jo emerge from the passenger side. She held a short canister in one hand and a tablet in the other. A crystal on a cord around her neck reflected prismatic colours in the watery autumn sunlight.

"Ladies, please return to your vehicle," the cop

called. "We have a potentially dangerous situation here."

Honore and Jo ignored him. Honore raised her own tablet and began to intone something that buzzed in my ears like a nearby bee, but I couldn't make out words. Flickers of magic aura danced in the frigid air around her.

The demon hissed, and I glanced back to him to see him bare sharp, white teeth before he turned and sprinted away in the direction he'd come from.

"Hey! Stop!" the cop yelled, and he started after the demon, even though I was sure he could see just as well as I could that it would be futile. The demon moved with—well, *inhuman* speed, and the cop would have to weave through multiple rows of cars before he could even really start running. I could have told him that, but odds were he wasn't going to listen to me. He dashed past us without a glance in our direction.

I stood up straight and Honore and Jo headed for me. "Acacia, are you all right?" Honore asked.

Oliver got to his feet then, brushing futilely at the mud and friction burns on his previously immaculate clothes. The grey flight jacket seemed to have escaped damage, but the knees of his khakis were a ruin.

"We're fine," I said before he could start to complain. "We think he must have intended to get in and see Chloe."

"Is that what you were doing here?" Jo asked in an icy voice. Belatedly I remembered they'd asked us to leave Chloe alone for now. Well, it was too late to do anything but brazen it out.

"Yes. We needed more information, so we stopped in to see how she was doing. We had no intention of bothering her if she wasn't up to it," I added defiantly.

"And was she? Up to it?" Honore asked. Her tone wasn't quite as chilly as Jo's, but it wasn't what you'd call warm, either.

"She seemed agitated," I said truthfully. "And she might have tried to cast a spell at us."

Jo's eyes widened. "She was conscious?"

"Not exactly." I was in the middle of explaining what had happened when the tall cop returned. He was speaking on a cell phone and he really didn't look happy. The distant sirens continued to grow closer, their wails fading in and out oddly through the surrounding buildings.

Jo slid the canister into her pocket. It looked to me like pepper spray, although unfamiliar sigils glowed faintly blue along the sides of the metal.

The cop ended his call and said to the four of us in general, "Would someone like to tell me what happened here?"

What was left of the grey car burned merrily, sending black smoke blooming above the parking lot, and the sirens had drawn a lot closer. I really, really wanted us all out of there before things got more awkward.

"I don't know," I said, putting as much frightened innocence into my voice as I could. "My cousin and I were just leaving the hospital when that guy started acting crazy. I think he must have shot the engine of that car or something. We were just trying to stay out of his way. Maybe someone inside saw something more."

The cop had nice grey eyes, but they regarded me with more than a little skepticism.

"Do I know you?" he asked. He looked from me to Oliver as if rifling through some internal memory storage.

"I don't think so," I said cautiously.

He turned to Honore and Jo. "You ladies all right?" He must have been too focused on the demon to have noticed the part the witches had played in the creature's sudden withdrawal.

Honore nodded and put on an innocent face. I noticed her French-Canadian accent became more pronounced. "Officer, this is frightening. What happened to that car?"

The fire truck pulled into the parking lot just then, killed the siren, and wove its way toward the burning car. "Do you need us to make a statement or something?" I asked. "Not that we saw much, but we could do that."

The cop looked at the approaching fire truck. I knew he'd have to go talk to the firefighters, too. "Give me your names, please," he said, calling up a notebook app on his phone. "Go into the station later today, or tomorrow at the latest, and just give your statements there, all right?" He took down names for all four of us, and phone numbers, too. I gave him the office number, and Oliver looked daggers at me because that left him having to give his cell number or raise uncomfortable questions about why we shared a number.

People opened the door of the hospital now and peered out, cautious and curious. I knew the officer was seeing multiple things he should be doing to control the crowd until another squad car arrived. The urgent wail of another siren drew steadily closer, so I knew that wouldn't be long. "Thanks, officer, we will. What's your name, by the way?"

I don't know what I asked him that; I didn't really need it. It just came out. Might have been those grey eyes. I thought they'd be nice if they weren't looking at me with such an unnerving level of suspicion.

"Detective Ames," he said. "Ellis Ames. Please don't forget to go in."

"We won't," I promised, and I thought I heard Oliver stifle a snort beside me. With a final dissatisfied glance over us, Detective Ames headed for the firefighters and the crowd outside the hospital door.

"Will you stop by the shop later?" Honore asked. "We should talk about this with the others."

I'd been thinking the same thing, so we set a time and the witches climbed back into their car, reversing out of the lot past an incoming squad car.

"We won't," Oliver mimicked in a ridiculous falsetto that sounded nothing like my voice.

"Oh, stop it," I said. "I was trying to throw him off the scent. The last thing we need are normal cops poking around in this and cluelessly taking on a demon. That was super bad timing, him showing up when he did."

"Tell me about it," Oliver said, "although he did provide a distraction. The demon had to split his attention between us and the good detective."

I said nothing as we finally hurried to the car and climbed inside out of the wind. I was wondering why the detective hadn't asked how, if we hadn't seen anything, I'd known to warn him when the demon threw—whatever it was, at him. Further up the parking lot, the firefighters had the car fire mostly under control, and police officers worked to keep back a growing crowd.

"So, what's next?" Oliver asked, after he'd buckled his seatbelt and sat waiting for me to start the car. "Back to the Internet to research best practices for confronting malevolent demons? I feel like that was a gap in our research earlier."

I stared at his fingers, nervously and repeatedly tracing the contours of the dog amulet. "What about your friend? Could she—or he—help us? I'd love to talk with someone who knows about the Practice before we meet with our clients again. Instead of relying on what we can dig up online."

"What friend?" Then he realized I was staring at

the amulet and began to shake his head. His fingers closed over the talisman, hiding it from sight. "Oh, no. We're not involving him in this any more than he already is."

"I just want to talk to him. If he had all this magical stuff," I waved my thumb with the wide protection ring on it in front of Oliver's eyes, "he can probably help us more than a dozen Practice chat rooms."

"No."

"Look, he doesn't have to get involved in the case. This will just be him talking to us, answering a few questions. Helping us figure out what's going on and what to do next."

Oliver glared at me. "Acacia, is there any part of my life that can stay private while I'm working for you?"

I turned the key in the ignition and reached over to pat his arm. "Of course there is. And I'll let you know as soon as I figure out what it is."

Oliver punished me for my insolence by refusing to tell me anything about where we were going or the witch we were going to meet until we reached our destination. We drove across town from the hospital and Oliver directed me to a street only a few blocks from the Olympia Investigations office. The area was mostly residential, but one of the houses had the intentionally uneven rooflines and mismatched windows of storybook architecture. It also sported a brightly painted sign mounted on the neat white fence bordering the road. Oliver pointed, and we pulled up in front of it and got out.

"*The Patient Frog*?" I read from the sign. In smaller letters underneath, it advertised *Metaphysical Provender*. I raised my eyebrows at Oliver.

"Don't be weird," he told me. "Remember who we are."

Well, he was right. Nothing should surprise me any more.

The barren stems of tall hollyhocks bowed along the path to the front door. A couple of months ago they would have been buzzing with bees, but now the seed pods rattled in the wind and only a few withered, curling leaves dotted the stalks. A second sign, on the door, proclaimed *Ring and Walk In*. Oliver pressed the button and a few muffled bars from the overture of *Wicked* sounded from inside. Oliver pushed open the door without waiting, and I followed him inside. We stood in what was probably a former living room but had been converted into shop space. Shelves lined the walls, overflowing with incense, oils, crystals, candles, polished stones, jewelry, plants, dried herbs, and assorted other occult paraphernalia. The bits of wall visible between shelves displayed multiple bright paint colours. A collection of small, mismatched tables scattered the room as well, as if frozen in place in the middle of a game of tag. Navigating this space in the dark would be nigh impossible. The room was as heavily scented as the coven's beauty shop had been, but it seemed both lighter and earthier. More essential, somehow.

And to my surprise, the space held a heavy infusion of magical energy just like the coven's wardroom, as if magic use was a common occurrence within these walls. Was Oliver's friend an actual *witch*? Or did he merely entertain a lot of Practitioner customers, who tried out charms, potions, and spells in the shop? I shot a sharp glance at Oliver, but he was studiously not looking at me.

A beaded curtain at the back of the room swished aside, and a man ducked through. He wasn't overly tall, about my height, with skin that might have been dark by way of genetics or a lifetime spent outdoors. His head was completely bald, and with his slightly protruding eyes, he did remind me a bit of a frog. I wondered distractedly if that's where the shop got its name. He was dressed in faded jeans and a tunic-style shirt striped in a marvelous assortment of bright colours.

"Oliver!" he called in a booming, friendly voice. "You're back! And you've finally brought Acacia to meet me, unless I'm sadly mistaken."

He deftly wove through the obstacle course of tables and shook Oliver's hand, then took one of mine in both of his. For his stature, his hands were huge, and mine was enveloped. His deep brown eyes were warm with evident delight as he said, "I'm so pleased to meet you, my dear. Oliver holds you in the highest regard. I'm

Robin."

"Acacia Sheridan," I responded automatically, then realized how ridiculous that was since he obviously knew who I was already. "It's nice to meet you, too. What a wonderful shop!" I knew that also sounded lame as soon as the words left my lips, but I was inwardly berating Oliver for not preparing me at all. Highest regard, my ass. I glanced at him and he offered me a smug smile. He was enjoying this.

But Robin sent a loving glance around the room.

"It is, isn't it? I enjoy what I do so much. Helping other people really is the most rewarding thing in life. But in your line of work, you understand that, too." He released my hand with another smile and turned to Oliver. "So, everything all right? You walked into the lion's den and emerged unscathed?"

There was a gentle note of teasing in his voice, but it was also a serious question. This man wasn't making fun of Oliver's fears. Then his gaze travelled down to Oliver's scuffed and muddied pants and my dirt- streaked jeans and his expression changed, turning grave.

Before he could ask anything else, Oliver shrugged. "It was fine. But we have some questions that Acacia thought you might be able to help with."

Okay, he was putting the responsibility for us being here squarely on me. That was fine. "I don't know how much Oliver has told you—"

But a frown had puckered Robin's forehead and he

put a hand up to hover next to my cheek. "And what's happened here?"

I touched my face automatically, realizing the marks of Chloe's fingers must not have faded completely yet—or perhaps a bruise was rising to mark the spot. "Oh, it's nothing. The witch who was hurt in the summoning—we tried to talk to her but she got a little freaked out. I don't think she even realized who I was—"

"Wait here," Robin commanded, and crossed to a shelf on the right-hand wall. He ran a finger along a row of small ointment pots, then selected one and brought it over to us, unscrewing the lid. He presented it to me. "You won't need much. Just lightly massage it in."

I swiped a bit of the pale pink cream onto my index finger and smoothed it over my cheek. It tingled on contact, then felt cool and soothing as I rubbed it into the mistreated skin. I realized with a start that the spot had been tender, aching slightly, although I'd been ignoring it with everything else that had happened. Now all the residual discomfort faded. I smiled. "Thank you! That feels wonderful!"

Robin tucked the small jar into my hand and closed my fingers around it. "The perfect remedy for small indignities, especially if there's malice behind them," he told me. "And don't even think about paying for it. A gift is a sacred thing."

I blinked and tucked the jar into my pocket. "All right, then thank you again. So this case we're on—"

"Tea!" Robin declared. "Tea absolutely must be the next order of business. Follow me through to the kitchen; it's a much more soothing atmosphere for the telling of distressing tales. We'll sit and have tea while you relate your experiences."

The man turned and vanished through the beaded curtain again. Oddly, I wasn't upset. If Oliver did that when I was trying to explain something to him, I'd be annoyed.

"Let's go," Oliver said. "Tea is a serious matter in this house." He followed Robin and I trailed after them. I admit I had a burning curiosity to see more of the place.

Beyond the curtained doorway, the house lost its occult trappings but none of its charm. We followed a wood-floored hallway past a cozy living room, where iron-railed stairs wound up one wall to the partial upper floor and presumably at least one bedroom. The downstairs hallway emerged into a yellow-walled kitchen with blue and white gingham curtains at the windows and an ancient-looking mahogany table at one end. Four mismatched but oddly complementary wooden chairs waited around it. At the other end of the room an actual cooking hearth sat inside a fieldstone surround. Space had been found for modern appliances, too, and Robin set a red enamel kettle on the stove as I walked in.

"Sit," he ordered genially, and Oliver complied, pulling out a chair at the table. I did the same. Hanging wire baskets held potatoes, onions, and other vegetables, and bunches of drying herbs tucked up near the beams of the vaulted ceiling. This was a kitchen in which someone actually *cooked*, and I thought of my well-used ancient microwave with a pang of guilt.

"All right," Robin said, spilling golden-brown muffins from a jar on the counter onto a floral-patterned plate and setting it on the table. "Your clients have a demon problem."

I flashed a look at Oliver as Robin bustled around the kitchen, pulling butter from the fridge, small plates from a cupboard and knives from a drawer. Oliver shrugged.

"That's right," I said as Robin laid everything on the table. "I don't know *how much* Oliver has told you—"

"Just the bare facts," Robin assured me. "So I would know what protections he might need. He didn't share anything confidential, I'm sure."

The scents of chocolate and banana crept into my perception, and when I reached for a muffin, it felt warm. But Robin hadn't heated them...had he? I glanced up sharply, and sure enough, a weak yellow aura of just-used magic limned his fingertips. I'd figured him simply for a supplier of magical items, but now I knew his involvement went much further than that—he was an actual Practitioner. The idea that Oliver could have a friend who was a witch had never occurred to me, given his past experience and his obvious discomfort with

Honore and the other coven witches. Oliver had said nothing about Robin's calling—probably so he wouldn't have to explain it to me. What a rat. But I'd have to deal with that later. I blinked and focused on what Robin was saying.

"I understand you don't have much to go on. If we knew the type of spirit that had been summoned, it would be a big help. Can you pinpoint where he's been appearing?"

"I didn't think to ask my clients that. They said they'd been able to locate him a few times through scrying but could never get to the location fast enough to catch him with a geas. We were trying to arm ourselves with more information before we actually go out looking, but then we encountered him ourselves today—at the hospital."

Robin raised his eyebrows. "Which explains your slightly rumpled state, I assume?"

Oliver nodded.

"All right. Any idea what he was doing there?"

"We think he was trying to get to the witch who served as the keystone in the summoning. She's still in that hospital."

Robin nodded thoughtfully. "You're probably right. But if they can tell you something about the other areas where he's been noted, there could be a clue there. And also a starting point for you two to start looking for him."

I felt stupid for not asking that seemingly obvious question. "We're meeting them tonight, so I'll ask. We're suspicious that one of the witches—the keystone—might have had dealings with this demon before," I said. "The others in the coven hadn't said so, but maybe they didn't know. We read online that a previous entanglement—I'm sure I'm not using the correct terminology—might explain why this spirit appeared and not the one they wanted, and why it attacked her."

The kettle whistled, and Robin got up to see to it, pouring the boiling water into a teapot painted with delicate roses. "That might explain it," he said, wrapping the teapot in a bright flannel cozy and bringing it to the table to pour. "That kind of connection can be hard to break if enough time hasn't passed. And a lot depends on the strength of the demon, the experience and will of the Practitioner...without more details all I can do is speculate."

"We'd appreciate any help at all," I said.

Robin wrapped his hands around his mug, contemplating the steam rising from the tea inside. "Let's make a fairly safe assumption: if the coven knew of the keystone's previous, recent connection to a demon—a demon they did *not* want to summon—they would have taken better precautions, or ensured that someone else acted as keystone. They would have known of the danger."

"So you think they didn't know," I said.

He nodded. "Unless they are lying to you about everything—in which case, why hire you at all?"

"Good question," I said, "and I don't have an answer for it."

"All right, let's assume they aren't lying to you about everything—although they may be lying to you about *something*, or holding information back. Witches are notorious for liking to play things close to the chest," he said with a smile. "But I don't think they'd take the chance of letting her stand keystone if they knew she had a previous connection."

"Why wouldn't she tell them, though?" I asked. "Or at least come up with some reason to avoid being keystone? She must have known it was dangerous."

Robin nodded gravely. "She must. Or at least suspected it could be an issue. Thus, the question must be, what did she hope to accomplish?"

I pulled a deep sigh. "The other witches may have an answer—if they'll tell me."

"It's the logical place to start. I assume the keystone herself is unavailable for questioning."

"Not for lack of trying," I said, "but for now, no, there's no help there."

"And not much here, I'm afraid," Robin said with a sigh. "Although I'm willing to help all I can. I just need more information."

"We'll see what we can get," I said. "We'll probably be back."

Oliver groaned, but I ignored him. Robin was too good a resource to waste. "One more thing before we go," I said. "Do you have any demon wards in stock?"

Robin smiled, and Oliver sighed and rolled his eyes. "Let's go back to the shop," Robin said, "I think I know just the thing..."

CHAPTER ҌIVE

Like good, responsible citizens, Oliver and I reported in to the police station and gave our statements about what had happened in the hospital parking lot. Yes, we kept it vague and played "dumb." We probably wouldn't have gotten away with it if either Detective Ellis Ames or my sort-of-friends, Detectives Sasha Crombie and Dmitri Crux, had been present for the interviews. Crombie and Crux pretended not to know about the peculiarities of my PI business, but in truth they were simply happy to turn a blind eye to anything that seemed a little too unusual and trust me to take care of it. I wasn't sure if that was complimentary or just self-serving. As soon as something happened that was serious enough, though, they knew and I knew that they'd have to take the blinders off. They'd be hard pressed to believe I didn't know more than I was telling when a car suddenly detonated in a parking lot where Oliver and I were standing. Detective Ames had been on the spot, and I felt reasonably certain he hadn't bought my wide-eyed innocent schtick, either. He just couldn't do much about it at the time.

Anyway, we gave our didn't-see-much-and-understood-even-less tales and left the station with only about half an hour lost. It was late afternoon now, and I had to admit the day was wearing me thin.

"I sure would like to take the rest of the day off," I told Oliver as we stood by my car in the station parking lot. The chill wind had calmed but the day remained cool, and I kept my hands in my pockets. The trees studding the edge of the police station lot still held onto most of their autumn colours, but a few red leaves crinkled under my feet. "But I promised to go and talk to the witches again. And now we have to ask them some tough questions about Chloe."

Oliver nodded and rolled his neck. "I wonder if we could do it after dinner? I need a hot shower and a change of clothes, and something to eat before I feel normal again."

"For some values of normal," I said with a half-hearted grin.

"Not even going to argue with you at this point," he said in a tired voice. "Do you think the witches will do anything about Chloe being alone in the hospital? And that guy maybe trying to get to her?"

I shrugged. "I assume they will. I thought I'd get to bring it up this afternoon. But I don't expect they need me to tell them she might be in danger after this afternoon."

Leaning against the side of my ancient Honda, I sent Honore a quick text asking if we could meet around 6:30 or 7. She agreed, and instructed that the shop would be closed but we could knock at the rear delivery door whenever we arrived.

"We have a reprieve," I told Oliver. "Actually, if you want to skip this one, you can. I think you've put in your hours today."

"I can be ready to go again for this evening," he said. "I'd like to hear what they have to say about the demon showing up at the hospital. And whether they're ready to be more forthcoming about Chloe."

"All right, hop in," I told him. "I'll drop you at your place and swing by to get you again later. But just remember, this is the job you didn't want to work on at all, and now I can't get you to take a break from it."

He made a face at me and we talked about other things as we crossed the city. I told him I'd see him in a couple of hours when he climbed out in front of his building, but I turned out to be wrong about that.

I'd cleaned up and was eating a slice of cold pizza fortuitously left in my fridge when my phone buzzed. The ID showed Detective Sasha Crombie's number in the call display. Surprised, I picked up. "Detective?"

"Hey, Sheridan," she said, but her voice sounded flat. "We have something I think you'd be—interested in."

I took the phone away from my ear and stared at it. The detectives were coming to *me* for input? This was new. And I wasn't sure I liked it. I listened again. "Okay, tell me what's up."

"I think you ought to see this," she said. "Okay if someone swings by and gives you a lift to a crime scene?"

"Uh, sure. I'm supposed to be somewhere in half an hour or so. Will this take long?"

"Is it at all possible for you to postpone whatever it is?" Detective Crombie asked evenly.

Well, this was sounding worse and worse. But the witches could wait until tomorrow morning. Maybe this couldn't. "I'll be here," I told her, and she said "Great" and broke the connection.

I sent quick texts to Honore and Oliver telling them something had come up and we'd have to reschedule, and they both replied. Honore said she'd gather the coven in the morning. I dumped the rest of my pizza in the trash, having lost my appetite, and glanced around the apartment, wondering if there was anything special I should be taking. Detective Crombie hadn't been exactly bubbling over with information for me.

In the end I shrugged into my jacket, checked that the ring Oliver had given me was snug on my thumb, and hung the amulet I'd bought from Robin around my neck, slipping it inside my t-shirt out of sight. It was a silver tray pendant with a blue-green cat's-eye stone set into the tray. Robin had described the distinct white band of reflective light marking the stone's centre as *chatoyancy,* and showed me how moving the stone made it appear that the line opened and closed like a cat's eye. He assured me it was a strong ward against evil and turned it over to show me the tiny sigils elegantly engraved on the pendant's silver back. He'd pressed me to take it as a gift, but I'd insisted on paying him for it. The pendant settled cold against my skin but quickly warmed. In my line of work, I could use all the protection against evil I could get. But I didn't need it to be so obvious that people would start asking awkward questions.

Anyway, I didn't want to appear too eager since the police were asking for my help for a change, so I stood at my window overlooking the street while I waited for the pickup, mulling over the problem of how to safely catch a demon who could blow up cars from a hundred feet away.

I'd just concluded that actually catching him was going to be the witches' job anyway, when a police car pulled up outside the building. I headed downstairs to meet them, pulling on my jacket as I went. I wasn't going to make Crombie and Crux walk all the way to my door when they knew I was expecting them.

Except when I stepped outside and headed for the cruiser, I realized that neither Crombie nor Crux had come to collect me. It was Detective Ellis Ames. My stomach gave a lurch. *The game is up.* He watched me approach the car with an expressionless face.

I made myself smile normally at him as I opened the passenger door and climbed inside. "Evening, Detective."

"Miss Sheridan," he was all he said, and put the car in gear.

"Oliver and I went in and gave our statements this afternoon," I blurted. I immediately wanted to bite my tongue, because if he was here picking me up about something Crombie and Crux knew I should be involved in, it was far too late to keep up my clueless innocent bystander charade. I wanted to wait and see how he was going to handle it, though.

"I read them," he said blandly.

I looked out the car window, wondering where we were going but sensing that maybe it would be better if I just stayed quiet.

Detective Ames wasn't going to let me do that. "You know," he said, turning the cruiser in the direction of the most northerly of the three bridges connecting the halves of the city bisected by the river, "I thought your name sounded familiar when you gave it to me today."

"Oh?" I said cautiously.

He tossed a glance my way and then put his eyes back on the road. "Crombie and Crux have mentioned you from time to time. They seem to think you're—"

I waited, but he didn't finish the sentence, as if he were searching for just the right word. "Special?" I suggested finally.

The corner of his mouth twitched, as if it wanted to smile. "Involved in some...unusual cases."

"Well, that's true," I said. "But let me point out that Crombie and Crux have never evinced any desire to poke into my 'unusual' cases too closely, so you might not want to take everything they say as gospel."

We'd crossed the bridge now, to the east side of the city. Oliver's apartment building was over here, and for a paralyzing moment I thought maybe something bad had happened to him. Then I remembered with relief that we'd texted *after* Crombie had called me.

"They actually admitted as much to me," Ames said. "They suggested that I might want to take the same approach."

"And what do you think of that suggestion?"

He drove in silence for a moment and then said, "On balance, I'm happier knowing things than not knowing them."

"But you can't be sure about that until you know what a particular thing is," I noted. "Then once you know it, you might think you were happier before you knew it."

This time he turned and looked fully at me. "Are you always this annoying?"

"Thanks, I like you, too," I said. "And the answer to that question depends entirely on who you ask." I knew exactly how Oliver would answer it.

He got quiet again after that, but we drove for only about another minute anyway. Then up ahead I saw the telltale flashes of blue and red lights, and I knew this was not going to be good.

Chapter Six

At first glance, it was a stereotypical crime scene—
yellow warning tape marking a perimeter and various
official vehicles parked haphazardly nearby. I saw the
ME's van and wondered if my friend Caro Lewis was on
the scene. I rather expected so. She was the head of the
department and liked to see things for herself.

I didn't make a move to leave the cruiser when
Detective Ames pulled it over and shut off the engine. I
turned to him. "Okay, I don't usually find myself at actual
crime scenes, so I'd like a little preparation about what
I'm doing here and what I should expect to see."

He nodded. "Fair enough. It's a homicide scene—
I'm sure you figured that much out already. Two bodies
discovered in the alleyway behind a club called Strange
and Wonderful. The place wasn't even open yet—they
unlock the doors at 8. Cleaner getting the place ready for
the night took some garbage out back and made the find."
He took a breath. "It's not pretty."

I swallowed past a dry mouth, suddenly glad I hadn't

finished the rest of my pizza. "And I'm here, because?"

Detective Ames blew out a sigh. "Because someone in the neighbourhood described seeing a guy that sounded a heck of a lot like our friend from the hospital today. And because I think there was more to that incident than you told me. Or mentioned in your statement. And because Crombie and Crux told me you'd want to help, as long as I didn't try to push you into it."

I had my own ideas about being pushed into it, considering that I felt Sasha Crombie had...maybe not lied, but certainly misled me about who was coming to pick me up. However, I could let that go for now. It seemed like Ames was being straight with me. I figured I could at least try to be straight with him.

"Fair enough. Yes, there was more to today's incident than I told you. But," I held up a finger and continued quickly when he opened his mouth, "you may or may not be happy with or even believe my explanation. That'll be up to you. I do want to help, though, if I can." I drew in a breath. "So I guess you'd better show me what happened."

He studied me for a long moment, then seemed to decide. "Let's go."

I kept pace with him as we made our way through the lowering twilight, into the alley behind Strange and Wonderful. I'd never been inside the club myself. I had it pegged as catering to a younger crowd. But every bar and club looked pretty much the same outside the back door.

A none-too-clean alley strewn with debris, graffiti-streaked walls, dumpsters piled with bagged trash, and an assortment of smells, mostly unpleasant. This one, while it had all those things, was also filled with differences. I stopped and took it in. Tented white evidence cards marked some of the litter, and a body lay mostly covered with a tarp near the club's back door. I caught a glimpse of a woman's white face under a spill of auburn hair and shuddered. A woman in a pale coverall, dark hair caught back in a short ponytail, knelt next to the body doing something I couldn't quite make out. Further down the alley, the surroundings flared briefly in the repeated flashes of a police photographer's camera as he took pictures near another tarp-covered form. Beyond him, a pair of beat cops stood guard at the other end of the alleyway.

Two more techs stood near the back wall of the building, examining what looked like paint spatters. I turned away a little too quickly. I knew after the first glance that it wasn't paint.

Detective Ames' hand caught my elbow gently. "You okay?"

I took a deep gulp of air and nodded. "No. Yeah. Just took me by surprise there."

"You don't have to look at the bodies if you don't want to—there's no reason to think you could identify them. Let's have a chat with the medical examiner." He raised his voice. "Dr. Lewis? Do you have a moment?"

The dark-haired woman in the coverall stood and turned toward us, a slight frown marring her smooth features. It disappeared when she saw me, though, and she hurried over.

"Dr. Lewis, this is—"

Caro ignored Detective Ames, throwing her arms around me in a hug. The Mi'kmaw woman was one of my best friends, but it was rare for me to encounter her at an actual crime scene. Intellectually I knew this was part of her job, but I usually saw her in her office in the hospital's chilly basement if I had a question about a case. "When I saw the bodies, I thought you might have an interest in this, but I didn't think they'd drag you down here for it," she said, and pulled back. She gave Ames a look that could be described as disapproving, if we were being generous.

"Okay," Ames said. "No introductions necessary, I see. Dr. Lewis, can you give Ms. Sheridan a run-down on what we have here? And I wonder if you'd explain what you mean about thinking she'd be interested when you saw the bodies?"

Caro sent him a challenging look. "You're the ones who brought her here, you must have a reason, right?" Ames looked like he wasn't sure what to say to that. Caro shrugged and went on. "Two victims, one male and one female, both in their mid-to-late twenties at a guess." She glanced over her shoulder at the nearby tarp and grimaced. "They might have been chased in here,

225

judging by some of the marks we found near the entrance to the alley. It was...messy. I might think they'd been attacked by a wild animal if—" She broke off.

"If what?"

"If we were further north, I'd suspect a *ki'kwa'ju*."

I must have looked blank at the Mi'kmaq word, because it was one I hadn't heard before. "Wolverine," she said. "Vicious animals, stronger than their size would make you think. The victims are badly cut up. A lot of blood spray, which you can see on the wall there." Caro nodded to the area next to the door. "I think whoever did it attacked the woman first, the man tried to run at some point, and the assailant brought him down like a coyote on a deer. At first glance, the wounds look more like claw damage than something done with a blade. They're ragged."

This must have been the first Detective Ames had heard about that. "We haven't had any reports of wild animals in the area, have we?"

Caro Lewis gave him a look as if he were dense. "I didn't say they *were* attacked by a wild animal. I said that's what it looks like."

"So it was a blade after all?"

She gave him a piercing look. "Those aren't the only two options. Do you even know why you have Acacia here?"

Detective Ames' grey eyes went wide, glanced

around the scene as if the answer lay in plain sight. "Okay, I'm starting to suspect that I don't. I'm clearly out of the loop here. Is there any way you two could see your way clear to bring me inside it? You'll notice I'm asking nicely."

Caro's lips twitched, suppressing a sudden smile. I knew she wasn't really annoyed with Ames, but she liked to exert control over what she considered "her" crime scenes. And she was protective of me, knowing I was out of my element here. "He's asking nicely, Acacia. There's a coffee shop just down the block; I passed it on my way. Why don't you go there, get a couple of coffees, and tell him what's going on. Then you can come back with my takeout coffee, and tell *me* what's going on."

Ames shook his head, and I didn't think he was going to go for it, but maybe Caro's reputation made him think twice about crossing her at a scene. As darkness fell, the air got even colder, and the thought of what had happened here chilled me further. I shivered. I don't know if that convinced him, but I didn't argue when Ames agreed to Caro's suggestion.

Ten minutes later, we found ourselves at a quiet table near the window of the shop, two steaming mugs on the table between us. I wasn't sure where to start, and I had to consider exactly how much I was going to tell him, so I curled my hands around my mug and waited for Ellis Ames to begin the conversation.

"I feel like we got off to a bad start," he said, after

sipping carefully at his coffee. "And I suspect whatever you're going to tell me isn't going to be easy. So let's just say I'm open to starting over."

I took a pull of my own mug and pondered how to go about this. If he was willing to meet me even halfway, that was a good thing. As long as that commitment lasted past the first few revelations. But obviously Sasha Crombie thought he could handle the truth, and so did Caro, and they must know him better than I did.

"All right," I said finally. "You know I'm a private investigator."

He nodded.

"Oliver, who was with me—he's my office assistant, and also my cousin."

"Okay."

I tapped my fingers against the side of the mug. "What's your feeling on things that are...let's just say, a little outside the normal range of experience for most people?"

Ames tilted his head and regarded me, frowning slightly. "What kinds of things?"

There was no easy way to say it. "Supernatural things. Paranormal things. Weird things."

He sat back in his chair with his lips pursed, but at least he didn't laugh. "I'm...a skeptic."

"Okay. That means this is going to be hard for you. I'm sorry." I took a sip of coffee. "Most of my clients are not normal humans. They exist right here among the rest of us, but most people don't understand their true natures, and wouldn't be able to tell them apart from normal humans anyway. Not just by looking."

He raised his eyebrows. "We're not talking about aliens here, are we? Like extraterrestrials?"

"Would that be easier for you?"

"Easier compared to what?"

I sighed. "My last three clients before this case were, in order, a ghost, a mythological goddess, and a vampire who lives a few blocks from here."

He studied his coffee cup, brows knit. He looked out the window for a minute, although all he'd be able to see against the early evening darkness was our reflections in the cozily-lit shop. Then he returned his gaze to me. "Honestly, aliens might have been easier."

I smiled. "Well, I haven't had one of them yet, but I'm not prepared to guarantee they don't exist. What I can tell you is that my current client—well, clients—are a coven of practicing urban witches, and their problem is that they've accidentally summoned a malevolent spirit. What some people might call a demon."

There was another pause while he digested this.

"I know this is a lot to take in." I had to admit, he appeared to be taking his promise to keep an open mind seriously.

He shook his head. "No, it's all right. I'm just rearranging my mental furniture. So that was a demon in the parking lot today?"

I nodded. "He caught us by surprise when he showed up."

"And I'm guessing the theory is that he's also responsible for the deaths of those two people. That's why Crombie and Crux put me onto you."

I shrugged. "We'll have to get more information from Caro Lewis, and I'll have to do some more research before I could even attempt to give you an opinion on that. Honestly, this is my first demon. And yeah, Crombie and Crux don't come right out and admit it, but they at least suspect there's something weird about most of my cases."

He tried a half smile. "But after vampires, surely a demon is a piece of cake?"

"To tell you the truth, the vampire was a pretty decent person, and we've become friends," I told him. "Vampires get a bad rap with the whole blood-drinking thing, but there's a lot more to them than that."

I had a sudden memory of Valia Northern attacking the thugs who'd been killing people from a local homeless shelter and shuddered despite the warmth of the coffee shop and the steaming mug in my hands. The blood-drinking thing wasn't something you could discount entirely, no matter how nice the vampire in question might be.

But we weren't here to talk about Valia. "I think the demon was at the hospital today looking for one of the witches who was responsible for summoning him. She's still a patient there following the ritual that went wrong. From what my investigation has turned up so far, she may or may not be somehow working with him, unknown to her coven sisters. When we chased him away, maybe he was just pissed off and took it out on those folks in the alley; maybe there's more to it and there'll be a connection when we know who they are. Like I said, I don't know much about demons yet. But I've heard stories from my grandmother, who *did* know a lot about demons, and let's say it wouldn't surprise me if a random rage-killing turned out to be the explanation."

Ames looked very solemn and nodded slowly. "Let's say for the sake of argument I believe you. I mean, you seem reasonably sane and in control of your faculties."

"Gee, thanks, glad I don't look like I've broken with reality today."

"I meant it as a compliment," he said with a half-smile. "But if what you say is true, we have to get this guy, and we have to get him fast. I still don't know how he did everything he did, but between blowing up cars without a bomb and ripping people apart, he's proven he's extremely dangerous."

"Agreed. That's my job for the witches—help them track him down. Oliver and I have a...talent for finding and recognizing these types of beings, so we're a logical choice. If we find him, the witches can put a geas on him—control him," I explained when Ames looked blank. "They'll send him back where he came from, but it's a complicated process, especially with one of them still in hospital. But the geas should contain the threat until they can do that."

"I don't suppose a good old-fashioned jail cell is going to be up to the task," he said, as if he'd already figured out the answer.

I shook my head. "You were in the parking lot for part of what happened today. I don't know the extent of his powers, but I don't think brick and mortar are any match for what he's packing."

I almost saw the lightbulb go on above his head. "And those two women who showed up in the car at the hospital—"

I nodded. "They were two of my clients. They were doubtful they could do much against him without the others, but they showed up willing to try."

It was Ames' turn to drum his fingers on the scarred tabletop. "And you want me to keep this quiet, right?"

I shrugged again. "Go ahead and tell if you think anyone will believe you, but I don't think that's likely. And if you want my opinion, sending beat cops after this guy is only going to get you dead cops."

"After what I saw in the alley, I'm inclined to agree with you," he said. He fetched a deep sigh. "So we're demon-hunting. Okay, that's a new one, but let's do it."

"We? Are you sure you're—"

His mouth pressed into a thin line. "I saw those bodies. I want to help get this guy. Thing. Whatever he is.

Now, how does Dr. Lewis like her coffee?"

"Black, one sugar, and a vanilla shot if they have it," I said. Detective Ames went to the counter to order it and I looked after him, considering. He'd taken all that surprisingly well. It might be nice to have a cop who'd actually work with us on this one.

On the other hand, it might just be a big pain in the ass. I rather expected Oliver to think so.

When he came back with Caro's coffee, we headed out into the now-black night.

The scene of crime team was winding down as Detective Ames and I returned to the back alley of Strange and Wonderful. Caro had packed up her bag and stood watching two techs maneuver the bodies into the back of a morgue van. She took the coffee gratefully and sipped it. She eyed Detective Ames, but spoke to me.

"Well, he's still upright, and still here," she said with a half-smile.

I nodded. "He took it pretty well, honestly." "I'm standing right here," Ames protested.

"And don't think we don't appreciate it," Caro said.

"So, what's the bad news? What's involved here?"

I sighed. "I think it's probably a demon."

Caro pursed her lips. "That's a new one," she said finally, without the hint of a smile.

"Unfortunately, I don't know as much as I'd like to about what that means," I said. "But my main job is to find him. That's what my clients hired me to do."

"It could explain the wounds," she said contemplatively. "Large, curved claws would do this kind of damage."

Detective Ames frowned. "I'm trying to stay on board here, but the guy I saw in the hospital parking lot didn't have any kind of claws. He just had hands."

Caro shrugged. "Demons and spirits aren't confined to one shape, Detective. A wolverine spirit, like *Luks,* could assume aspects or attributes of the animal if it wanted. It lines up with my impression of those wounds."

I really had to go and talk to Robin again, ask him if he'd give me a crash course on demonology. Even Caro knew more about these things than I did.

"I'll keep my report as generic as I can," Caro told us. "Drop by tomorrow afternoon and I'll tell you anything else I find. Now I'm going home to finish my dinner."

"Thanks, Caro," I told her. "I'll let you know if anything else happens."

"I hope you rein this one in quick," she said, and squeezed my arm. "And watch yourself, Acacia. This one's nasty."

As she walked away, I instinctively put a hand up and touched the protection pendant around my neck.

The silver had warmed in proximity to my skin, so I was hardly aware of it anymore. Through my shirt the smooth roundness of the cat's-eye gem felt small and insignificant. Could it really help if I came up against rending claws and the fierce rage of a demon?

Beside me, Detective Ames had stuck his hands in his pockets, also watching Caro Lewis walk to her car. "And to think I was worried this might be a serial killer," he said laconically.

I shuddered. "Let's hope not."

"I guess I'd better get you home," he said. "Not much more to see here, I guess."

I came out of my reverie. "Let me have a look around," I said. "Now that the bodies are gone, I might be able to pick up on something."

Ames shrugged. "Whatever you think."

I made myself turn and face into the alley again. The two cops at the far end were shadowy outlines now, and only two crime scene techs remained, making final notes. I walked toward the guards, letting my gaze sweep left and right along the alleyway. If the demon had really been here, if he had used a shifter ability to take on the aspect of the animal, there might be a trace left that I could identify. Nothing so obvious as the riot of scent and colour in the witches' wardroom, a place where magical residue permeated the space. But I might catch a whiff—

I stopped. I stood near the place where the woman's body had lain. I hadn't ventured this far into the alley when we'd first arrived. But there was something here...just a hint of a dark, oily scent I recognized. I knelt and put a hand on the cracked pavement, being careful to avoid the dark splotches of drying blood. If I squinted, a faint reddish tracery of magic signature glowed on the ground, possibly in places where the demon's feet had touched down.

"He was here," I said in a low voice, and then repeated it when Ames didn't seem to hear me. "He was here."

The detective knelt beside me, following my gaze. He shook his head. "I don't see anything. How do you know?"

"It's nothing that would stand up in a courtroom," I said. "But it's what Oliver and I do. We can see people for what they are—a ghost, a vampire, a demon, whatever. We can sense the use of magic and magic abilities." I shrugged. "Stuff like that."

He snorted a soft laugh. "Yeah, stuff like that. Stuff I would have laughed at before this afternoon."

I looked over at him. He was staring at the ground as if thinking if he looked long enough, he'd be able to see the magic, too. "You saw something, or felt something, at the hospital today, didn't you? Even if your mind wouldn't let you process it right then in the middle of everything happening."

He bobbed his head, not looking at me. "I waited while the Fire Marshall investigated the burning car. I talked to the fire fighters. No-one could figure out how the fire started. It didn't make any sense. Finally, they said it was electrical, but we all knew no-one was satisfied with that." He pulled his shoulders up toward his ears and let them fall back again, as if trying to ease tension in his back. "But it was really when you warned me to get down. I thought the guy had a gun or something I hadn't seen, but I...I *felt* it go over me, you know? Whatever he threw at me—energy or evil or magic or whatever we're going to call it—I *felt* it." He shuddered. "I'd never felt anything like that before. And I sure as hell didn't like it."

"Haha, I see what you did there," I said. "Sure as hell? Demon?"

He looked at me with one eyebrow raised.

"Sorry, just trying to lighten the mood," I said with a sigh. "Yeah, I get it. Weird feelings I get from supernatural creatures don't freak me out personally anymore—well, unless they're the kind that are trying to kill me—but I understand that they'd make an impression. You were lucky. Most people probably wouldn't have time to think about it afterward, because they'd be dead. Welcome to your first taste of magic."

"Well, I'm not-dead because of you," he said lightly. "So thanks."

"You're very welcome."

I stood and continued down the alley, sensing the same energies when I reached the place where the demon had taken the man down. "It's either the same demon or one with the exact same signatures, and I don't even know if that's possible. I'll try to find out tomorrow."

"Please don't tell me there's a chance there are two of these things in the city."

"Highly doubtful," I said, and smile reassuringly at him. "And now, I think I'm ready to go home."

We climbed into the car and I felt weariness hit me like a wave. Ever since I'd received the call from Crombie, I'd been on high alert without even realizing it. We didn't say much on the drive back to my apartment building, mostly because I was fighting to stay awake. We were almost at my apartment when Detective Ames asked, "So, what's our next move?"

That jolted me awake. *Our?* Oh, right. The detective wanted in on the investigation. "Well, I'm meeting with the witches in the morning. I'm not sure if it would be wise for you to come along on that or not," I said, giving him a rueful smile. "They're my clients, and it's a pretty unusual situation for me to be sharing even that much information with the police. Once I tell them about the murders, I'll explain that there'll have to be some police involvement, but I need a chance to break this to them first."

He nodded. "Understood. But you have my number. Will you let me know what you're going to do after you talk to them? I don't want you—I just want to be in the loop, all right?"

I wondered what he'd been about to say, but I was too tired to push it. I nodded. "Sure. I'll call you when I know something more."

He glanced at my building. "You okay now? Want me to walk you in?"

I shook my head. "I think I'm fine. I know you're not going to drive away until I'm inside."

He chuckled. "You got me. Thanks, Ms. Sheridan. And thanks for being straight with me about— everything."

"Thanks for not calling me crazy," I returned lightly, "and you might as well make it Acacia. I'm not much for formalities."

"Great. I'm Ellis, then."

"Goodnight, Ellis." I got out and walked to my building, glancing around as I always did, but not feeling particularly concerned. I didn't expect the demon to come after me here; after all, how would he figure out where I lived from the brief encounter we'd had?

I still turned on all the lights in my apartment and searched it from top to bottom after Detective Ellis Ames had driven off in his car. You can't be too careful where demons are concerned.

239

Chapter Seven

Oliver and I arrived at Seven Sisters Health and Beauty at the appointed time the next morning. Jo let us in and turned the "Open" sign on the door to "Back Soon," then led us back to the wardroom. The six unhospitalized coven sisters were present: Honore, Jo, Blanche, Sasha, Gennai, and Trina. Blanche had been the one stirring the big pot and wearing the Hello Kitty bandanna yesterday; Trina had the blonde highlights and multiple piercings. The general mood of the group was grave. More than one of them showed the red-rimmed eyes of someone who'd been crying. They must have heard about the murders.

"I take it you've heard the news," I said, once they'd brought a couple more chairs to the boardroom table so we could all sit around it.

"I don't understand how this could happen," Honore said in a voice that threatened to break if she didn't keep tight control of it.

"He must have been angry about what happened at the hospital," I ventured.

The witches looked puzzled. "Who?" Jo asked. "Um, the demon?"

"You think he took her?" Blanche breathed. "I was afraid of that."

I held up my hands. "Whoa, whoa. What are you all talking about? I'm talking about the murders last night."

"Murders?" Gasps ran around the room and the women looked startled. "Who was murdered?"

"Not Chloe?" Honore rasped.

I shook my head. "No, not Chloe. A man and a woman behind a club on the east side of the river. I don't know their names, but the woman had red hair. Why would you think it was Chloe?"

"Because she's gone!" Jo blurted. "She disappeared from the hospital sometime during the night. That's why we're upset!"

"She wasn't in any shape to walk out of there on her own," Oliver said. "Not when we saw her yesterday."

"I know," Honore said. "The nurses can't understand it. Gennai went around this morning with a healing philtre, and Chloe's room was empty. Everyone on the floor swears she was there whenever they checked through the night, and no-one saw her leave."

I chewed my lip for a moment and said, "Well, this complicates matters." I glanced at Oliver and he shrugged. I still had to ask what I came here to ask. "However, I still have to ask you some things about Chloe."

The witches glanced at each other. "What things?" Trina asked.

I took out my notepad. "Do you think there's a chance Chloe might have summoned this particular demon at some time in the past? Specifically, the recent past?"

Jo looked confused. "Without us knowing? I don't think so. And why would she do that?"

"I don't know," I admitted. "But Oliver and I did some research." I told them what we'd found about the binding entanglement between a summoner and a spirit. "It seemed to us that could explain why this particular demon appeared when you didn't expect him."

Honore and Jo shared a quick look I don't think they wanted me to see, but I was trying to watch all their reactions closely.

"What?"

Honore made eye contact with each of the other witches before she answered me, as if asking a silent question. She must have received an answer, because she said slowly, "We did have a little...trouble, with Chloe a few months ago."

I perked up, interested, and Oliver did, too. "What kind of trouble?"

She was obviously reluctant to explain, but she did.

"We got it sorted out. She saw that what she was suggesting was wrong. It was just...Chloe wanted to try some things that not all of us were...comfortable with."

"Dark Practice?" Oliver asked in a harsh voice.

Honore shook her head. "No, not Dark. We'd never agree to that."

The other witches added their support, but then Jo said, "But if we're honest, perhaps trending that way. Methods of utilizing energy that the rest of us couldn't condone—using animals."

Oliver made a disgusted noise in the back of his throat.

Jo turned to him. "Yes. I agree. As did all the rest— that there was no place for that in our Practice."

Trina said, "Chloe backed off pretty quickly. She said she hadn't thought it through, that she was just thinking we could do more good in the community if we could increase our energy output."

I pursed my lips. "And you think she accepted your refusal to consider her suggestions?"

Honore glanced at the others. "I really thought she did," she said. "You have to know Chloe. She can be a little...impulsive. She does things without thinking them through sometimes. But she has a good heart."

"Impulsive to the point of being reckless?" I pressed. "Would she go behind your backs to follow her ideas if the rest of you didn't agree?"

No-one answered. Blanche licked her lips and said

finally, "She might. Maybe she got herself into something she didn't intend."

"Can you find her?" Jo asked. "I know we haven't even found the demon yet, but maybe we should try to find Chloe first."

"The demon has started killing people," I reminded them. I knew it sounded harsh, but it was the truth. "I don't think we can let up on trying to find him. And Oliver and I will be no better than anyone else at finding Chloe. She won't stand out to us as a magical being unless she uses magic where we can see her. I think we'd better continue to concentrate on the demon. And there's something else," I told them. "Last night's murders open up a whole new problem—police involvement."

Sasha, who had been quiet this whole time, said, "The police aren't going to buy a story about a demon."

"I've found one who will," I said, "and he wants to work with us on this. The Medical Examiner is a friend of mine, too, so we should be able to keep the supernatural element out of it—but only if we get to the demon and shut him down soon. Now, I want to have a look at Chloe's apartment."

"What? Why?" Honore asked. "Do you think she'd go there?"

"I checked when I left the hospital," Gennai said. "I don't have a key, so I couldn't go in, but she didn't answer when I knocked. There was no sign she'd been there recently."

I shook my head. "I want to see if there are any clues to what she might have been doing without your knowledge. We know another Practitioner who might be able to help us, too, but he needs more information about what ties Chloe might have had to the demon. And what kind of demon it might be—the areas you've tracked him in, where he frequents—" But they'd stopped listening to me.

"Another Practitioner?" Jo demanded. Her pale face had flushed with anger. "Why would you go to another Practitioner?"

"Honestly? Because I felt you were holding back on us," I said. "And as it turns out, you were. You can't expect me to help you if you don't tell me what I need to know."

"That's unacceptable," Blanche said flatly. She was frowning and her eyes had darkened. I wondered briefly at the wisdom of angering a bunch of witches. Even witches who wore Hello Kitty bandannas. "You've overstepped your bounds. We thought we could expect confidentiality from you."

"And you can. I've told the other Practitioner no names or details about you personally," I said. I was careful to say "I" because I honestly didn't know what Oliver might have told Robin; but they didn't have to know that. "Now, please tell me where the demon has been when you've successfully scried him."

245

Honore looked a bit sulky, but she did answer. "Almost always around clubs or bars. He seems attracted to night life."

"And it was behind a club that the murders happened," I said. "That ties in. Now, what about Chloe's apartment?"

There was silence for a minute or two. I waited them out. Finally, Honore said, "I have a key. I'll let you in."

Jo glared at her, but Honore only shrugged. "What else are we going to do? He's killed two people. If this will help..."

Trina said, "Honore is right. Stopping him has to be our top priority."

"And finding Chloe," Sasha said. Her eyes had filled with tears again.

"With luck, we'll be able to do both," I said. "What time can you meet us at Chloe's apartment?"

Honore had to go home to fetch her spare key for Chloe's apartment, so we agreed to meet at one o'clock, right after lunch. That gave me time to dither over whether to call Detective Ellis Ames and tell him our plan.

"Keep him out of it," Oliver advised. "You know we've always had better luck when we avoid 'official' channels."

"I know. But this time feels different," I said. "I feel

like we need protection for this."

Wordlessly, Oliver held up the amulet around his neck.

I shook my head impatiently. "I'm not afraid of our clients—or at least most of them. Not so sure about Chloe at this point," I admitted. "It's the demon. I feel a lot more comfortable having a guy with a gun around if there's a possibility of running into the demon."

Oliver still looked skeptical. "Didn't seem to do much good in the hospital parking lot yesterday."

"Yeah, but the good detective didn't know what we were dealing with at that point. Now he's up to speed and he honestly seems okay with it."

"Do we even know if demons are susceptible to mundane weapons?"

"No, but we could call Robin and ask him."

Oliver pulled a deep breath and let it out. We were sitting in my office, me at my desk and Oliver in the chair opposite. He'd made coffee as soon as we came in, and we both sipped gratefully at the hot brew as we talked. "Well, it's up to you. I don't know if Honore is going to be happy to see him when we show up at the apartment, but there won't be much she can do about it at that point."

I picked up the phone. Ellis Ames answered after one ring. "Miss Sheridan? Acacia? What's up?"

"Hey, Detective," I said, making my voice casual. "We're going to check out the apartment of the witch who was in the hospital."

"Was? She's been released?"

"Not exactly. Apparently, she left the hospital sometime last night—on her own, or with help. We don't know. No one's seen her since."

I heard the tick of computer keys through the phone. "She's not in the missing persons system," he told me.

"Probably hasn't been long enough yet," I said, "and I don't know how the witches are treating it. Anyway, we're going over there to have a look around her apartment, with the permission of one of her coven sisters. Do you want to come?"

There was a pause, and then he said, "Yes, of course. Sorry. Kind of threw me there when you said, 'coven sisters.'"

"Welcome to my world. We'll be there at one o'clock; here's the address." I gave it slowly, allowing him to write it down, and then we ended the call.

"I hope you know what you're doing," Oliver said as I put my phone down.

"No more than usual."

"We're in just as much trouble as I thought we were, then. You want me to call Robin?" "That's all right. I'll do it."

"Suit yourself." He took his coffee back to his desk.

When he'd closed the door of my office, I pulled out the little paper card with Robin's phone number on it. I was a little surprised that Oliver hadn't insisted on calling Robin himself—he still seemed touchy about Robin's involvement in the case. But maybe he was coming to terms with it.

Robin picked up on the third ring. "The Patient Frog, how may I help you?"

"Hey Robin, it's Acacia Sheridan," I said. "I have a little more information on the demon—some of it pretty bad."

"I'm sitting down already," he said, and I could hear the smile in his voice. "Let's hear it."

I told him about last night's murders and what I'd seen and felt in the vicinity. He was appropriately horrified. "The witches said that the other times they've tracked him, it's always been near clubs or bars," I added. "Do you think that's significant?"

After a pause, he said, "I do. Seems like he's drawn to the energy and vitality of night life, and no doubt the frisson of sexual energy as well."

"So, some kind of incubus?" I felt my cheeks heating up, which was ridiculous.

Robin chuckled through the phone. "Much of the traditionally accepted lore about demons is overblown and just plain wrong," he said kindly. "It's been twisted and molded to shoehorn it into various religious archetypes. Demons are, fundamentally, spirits who seek to increase their power, much as a lot of humans wish to do. They undertake it in different ways, and thus become more 'attuned,' shall we say, to different venues of acquiring that power. A demon who, loose on Earth, frequents such places is usually looking to tap into the energy of youth, vitality, and sexual vigor."

"Okay," I said slowly, "so how does knowing this help us?"

"Well, it tells you where to look for him," Robin said gently. "But it also tells you that he may come in the guise of a seducer, or he may prey upon couples for their combined energy. The fact that he killed that man and woman last night lends credence to this supposition. If you find out they were indeed romantically or sexually involved, it will be even more certain."

"Does it tell us how to fight him? What his weaknesses are?"

"To some extent, yes. Energy bonds that are not of a romantic nature will strongly counter his magic. Amulets with an air or water attunement will absorb his energy and protect you from his attacks. Fortunately, the cat's-eye you got from me will do nicely."

"Will a bullet stop him?"

There was a pause before Robin answered. "Probably not. It could slow him down, but I wouldn't depend on it as a final solution."

"Good to know," I said, although it wasn't the answer I'd been hoping for. "The magic stuff is beyond me, but I'll pass it along to my clients, shall I?"

"Absolutely," Robin said. "And if you stop by my shop, I'll give you a couple more items I think might be particularly helpful."

"Thank you," I told him sincerely. "We'll stop by on our way to the apartment."

When we arrived at Chloe's apartment building a few minutes before one, Ellis Ames was already standing outside. It was a small block building, just four floors, with clean white and grey brick facings and what looked like a railed rooftop garden area. The landscaping was neat and conservative in a way that said it probably cost more than you'd think. It occurred to me that the market for magical beauty products must be more lucrative than I would have expected. Honore pulled up in her car as Oliver and I walked to the door, and I was suddenly struck by the contrast between this upscale building where Chloe lived, and the outdated car Honore drove. I wondered if there was really a disconnect there, and what accounted for it. Honore looked suspiciously at Ames as she approached us, so I tried to head off any trouble.

"Honore, this is Detective Ames," I said. "He's assisting with the murder investigations." I thought if I reminded her just how serious things had become, she might not protest his presence.

I guess it worked, because she simply nodded and led the way inside the building. It was just as clean and well-appointed as you might expect from the outside, with hardwood floors and the feel of an upscale hotel lobby. We took a smooth, silent elevator to the third floor, and Honore led us down a demurely-carpeted hallway. A window at the end of the corridor flooded the space with light. A table in front of the window held a large, leafy plant, and I would have laid good money that it was real. I scanned the area for any residual magical energy but found none. There were no other indications of anything amiss, either.

Honore stopped outside apartment 302 and knocked, waiting to see if there might be any response. When none came after a couple of minutes, she fitted the key into the lock and pushed the door open. "Chloe? It's Honore," she called, one last nod to the hope that her coven sister might be inside.

There was no answer.

Although it wasn't huge, Chloe's apartment had a spacious, airy feel and an open-concept layout. A double-long violet sofa dominated the living room area, offset by a couple of elegantly-carved wooden armchairs grouped conversationally across a glass- topped coffee table. One corner held a desk and computer. The white kitchen was clean and tidy, although not with the staged-for-a-magazine-shoot air of a place that didn't get used. Only two doors opened off the main kitchen/living space, so I guessed they had to be bedroom and bath. The whole place resonated with magical energy, much like the wardroom at the coven's shop. Chloe might not do magic in the hallways of her building, but she didn't hold back here.

"So, what do you want to see?" Honore asked in a flat voice. She was obviously not happy we were here, but she'd agreed to cooperate.

I turned in a circle, taking in the room. "I just want to see if there's anything here that might give us some insight into what Chloe might have been doing, or anything that might tie her to the demon. The more we know about him, the better the chance we have of finding and containing him."

Honore leaned back against the kitchen counter and crossed her arms. "Feel free," she said, but it was obvious she wasn't willing to go so far as poking around in Chole's things herself.

I turned to Oliver. "Let's just see if anything jumps out." He nodded and moved toward the computer at the other end of the room. I went to the nearest door and opened it. As I suspected, this was the bathroom, and I gave it only a cursory glance. I moved on to the bedroom.

Like the rest of the apartment, this room felt permeated with magic. The bed was a gorgeous four-poster and the room was neat and tidy. On the hardwood floor in one corner, a pentacle had been inscribed with what looked like chalk. Someone had dragged something across it, breaking the lines, although not erasing it completely.

I left it alone, but I did snap a picture on my phone to show Robin later. The tops of the night table and the dressers held nothing out of the ordinary, and although I didn't really want to, I opened each bureau drawer and gave it a quick once-over. The closet held the usual array of clothes on hangers, a few items on shelves, and a small jumble of things on the floor. Nothing of interest. I looked underneath the bed. The floor was spotless, not a dust bunny in sight. Chloe was a good housekeeper or had efficient maid service. However, a wooden box had been tucked under the head of the bed.

I reached under and slid it out into the light. Sigils carved into the wooden top told me this might be a spell box—a container for all the elements of a spell, meant to lend it an enduring quality. Robin had showed me some beautiful and intricate examples in his shop and explained their purpose. Cautiously, I raised the hinged lid. Inside, a collection of small bottles nestled alongside a bundle of dried and crumbling herbs. A black wax candle showing signs of much use lay in the bottom. The bottles had been smashed, however, and the candle snapped in half.

I was about to leave the room to get Honore when I noticed that the night-table also sported a shallow drawer. I pulled it open and that oily feel of the demon's presence rolled out and hit me. The drawer held an electronic tablet like those we'd seen at Seven Sisters.

"Oliver," I called, "come in here a minute, would you?"

When he came in, I pointed to the open drawer. He

glanced in and said, "Definitely feel something coming from there. And it has the same flavour as the demon." Gingerly I reached in and picked up the device. As I turned it over to look at the back, Oliver gasped and took a step back.

Etched into the silver metal of the tablet's back were arcane symbols. Droplets of black candle wax formed small, intricate designs like the perfectly placed dots in a henna tattoo.

I glanced up sharply at Oliver. "You recognize this stuff?"

He nodded, his lips set in a firm white line. "Yes," he said bluntly. "From my previous unfortunate encounter with a witch."

His reaction had suggested as much. "What do they signify?"

"Dark magic, the kind that drains life energy from other beings." His tone was sharp and definite.

I pressed the button to turn on the tablet and Oliver drew in a sharp breath.

"I don't think it's dangerous in my hands," I said. "I don't know anything about this stuff."

"You might be surprised," Oliver muttered, but he stood his ground.

When the tablet screen came to life, however, it was at the setup screen, as if it had been reset. I showed Oliver the spell box and the ruined pentacle.

"Maybe Chloe's been trying to reverse or undo

something?"

I called to Honore to join us, and when she entered the room, Detective Ames was right behind her.

"I think the conclusion that Chloe was dabbling in dark practice is inescapable," I suggested. I showed them what I'd found.

Honore looked inside the box and then glanced at the five-pointed star inscribed on the floor. "I think you're right about the dark practice," she finally admitted. "But I did think we'd convinced her to stop." I handed her the tablet. Honore turned it over in her hands, studying the engravings on the back. She pressed her lips into a thin line, frowning. "But the tablet has been wiped or reset. And the other things wrecked, too. Maybe that means she was done with it and had changed her mind."

"It's entirely possible," I agreed. "But maybe if she thought that was enough to break her connection to the demon, she was wrong."

"Knowing Chloe over the past couple of months, I don't think she was still trying dark practices."

I nodded. "Okay, so let's say we give Chloe the benefit of the doubt. She summoned the demon here, experimented with what he had to offer, then changed her mind. She breaks the pentacle, smashes up the stuff in the spell box, and wipes the tablet. Some time goes by. She thinks her bond with the demon has been broken, and agrees to stand as keystone again because she believes it's safe. Would that make sense?"

Honore thought about it, her brow furrowed, but eventually she nodded. "I think so. Chloe is a strong practitioner, but she's not the most particular or cautious. She tends to play the rules a bit fast and loose sometimes. She might think enough time had passed for safety without actually doing the research or counting days."

The sound of a door slamming broke the silence that fell after Honore finished speaking. I pushed past the others and ran out into the main living space, although Ames had reacted more quickly and was ahead of me. The room was empty. I crossed and pulled open the apartment door. No-one in the corridor. The elevator wasn't moving, the light glowing steadily to illuminate the number 3.

But there was a door to a stairwell at the end of the hall. I ran to it, pulled it open, and heard hasty footsteps descending the stairs. I motioned to Ames and pointed into the stairwell. He ran over and started down, making more noise than I'd hoped he would. Still, it was nice to have someone else to run after whoever had poked their nose into Chloe's apartment. I followed more quietly and heard the stairwell door at the bottom slam shut.

When I emerged into the foyer, it was empty. Ames opened the outside door and strode in, looked frustrated. He shook his head. "Whoever it was, they disappeared. I think they might have had a car waiting, maybe a taxi."

"Hmm. Or it if was the demon, he might have used magic," I said.

Ames shrugged. "Are we learning anything?"

"I think so, but let's go talk to Honore to make sure," I told him, and we climbed back up the stairs instead of waiting for the elevator.

Honore and Oliver were back in the living room, Honore still holding the tablet. I shook my head as we entered. "Whoever it was, we lost them," I said.

Oliver said, "Honore has an idea."

I grinned. "I was hoping that might be the case."

chapter eight

"I'll have to speak with the others first," Honore said slowly, "but I think this could work."

Not feeling comfortable making ourselves at home in Chloe's apartment—especially since we didn't know if she might have overheard us in there—we'd retired to a nearby coffee shop, The Friendly Bean, to discuss Honore's idea. Honore ordered something herbal and spicy, Oliver asked for cappuccino, Ellis Ames went with black coffee with half a sugar (to which I thought, why bother?), and I had a creamy, sweet dark coffee. We'd taken the tablet with us, Honore tucking it into her bag for safekeeping. Everything else at the apartment, we left as it had been when we arrived.

"So, what's your idea?" I asked.

Honore tapped her bag, indicating the tablet. "We use this to summon the demon. Forget having to track him down; with this, we can make him come to us."

"But I thought the tablet was wiped," Ames

259

protested.

Honore nodded. "It was. But we can find out what Chloe would have had installed on it for this kind of summoning—for what she was doing," she said. "The important part is that the glyphs on the back are intact. She would have put those there to single out this particular spirit. Chloe got the demon without this tablet because of their entanglement, but if we summon using the tablet, even without Chloe, we should get him."

"Should?" I asked, picking up on the word. "Sounds like it could be dangerous if you're wrong."

Honore lifted her chin. "I'm not wrong. And I'll consult with the others before we do anything."

"Wouldn't Chloe have known that breaking the glyphs on the back would be more important for breaking the bond to this demon than the apps or whatever on the tablet?" Oliver asked. He'd been very quiet since we'd found the tablet, but he seemed to be coming back to himself now. Seeing those glyphs had been a shock to him, I could tell.

"As I said, Chloe doesn't always do the research—she goes with her gut, or what seems right to her. I think she figured that erasing the tablet meant it couldn't be used, and if it couldn't be used, this demon had no connection to her. Especially in conjunction with wrecking the spell box and the pentacle, too. But that bond must have been a little more difficult to sever," Honore said. She turned her mug slowly around and around on the table. "I'm guessing at a lot of this, but I think I'm right."

"So if you summon him using this tablet, but do it at your wardroom, you think you'll be able to contain him long enough to get the geas in place?" I asked. Ellis Ames threw me a grateful look. I thought he must have been wanting to ask something similar but wasn't sure he had the terminology to do it.

Honore nodded slowly. "I think so. We can prepare for the arrival of a hostile entity. We just weren't expecting that the last time. There is one catch, though," she added.

I raised my eyebrows.

"What's that?" Ames asked.

"You need a seventh," Oliver said. "You're still missing Chloe, and she wouldn't be in any shape to stand in even if we could find her."

"Right," Honore said. "We'll have to reach out to the community, try to find someone willing to stand in. Not as keystone, I can do that, or maybe Jo...but yes, we need a seventh practitioner to make it work."

I opened my mouth to say that Robin might do it, then shut it again. Oliver would skin me alive if I offered up his friend without even checking with him first, and he'd be absolutely right. Honestly, Oliver might skin me alive for even suggesting that we talk to Robin about it.

Then he surprised me. "I might know someone," he

said. "I can ask him—if you don't mind a male witch. I know some covens are particular about gender makeup."

Honore looked grateful. "No, that wouldn't matter to us," she said. "Is it your friend who already knows about the demon?" I got the feeling that she thought the fewer people in the Practice community who knew about their situation, the better.

Oliver nodded. "He hasn't done coven practice for quite a while—he's a bit of a lone wolf—but I can ask him." He smiled at Honore as if he hadn't been scared to death of her only a couple of short days ago. I wasn't sure what had come over him to account for the change, unless it was the fact that coming up against the dark practice he'd feared encountering had actually lightened his mental load. Sometimes once the worst fears are confirmed, then you stop worrying and start dealing.

"Now, what about Chloe?" Honore asked. She turned to Ellis Ames. "Do we need to file a formal missing persons report now? What can we do to try and find her?"

Ames looked from me to Honore. "Well, if I understand what Acacia's told me, can't you use...um...magic, to find her? Like you used to find the demon?"

Honore stared at him for a moment, then broke out into laughter. The rest of us stared at her, not getting the joke. Just when it was starting to sound a little hysterical, she quieted, shaking her head and chuckling a few times. Then she said, "Detective, thank you. We've been so preoccupied with the demon, it never occurred to me to scry for Chloe. But it's possible one of the others has thought of it and found her by now."

She stood abruptly. "I should get back and find out about that. And ask them what they think of my plan." I stood, too. "I know you don't technically need us any more to find the demon—if this works—but I feel like we should be there when you try. Just in case...well, just in case anything goes wrong. And if Oliver's friend agrees to help, that's another reason I'd like us to be present."

"Of course," Honore said. "Well, you'd have to wait in the kitchen for some of it—we wouldn't perform the entire ritual in front of non-practitioners—but we can work something out."

She looked so relieved to have a plan that I simply said, "That's fine. I'll call you later this afternoon and see what you've decided."

She nodded, thanked us again, and left. I sank back into my chair. "Is this a good plan or a crazy one? I can't tell anymore."

Ellis Ames lifted his hands, palm out. "Don't look at me. I stopped trying to figure out what's crazy and what isn't when I realized I had to accept the existence of witches, demons, and who knows what else in my city."

Oliver pursed his lips, considering. "If Robin will go along, and if they're sure they can contain the demon, and if the summoning works the way Honore seems to think it will—"

"That's a lot of 'ifs'" I said, draining the last of my coffee.

He pulled in a deep breath and blew it out in a sigh. "It really is," he agreed, "but I do think it's a good plan." I turned to Ames. "Why did you put her off filing a missing persons report on Chloe? I would have thought you'd want to do that by the book."

Ames shrugged. "We don't know if she's with the demon, if he got her out of the hospital, or what's happening with her. And there aren't a lot of other officers I'd feel comfortable bringing in on this, besides Crombie and Crux. They're already in, after all."

I shook my head. "They're not really 'in'," I said. "They just know there's something they don't want to be 'in', so they look the other way when it comes up."

Ames sighed. "Anyway, if the witches can find her themselves, it makes things a whole lot simpler," he said. "The hospital will be able to just let her disappearance go unexplained, if I go tell them she's been found and give them a stern talking-to about keeping better watch on the patients in their care. If the demon—or Chloe herself—used magic to get her out of there, they can't deal with that. Not stopping it or understanding it. So the more quietly we can make this all go away, the better for everyone."

I considered him. "You're an unusual cop."

"Coming from you, I think I'll take that as a

compliment," he said and gave me a smile that went all the way to his eyes. "Now, can I buy us a box of doughnuts to go, and come wait at your office until we hear from Honore? I don't think I can go back to the station and face paperwork right now."

"People bearing doughnuts are always welcome at the Olympia Investigations office," I told him warmly. "Even cops. Make sure there's a lemon-filled, would you?"

The rest of the afternoon passed in a blur from there. We ate doughnuts and drank coffee back at the office, and Oliver and I told Ellis stories of a few of our cases. He seemed genuinely interested, which was a pleasant change. Not that I tell many people about my work and why I do it, but the odd time I have, it hasn't always gone down well. Caro Soles is one of the only non-supernatural beings who's accepted the strangeness of my world with equanimity. I credit her own strong cultural belief in a spirit world for her open- mindedness.

Anyway, we'd polished off most of the doughnuts and I was wondering how much exercise I'd have to do to work them off, when Honore called. Apparently, it had taken a long and not unchallenged debate, but the coven had agreed to try the summoning. They'd also scried for Chloe without success, but that could mean any number of things—including that she was dead, unconscious, or had been possessed by the demon. I decided not to dwell on those possibilities and instead believe that she was actively blocking their efforts with a concealment spell or charm, for her own inscrutable reasons. Or was being hidden by the demon himself.

It surprised me that Robin had agreed to help with the ritual, although admittedly I'd only just met him. I didn't know him as well as Oliver did, and Oliver seemed worried but unsurprised. When I asked him about it, Oliver sighed and said, "Robin likes to play the lone wolf as a Practitioner, but he can't stand to see anyone in trouble." It was a risky undertaking, and Robin's immediate agreement to help made me like him even more. I resolved to patronize his shop on a regular basis from now on. The summoning was set for seven o'clock that evening.

Once the doughnuts ran out, Oliver, Ellis and I ordered Chinese takeout and ate it at the office. Spending most of day there with Ellis made me realize how much the place needed a coat of paint and a general spruce-up. I realized I'd been thinking that for a long time now and putting it off. If we cleared this case tonight, I swore I was going to buy paint with some of the fee. And upon further consideration, hire a painter with some more of it. The idea of me and Oliver trying to paint the office together without killing each other defied my imagination.

With no small amount of trepidation, we arrived at

Seven Sisters Health and Beauty just before seven. The shop lay mostly in darkness, with only a few ghostly night lights burning to dispel some of the gloom. Jo opened the door in answer to our knock, looking not entirely pleased but resigned. "I hope this works," she said in a slightly accusing tone, as if I'd been the one to suggest it.

"Honore seemed confident you could all make it happen, or I don't think she would have broached it to us," I said, just to clarify whose idea this had been.

She nodded and, with a slightly suspicious look at Ellis Ames, led us inside. I introduced Ellis and Jo, and she shook hands with him graciously enough. Then we followed her through to the kitchen.

Tonight, the stoves were cold and the counters clean and tidy. The bright overhead lights had been replaced by the glow from a few under-counter task lights, lending the room a restful air. Although a pleasant mix of herbs and other scents filled the space, it lacked the heady resonance of potions in mid-brew. *Even if they were only mundane beauty potions*, I thought with a smile. Then I wondered just how much magic might be infused into those products. Maybe the Seven Sisters were onto something.

Honore and Robin stood talking at the end of the kitchen, near the door leading into the wardroom. Robin's face lit up when he saw us, and he hurried over to shake Oliver's hand and give me a hug. "Oliver! Acacia!

Thank you so much for being the vector that led to my meeting these wonderful compatriots! I'd almost forgotten how lovely it is to have fellow Practitioners to talk with!"

Honore gave a somewhat bemused smile, and I got the impression that Robin had descended on the Seven Sisters like a whirlwind. I wondered how they had not been acquainted before this and made a mental note to ask Oliver about it later. This was no time for delving into Robin's personal life.

"If you three will stay in here for about ten minutes," Honore said, "then you can come through into the wardroom. We'll have the ritual well underway, so just keep back from the mandala and our circle and you'll be able to watch the proceedings."

I swallowed. "What should we expect?" I asked. "Like, when the demon appears?"

She raised her eyebrows. "Honestly, I'm not entirely sure. He may accept the geas peacefully enough, or he may try to fight it. Either way, he'll be contained inside the inner ring of the summoning circle, so there won't be any danger to you. Just don't disturb our concentration or break the circle and it should be fine. Make sure you stay *outside* the mandala once we've started," she said with emphasis.

I hoped it was as simple as that, but I still felt better having Detective Ames along. As long as he didn't freak out when the demon appeared. That could send things down a whole different road, and I didn't like the idea of travelling it.

"Any luck scrying Chloe?" I asked Honore, to get my mind away from that troubling scenario.

Her face and shoulders sagged. "No. We tried several times, but we can't get a reading. Maybe she's out of range, or somewhere shielded."

I didn't mention the trouble they'd also had keeping a read on the demon, or ask whether the two could be related. I was sure she'd already thought of it. This wasn't the time to distract her any further.

Honore and Robin took their leave of us then, leaving us in the quiet, dimly-lit kitchen. I leaned against a counter and crossed my arms, checking the time on my watch. "Why do I feel like this is going to be a long ten minutes?"

"It's the curiosity that's killing you," Oliver said. "You're dying to know what's happening on the other side of that door."

"Well, I know I am," Ellis Ames said. "Even if I'm half-terrified to know at the same time."

I liked him better for that simple admission than for anything else he'd said since I'd known him.

We waited quietly for the rest of that ten minutes, only the slightest murmurings reaching us through the door to indicate the beginnings of the ritual. When my watch proclaimed the ten minutes were over, I squared my shoulders, pushed off the counter and said, "Shall we?" Oliver and the detective nodded, and I gingerly pushed open the wardroom door.

Inside, the room had been transformed. A multitude of candles burned inside the mandala and on the boardroom table and credenza, limning the room in a warm, buttery glow. Their combined light illuminated the mandala and the seven figures gathered around the curving circle of its outer edge, throwing a myriad of intersecting shadows across the floor and walls. The candles flickered in unison as I opened the door, even the small breath of a draft sending the flames bobbing and dancing and the shadows leaping crazily. They quickly steadied, however, as Oliver closed the door behind us.

Paler, blue-white electronic light shone from the screens of the tablets the witches held, painting their faces ghostly. None of the Practitioners wore robes or cowls or anything an overly-imaginative mind might assume for witches at a summoning—they all simply wore street clothes, which lent a much-appreciated element of normalcy to the otherworldly scene. Dotted around the room and throughout the mandala, smoldering clusters of dried herbs stood upright in colored glass vases, sending heady smoke into the air. I picked out the scents of sage, dill, and sweetgrass, but the rest was simply a morass of mixed aromas.

None of the seven, Robin or the six remaining coven sisters, had turned to look when we opened the door and entered the room, their concentration focused on their work. A low, murmuring chant rose from all seven of the Practitioners, and if I squinted, I could discern a dim, greenish glow surrounding each tablet. This bore no relation to the light from the screen—it must be a manifestation of the spell energy being drawn from the power of the online world. *Cat videos*, I thought with an inner smile.

I was distracted from that thought almost immediately, though, as the inner circle of the mandala began to glow with a pulsing amber light. A mist shimmered above it and I realized it must be the demon, beginning to take form. I took an involuntary step backward and felt someone grasp my hand. I looked over and saw that it was Ellis Ames. His eyes were fixed on the coalescing mist, but his fingers tightened around mine.

I thought I understood. His understanding of the world had been challenged in the last few days, and what he'd accepted in the abstract, he was about to witness in reality. Anyone might want a hand to hold at a moment like that.

And then the door to the kitchen flew open and a wild-eyed, wind-blown Chloe screamed, "What the hell are you doing?"

CHAPTER NINE

The candle flames fluttered in the sudden change of air, shadows diving and pitching around the room again. Some of the candles guttered out. The lazy, upward-drifting streams of smoke from the smoldering herbs shuddered and fragmented, embers flaring like baleful orange eyes in the dim light. The coalescing mist of the demon spirit trembled and convulsed.

To their credit, none of the witches panicked. Tablet screens twitched, sending shadows dancing weirdly over faces, but the chanting voices faltered only slightly before rebounding. That was good, because as I found out later, Chloe made her entrance at the most sensitive part of the summoning—when the demon was partially formed. Whether they knew they couldn't afford to let go of their concentration or they trusted the remaining three of us to contain Chloe, I didn't know.

"Contain Chloe" was precisely what Ellis Ames and I thought, however. After an initial moment of shock, he and I both started for the doorway where she stood. Even in the dim light of the wardroom and the kitchen behind her, it was evident that Chloe was not in the best shape. She'd ditched her hospital gown somewhere and wore a pair of torn black tights and an oversized fisherman's sweater. Her feet were shoved into scuffed ballet flats that looked a little too big for her. Her blonde hair had been caught back at the nape of her neck, but still looked sweat-damp. Much of it had come loose and dangled wildly at the sides of her face. The bandages remained on her left hand and forehead, but now they were dirty and straggling.

All this I took in at a glance, but it was her eyes that took most of my attention. They were wild and frantic, the whites showing like those of a frightened horse.

But she wasn't frenzied enough to miss our presence. As soon as Ellis moved in her direction, she sprinted into the room, circling away from us around the mandala and the ring of witches. She must know we wouldn't risk breaking the circle. I heard her voice rise above the coven's steady chant, intoning words that sounded all too familiar to me. In fact, they sounded suspiciously like the beginning of the spell she'd cast in the hospital. We had to stop her, and fast. But we couldn't chase her around and around the huge mandala like characters in a cartoon.

"Go that way!" I hissed to Ellis, pointing after Chloe. I ran around the circle in the other direction, figuring if we split her attention and came at her from two sides, we'd catch her between us in the middle. He got the idea right away and went after her.

Chloe was too crafty for us, though. She didn't stop on the other side of the circle but sprinted all the way to the far end of the room. She turned, put her back to the wall, and shot a hand out toward Ellis Ames.

"Down!" I called, remembering the explosion Oliver and I had heard come from the hospital room. Whatever Chloe was about to throw at Ames, it wouldn't be good.

I like a man who listens. Ellis threw himself sideways and down, sliding across the polished floor to bump into one of the credenza's legs. A flash of light blossomed where Ellis had been seconds before, and bits of concrete shrapnel peppered up from the point where Chloe's magical energy impacted the floor.

I slowed and ducked, covering my face instinctively although the shrapnel probably wouldn't reach this far. Unfortunately, my reaction gave Chloe the time to cast another spell. This one was quick; I heard a single, low-voiced word slither over my hearing and felt a tug in my chest as if someone had tied a string around my heart and jerked it. I gasped and staggered, going down on one knee. I heard Ellis grunt as if someone had gut-punched him.

Chloe. I had to reach her. The string around my heart had vanished after that single yank, and I gasped, trying to fill my lungs. Somehow, I got to my feet, staggered, then ran. I ran straight at Chloe and lunged for her. With her back against the wall, she had nowhere to go, and we landed on the floor in a tumble. My elbow hit the wall and I felt a flash of pain and then numbness. Chloe's scream of rage split the air and almost deafened me since I was so close to her face. She fought like a wildcat then, scratching and struggling and swearing at me in French.

I grappled with her flailing arms, wondering where the hell Ellis was. Surely he'd had time to get to his feet and come help me?

Then I felt it. Or rather, I smelled it first—the dark, oily scent I now associated with the demon. On the heels of the scent came a chill that struck to my bones, and a wash of omnipresent, lowering darkness. I assumed this meant the demon had fully arrived, but I hadn't expected his presence to be so overwhelming— not when he was confined within the mandala's containing circle. Maybe Ellis had been overcome by the sensation, I thought raggedly as I tried to keep Chloe's clutching hands from reaching my face. If that was the case, I needed him to snap out of it and come help me.

"Ellis!" I managed to yell. "Detective Ames!"

There was no answer.

Then Chloe stopped fighting me, jerked once and went limp. I fell across her as she collapsed, then pushed myself up to look around. The room had darkened; most of the candles had been extinguished, and most of the blue-white light from the tablet screens was gone, too. The silence hit me. The witches had ceased their low chanting. That felt wrong. Wrong, and dangerous. Squinting, I pushed myself away from Chloe and tried to see into the mandala.

Something dim and red pulsed at the centre, and I realized it was the floor of the mandala's central circle. It glowed as if red-hot, but the figure standing in it didn't seem to find it warm. A faint green glow encircled the red, though—the outer perimeter of the containment circle. For now, at least, the witches' power held. A voice slid around the room, like a snake's tongue tasting the air for prey. It wasn't a harsh voice, but it grated across my eardrums with a sickening pressure.

"Thank you for inviting me," it said. "This seems...intriguing."

That's when I made sense of the *wrongness* of the scene before me. Where there should have been seven standing figures with the demon in the centre, I could make out only three upright bodies. Something cold clutched at my gut. *Where was Oliver? And what had happened to the others?*

Ellis Ames slid up next to me in the darkness. His breath sounded harsh and fast, but he kept his voice to a whisper as he asked the same thing. "Where is everybody?"

"I don't know. But we need to find out." I thought

of something. I slipped Oliver's protective ring off my thumb and passed it to Ellis. "Put this on."

He let me press it into his palm, but asked, "What is it?"

"Protection," I said tersely. "Just put it on." "What about you?"

"I have more," I said, touching the amulet still around my neck, under my shirt. "Put the damn thing on." He didn't argue again, so I assumed he'd done as I asked. Staying low, I crab-walked slowly toward the mandala and the space where, if I remembered correctly and hadn't gotten completely disoriented by the darkness, Blanche should have been standing.

I saw the light of her tablet first, a faintly-glowing rectangle outlined on the floor. The device lay face-down, the uneven surface of the mosaic tiles allowing light from the screen to creep out around the sides. As I got closer, I saw the outline of a limp hand limned by that light.

A woman's halting voice began to pick up the chant again—Honore, I thought. Robin's voice joined her from across the circle, and then one I thought was Jo. Thank goodness. They were getting things back on track. Maybe Ellis and Oliver and I could figure out how to help the others. I put a hand out, reaching tentatively to touch Blanche's arm. Her skin felt warm, but she didn't respond. I shook her arm.

"*A geas*?" came the oily voice again, the one I knew

was the demon. "Oh, I don't think so, little mice."

From where the demon stood, a wave of purple light washed out, expanding like ripples on a pond. When it reached me, I had the sudden sensation of a thousand spiders crawling over my skin. A momentary pressure constricted my heart and beat against my eyeballs and eardrums. Behind me, I heard Ellis draw in a sharp breath. The feeling passed as quickly as it had come, though. Across the mandala from me, I saw the purple light flow over and around Robin, but it didn't seem to touch him. Honore, Robin and Jo continued to chant.

"What was that?" Ellis whispered.

I shrugged, although I knew he couldn't see me well in the dark. "Some kind of spell," I said, "but I think he's weak as long as he stays contained in the circle. My amulet and that ring I gave you probably protected us, too." I knew Oliver had his own protections, but I was worried about him. *Where was he?* The witches must have had their own defenses. They hadn't all worked against whatever had laid more than half of them low, however. That spell Chloe had cast? The timing seemed right. Whatever. I didn't have to understand what had happened. We had to get them conscious and up. I leaned forward to find Blanche's shoulders and give her another shake, but Ellis laid a hand on my arm.

"They said don't break the circle," he said. "Stay outside the mandala. I guess that still counts, right?"

Damn. He was right. I had leaned into the circle, but

I hadn't touched down inside it. Nothing bad had seemed to happen, so I figured I hadn't crossed the line. "Okay, just help me drag her closer to us. We don't touch inside, and we don't move her outside the perimeter."

Beside me, Ellis nodded, and together we edged Blanche closer. I ran my hands over her head and face, but I couldn't feel any injury. The pulse in her neck beat strong and regular under my fingertips. "I think she's just unconscious," I said. I tapped lightly on the woman's cheeks, but she didn't respond. I gave her what might be construed as a slap, but still nothing. It didn't seem wise to assault a sleeping witch any further than that.

"Maybe someone else," Ellis suggested.

We started to half-crawl around the circle when red light flashed in the centre and the demon's voice came again. This time it sounded less amused. An edge of frustration leaked through his words. *"I will not be contained, nor bound. You are too weak to hold me, and I have...tasted the pleasures of this world."*

Honore, Robin, and Jo kept up their chant, but I knew without the other four witches there was probably no hope of setting the geas on the demon. It was up to me, Ellis, and Oliver to get the other women on their feet. I just wasn't sure how to do that.

The central ring flared a brighter red for a moment, then faded again. The green light around it pulsed and then steadied. The demon was testing the strength of his bonds. The three witches' voices faltered out of step for a word or two, then re-harmonized.

"Forget the others for now," I hissed to Ellis. "I have to talk to Oliver."

I hoped to find Oliver working on waking the sleepers, but instead I found him pretty much exactly where I'd left him. He slumped against the wall near the door to the kitchen. In the unsteady light of a single candle still burning nearby, I could see his eyes were closed, his hands clenched into fists at his sides. His breath came in short pants. I touched his arm and he flinched. "Oliver," I whispered, "what is it?"

He shook his head a little. "Chloe," he croaked. "She pulled—did you feel—"

I squeezed his arm and nodded. "I did. But only a little, right? Robin's protections worked. She pulled some energy from us, but not much. We're okay."

He breathed deeply and exhaled, then nodded, eyes still squeezed shut as if he could hide. "I don't know what's happening."

"Four of the witches are down," I said. "Maybe from Chloe's spell, I don't know. But we have to wake them up somehow."

"Without breaking the circle," Ellis added. That instruction had certainly made an impression on him.

"What did she do to them?" Oliver asked.

I shook my head. "I don't know. They seem fine, just asleep. We need to wake them," I repeated.

A low growl filled the room, and I turned to see the

mandala's centre pulse a brighter red again. This time the green light retreated, almost fading out before it flared back. We were running out of time.

Oliver opened his eyes suddenly and grasped my arm, pulling me toward the kitchen door. I thought he was trying to leave, so I pulled back. "We can't leave Robin and—"

He shook his head impatiently. "We need something in there," he hissed, and pulled again. This time I let him take me into the kitchen, Ellis close on our heels.

As soon as the door closed behind us, Oliver said, "Peppermint oil—they've got to have some here. Smelling salts would be better, but peppermint is strong. It might wake them."

"Worth a try," I said, and the three of us rummaged through the cupboards. Oliver finally found a small bottle marked *Peppermint* and unstoppered it, dropping some of the oil on two wads of paper towel and handing one to each of us. Quietly, and opening the door as narrowly as possible, we slipped back into the near-dark room and split up, moving out around the mandala.

I wasn't sure which of the witches was closest to me—Trina, I thought as I knelt near her, careful not to cross the boundary of the circle. The meagre candlelight glinted off her many piercings. Fortunately, she had fallen close to the mandala's edge, and I only had to turn her head a little toward me. I put the minty toweling under her nose and willed it to work.

After a couple of breaths, it did. Trina jerked and flinched her face away, one arm flailing out and almost hitting me in the face. I leaned close and whispered, "You have to get up and resume the spell. They need you."

After a couple more disoriented seconds, she seemed to grasp what I was saying. She sat up, feeling around for her tablet, but she couldn't find it.

"Never mind," she said finally. "This is wasting time. I'll draw on my own energy." She got shakily to her feet and took up the chant along with the others. Her voice was weak, but it strengthened as it joined the others.

I heard another voice return to the chorus. Red flared at the axis of the mandala again, and this time a bright wall leapt like flames around the demon. He growled again, louder now, a sound so furious and primal that a knot like cold iron formed in my gut. I edged around to where I knew Blanche lay and thrust the peppermint-soaked paper under her nose. She sputtered and coughed. "Blanche," I whispered, "you have to wake up."

Like Trina, she came around quickly and grasped the situation. She found her tablet, still glowing, and put out a hand for me to help her up, already beginning to mouth the words of the chant as she found her way in. The demon pushed against the boundaries of the inner circle again, red light flaring as he did so, but this time the encircling green was brighter with the power of the revived coven sisters. We were almost back to full strength, and he must have known that he wouldn't be able to hold out against the full coven.

Then a shriek of hysterical laughter cut through the chant, and my heart went cold.

We'd forgotten about Chloe.

CHAPTER TEN

This time, Chloe didn't waste time with spells. She bolted straight past me and into the mandala.

If I hadn't been still helping to steady Blanche, I might have realized what Chloe was doing in time to stop her. As it was, I stood dumbly as she darted directly to her demon.

And all hell literally broke loose.

When Chloe broke the circle, the witches' chant cut off as if it had been guillotined. Crimson light blossomed out from the central rings like an eerie red tide, illuminating Chloe where she had come to rest, with her arms wrapped around the figure of the demon. He raised a hand and caressed her hair, its pale blonde now limned by a hellish red glow. I stared in horror at that hand, as the realization struck home that this was the demon without his illusory veneer of humanity, as we'd seen at the hospital. Now the fingers stroking Chloe's hair were elongated and knobby, with long, cruel-looking claws.

"Shit," Blanche said succinctly. "We have to get back."

Half-dragging the witch, I backed up to the wall near the kitchen door. Oliver and Gennai were already there. Without any apparent consultation, the two witches began a new spell, one I hoped would be protective. I peered into the fiendish light searching for Ellis, but there were too many moving shadows to pick him out.

"Well, this is stupid," Oliver muttered, and smacked his palm on the wall. He'd obviously noticed a light switch, because the overhead lights sprang to life, illuminating the room with pale, cool fluorescence. Startled faces turned to us, then almost as one, turned back to the demon.

The light was a mixed blessing. It robbed the situation of a certain amount of creepiness and let us see where everyone was and what shape they were in.

Unfortunately, it also let us see the demon.

He towered a good two feet over Chloe, which I'd discerned even before Oliver hit the lights. However, I hadn't had such a good look at the taut, leathery skin of his face, or the way his lips didn't seem quite big enough to cover the hideous-looking teeth filling his mouth. I hadn't had to contemplate the slit-pupiled, yellow irises of his eyes as they darted around the room with a malevolent glare.

And honestly, I hadn't needed to see that.

Ellis backed up to the wall near us. He had his gun in his hand, but Sasha, whom he'd helped over, snapped, "Put it away, Detective. It won't do much good against him and you might hurt one of us." She turned from him and joined Blanche and Gennai in their spell-weaving.

He turned wide eyes toward me. "A gun won't hurt him?"

I shrugged. "They're the experts," I said. "I'd believe them."

Muttering, he stuck it back in his holster. "Now what?"

As if in answer, a shimmer appeared in the air in front of us. Glancing sideways, I saw that Robin had backed a few feet away from the mandala, and had pulled an odd-looking stick from somewhere—he hadn't had it before, not that I'd seen. He held it pointing down at the floor, and now a slightly iridescent, lustrous wall separated us from the demon. Only those of us on this side of the room, unfortunately; me, Oliver and Ellis, Blanche, Sasha, Gennai, and Robin himself. Honore, Jo, and Trina, on the opposite side of the mandala when Chloe broke the circle, had backed to the far wall.

Apparently intrigued, the demon left the inner circle—with the boundary of the mandala breached and the witches' spell disrupted, nothing contained him there any longer. Chloe stumbled a bit as he broke away from her, and I heard Honore call her name. Chloe appeared not to hear her, following the demon. He strode to the shimmering wall, the claws on his feet *ticking* incongruously across the mosaic tiles. He reached out a finger to touch the barrier. Where the claw made contact, electricity sparked and he drew back. The corners of his lips pulled up in a smile that was more of a grimace, considering that mouthful of teeth. "You'll keep," he hissed, then turned and threw a roil of dark energy across the room toward Honore, Jo and Trina. I saw it catch Chloe and knock her back a few steps, but the demon didn't seem to notice—or care.

Jo countered with something similar to Robin's wall, however. She held a small disc out toward the demon's attack, and the dark energy funneled into it, whirlpooling into the disc before it could reach the witches.

The demon threw back his head and laughed. "*Use all the tricks you have,*" he rasped finally. "*You'll run out eventually.*" Then his eyes fell on Chloe, and he tilted his head at her, considering. He grinned evilly. "*On second thought, maybe I don't want to wait.*"

I heard Robin's indrawn breath, almost a gasp. He must have known what the demon intended, but it happened too fast for him to do anything—if there was anything he could have done. The creature took two steps toward Chloe and caught her in the crook of his left arm. He spoke a single, guttural word in a language I didn't recognize, then slashed her right arm open with one swipe of a hooked claw. Blood blossomed from the wound.

I know I yelped in surprise and horror, but it was drowned out by the screams of Chloe's coven sisters. After a confused few seconds, though, I realized they weren't screaming in horror, as I was—they were screaming in pain. Every woman had gasped her own right arm, shrieking as if they, too, had felt the demon's claw slice their skin. Trina had gone to her knees, and Gennai fell against the wall beside me. I turned to help her, but I felt a hand on my shoulder. I turned and saw Robin, his face grave. At least he'd been unaffected by the demon's action.

"Acacia," he said in an urgent voice. "I need you. We only have one chance."

"What did he do to them?" My voice sounded very small, even to me.

"Tapped into their vulnerability—Chloe's connection to the coven," he said. "I didn't know—look, I'll explain later. We don't have time."

I nodded, tried to snap myself out of my stupor.

The demon advanced toward the other three witches, dragging Chloe with him. Blood dripped off her dangling arm, leaving a horrible trail across the mandala. She appeared to have fallen into unconsciousness.

"You have your amulet?" Robin asked me.

I nodded.

"Oliver's okay...what about him?" He nodded toward Ellis Ames.

"He's got a ring...the one you gave Oliver earlier," I said.

Robin nodded once. "They'll do. Will you help me power a spell?"

"Um—sure, I guess. What do I have to do?"

"Get the detective's permission, too. I must have a word with Oliver. Try to distract the demon for a minute."

"I—what?" But Robin had bent toward Oliver, talking low and urgently. Oliver looked pale.

I turned to Ellis. "He said we have to distract the demon."

I felt sorry for the poor detective in that moment. He'd been so willing to accept everything I'd told him about this world he'd been so blissfully unaware of before this case, and I knew he was really trying. But the past few minutes had stretched his aplomb to the breaking point and beyond. He gaped at me.

"We have to distract the demon," I said, louder. His eyes looked a little glazed. Still handsome, but it was like someone had switched the light off behind them. "Detective!" I shouted. "Ellis!" And I reached up and slapped him.

I'd held back when I was trying to wake Blanche, but I didn't now. My hand stung from the impact. But it worked. Ellis' eyes cleared. He pulled his gun again.

"You think this will do it? Even if it won't hurt him?"

"Give it a try. Robin said a bullet might slow him down." With luck, even a demon couldn't entirely ignore being shot in the back. "Oh, and will you help power a spell for Robin?"

"Whatever, sure. I just want to get the hell out of here." Ellis took aim and pulled the trigger. The sound echoed around the room and I instinctively put my hands over my ears. I saw the demon jerk and stumble forward, so at least it should get his attention.

It did. He turned with a snarl and dropped Chloe. Claws out, he lunged toward us. The shimmer wall was still there, but I wasn't sure I trusted it to hold back this charge. I didn't want to watch it fail.

Luckily, I didn't have to. Suddenly Oliver was there, putting an arm around my shoulders and one around Ellis'. "This is going to hurt a little," he said. "Just brace yourselves, okay? Take my hand."

"What do you—" I started, but that was as far as I got. I heard Robin intone a few words in that otherworldly language, and then the amulet around my neck buzzed against my skin like a phone on vibrate.

"Hold hands," Oliver ground out between clenched teeth, and I felt his fingers twine through mine. Ellis reached over and took my other one, and we formed a circle of three. I felt pitifully unequal to the task that even the seven witches hadn't managed.

Then the pull hit me. This time it wasn't just on my

heart. The strings had been tied around my brain, my heart, my gut, and Robin was tugging on them all at once. I blinked and shook my head, but Oliver squeezed my hand tighter. "Try...to...relax," he managed. Ellis Ames groaned, and I thought he might break my fingers, he was clutching them so hard.

But beside us, Robin's calm voice continued. He'd dropped the stick—or wand—he'd held earlier, and now a glass sphere about the size of a golf ball rested in the palm of one outstretched hand. Miniature bolts of multicoloured lightning crackled inside it, and the entire sphere glowed with an azure aura. As the sphere brightened, I felt the pull on my energy strengthen. My legs began to tremble and I tried to lock my knees. I wondered how long I could stay upright as the strength drained out of me.

The demon roared. Out of the corner of my eye I saw him impact our protective wall. It sparked and hissed, undulating but holding. Robin raised his voice and the sphere higher. The demon blasted a torrent of dark energy toward us and the barrier held, stretched...and buckled. The wave rushed over us like roiling smoke and my amulet went cold, biting icy fingers into my flesh. When the cloud cleared, though, I felt like it had barely touched me. Ellis and Oliver looked shaken but still standing, although Ellis had half-collapsed against the wall behind him. My hands were slick with sweat and I fought to keep our circle unbroken.

The demon reached for the sphere in Robin's hand and I imagined him crushing it like an egg. But Robin spoke a final, reverberating word that crashed up against my eardrums and left them ringing. A final pull of energy felt like I was turning inside-out and I gasped aloud, dropping to one knee.

Then the sphere's azure glow brightened to blinding, and I squeezed my eyes shut against the light. The demon screamed once, a sound reverberating with hate, and then it cut off abruptly. The pull released at the same time, as if all those strings had been cut with one swipe of a knife. Oliver and I sagged next to Ellis, panting. I heard a thump. Robin had collapsed. I half-crawled to him and put a hand on his head. He didn't open his eyes, but the corners of his mouth pulled up in a smile.

He croaked, "We did it."

The sphere lay beside him on the floor, its azure glow extinguished. Inside the glass, a dark blot swirled and circled as if trying to get out. I didn't even want to know the explanation for that.

I put one hand on my chest, where my heart beat heavy and slow as if it had settled to the very bottom of my ribcage. Oliver dragged himself across the floor to join us. Beyond him, Ellis lay on his back, gulping deep breaths. Oliver looked as ragged as I'd ever seen him, but maybe a little triumphant, too.

"I never, ever want to do that again," I told him.

"I warned you about witches," he croaked, and collapsed next to Robin.

EPILOGUE

A week later, I sat back in my desk chair and sipped coffee, enjoying the simple pleasure of the spreading warmth as I swallowed. I'd given Oliver a few well-deserved days off, and the office was quiet. I'd just hung up the phone from talking to Honore Martel. The coven had paid my fee in full and added something extra to acknowledge that maybe Oliver and I had gone beyond the call of duty. Chloe had landed back in the hospital, but they'd stitched her up. With the demon gone, she'd come back to herself, asserting that the demon had been controlling her ever since the fateful summoning- gone-wrong. On the questions of whether the others believed her, and whether she would continue as one of the Seven Sisters, Honore hadn't given me a straight answer, and I didn't press her. The coven would have to work those things out for themselves.

Robin, too, had needed a couple of days in the

hospital, but he was home again and tending to his shop. I stopped by to check on him the day he was released, and we had tea together. He told me some things that gave me pause.

"That's what happened to Oliver when he was younger, wasn't it?" I asked as we shared an entire half of a fresh-baked apple pie. With my mouth full of flaky pastry and tangy-sweet apple, I didn't feel the slightest twinge of guilt. "A witch used his life energy to power spells. But not with his consent."

Robin nodded gravely. "And without the protective items you all had. That would have made it far worse. It's a terrible thing to do to someone, even in the circumstances of the other night," he said, frowning. "Believe me, Acacia, I didn't enjoy doing that. But I couldn't see any other way."

I took another heavenly bite of pie and chewed slowly, following it with a sip of sweet tea. "I wouldn't want to do it again," I said. "But it worked. The demon's gone, and no-one else died. We're all okay. It was worth it."

"Demons are a lot of trouble," Robin observed. "I hope that's the last one I ever encounter."

"You and me, both," I agreed. I almost said something to the effect that I hoped I was through with witches, too, then remembered who had served me this amazing pie. There were witches, and then there were witches. The ones like Robin offered more than toil and trouble.

"I'm glad Oliver had you to talk to about his experience," I said. "He's never told me any details beyond what I pieced together myself."

Robin chuckled. "He's never told me much, either. I think he keeps those details close to his chest. I wish he *would* talk to someone about them. It would probably be healthier."

I frowned. "Then how did you know? About what happened to him?"

"Who do you think put a stop to the witch who was using him?" Robin asked with a rueful smile.

But he wouldn't say anything more about it.

The phone rang in my office again, jolting me out of my reverie. I let go of the memory of the pie with some regret and picked up.

Ellis Ames said, "Hey, how are you? Still recovering?"

"I'm doing pretty well," I said, "How about you?"

I heard the smile in his voice. "Apart from having to convince myself every morning that it was real and I didn't just dream it, I'm fine."

"Crombie and Crux give you the third degree?"

He chuckled. "You were right. Those two are much happier not knowing the details. They know it, and now I know it. So, we have an understanding."

"What about the higher-ups? They're never going to clear those two murders off the books."

"I know." He sighed. "But your friend Dr. Lewis has them convinced that there's no useful forensic evidence, so I guess it will go into the cold case file. No comfort for their families, though."

"They wouldn't be any happier if they knew the truth."

"I think you're right." He was quiet for a moment, then said, "On a brighter note, would you have any interest in going out for coffee on the weekend?" His voice was casual, but there was an undertone of seriousness. "I...don't have anyone else to talk things over with, and I feel like I still need to."

"Um...sure," I said. I liked Ellis Ames and his warm grey eyes. I hoped he wasn't just using me as a therapist while he came to terms with the existence of witches, demons, and other supernatural elements in his otherwise mundane world. But I could stand to drink some coffee while we figured that out.

I found myself smiling. Maybe the witches had brought me more than toil and trouble after all.

THE END

SHERRY D. RAMSEY

~BONUS STORY~

SUBORDINATE CLAUSES

An Olympia Investigations Christmas Story

It was half-past noon on a blustery day two weeks before Christmas, and my good friend Caroline Lewis and I toasted each other across the coffee shop table with matching mugs of steaming coffee.

"Here's to us!" Caro said, clinking her mug against mine without spilling a drop of the precious contents. "We are victorious!"

"And unscathed," I added. "Although I thought that woman was ready to take you down for the last jar of Vanilla Snowmelt Body Scrub."

Caro shrugged and sipped her coffee. "My mother will be just as happy with a Sugarmint Cookie Triple-Wick Candle. I could afford to be magnanimous."

I nodded. "The main thing is, we are—"

"Finished—"

"Christmas shopping!" we said together, grinning madly at each other. Never in the history of our friendship, which meant seven or eight years, had we both managed to complete our holiday shopping missions this early in the month. Coffee and two luscious eclairs seemed an appropriate reward.

I was savouring the first bite of mine when the elf stepped up next to the table. "Acacia Sheridan?" he asked in a surprisingly deep, raspy, smoker's voice, and I almost choked on the whipped cream and chocolate confectionery.

"Are you all right?" Caro asked with concern. "Make the sign for choking if you need the Heimlich maneuver." She demonstrated, putting her own hands to her throat, and half-stood from her seat, but I managed to wave her back to a sitting position as I coughed. Caro was the local Medical Examiner and I knew she could perform the procedure perfectly well, but I just needed a minute to catch my breath.

"Sorry," the elf rasped. "I didn't mean to startle you."

Caro watched me closely, and ignored the elf completely. That would be difficult to do, even if your best friend might be choking to death across the table. He was an absolutely stereotypical Christmas elf, straight from a kids' book illustrating the North Pole workshop. Conical green hat with the point cocked askew. Silver bell dangling from it, chiming softly when he moved his head. Dark green tunic above red and white candystriped leggings. Black booties with extended, curling toes and a bell on the end of each one. His face was half obscured by a thick, wavy, white beard above which brown eyes peered at me.

He stood approximately three feet tall and was limned with a faint glow that had nothing to do with the Christmas lights decorating the coffee shop.

Now, all this is not quite as unusual as it might seem. I have the particular ability to see and communicate with all sorts of supernatural creatures, a "gift" from my grandmother, Nonna Pia (short for Olympia, and the namesake of my business, Olympia Investigations). My cousin Oliver inherited the same dubious gift, and I took the ability and opened a P.I. business wherein most of my clients are of some supernatural persuasion. Oliver being out of work, I hired him on as my assistant. Some days that works better than others, but for the most part we get along.

The thing is, most supernatural creatures live and move amongst humanity generally unnoticed, their unusual characteristics invisible to normal folk. Most people don't see the shadowy wings hovering behind a vampire's shoulders or smell the oily chemical scent of a demon; they see ostensibly normal people. But in a few rare instances, the supernaturals are simply invisible to everyone else. I wondered if that was the case here. I knew this guy was a supernatural from the telltale glow— well, and the fact that he was an elf—but what did others see?

"Caro," I said when I'd stopped gasping for air and could breathe again, "do you see anyone standing next to our table here?" I didn't want to point, so I gestured with my head and eyes toward the elf.

She examined the indicated space thoughtfully, then pursed her lips and turned her dark brown eyes back to me. "No, I don't. Should I? Is it a *sg'te'gmuj*?" she asked with interest.

I knew the Mi'kmaq word for "ghost," so I shook my head. "I don't think so. More like...an elf? A Christmas elf?"

Caro frowned, peering harder at the spot where the elf stood. The polite look on his face had begun to harden into impatience.

"Just one moment," I told him, trying not to look like I was speaking to thin air for the sake of the others in the coffee shop.

Caro leaned back and shook her head. "*Meskeyi*, Acacia. Sorry. I can't see anyone there."

I sighed. "All right, it looks like I'm going to have to head back to the office. I think I have a client, but it's going to look weird if I talk to him here and no-one else can see him."

The elf spoke up then. "Ms. Sheridan, please finish your treats. I'll stand next to your friend here and it will look like you're speaking to her."

I glanced longingly at the I. The firm chocolate shell glistened under the festive lights in the window as it warmed and softened in the heat of the shop.

"He says he'll stand next to you and talk to me here,

and no-one will realize I'm not speaking to you," I told Caro. "Are you up for that?"

Caro's eyes twinkled. She's very tolerant of my abilities and my unusual clients, moreso than I have any right to expect. "Go ahead," she agreed. "This should be interesting."

The elf stepped back to stand next to Caro's chair. His head barely reached to the height of the table, so this wasn't going to work perfectly. I'd appear to be talking to Caro's right elbow.

I took another bite of I and raised my eyebrows at the elf encouragingly. Caro sipped her drink, looking amused.

"My name," the elf said solemnly, "is McJingles. I've come—"

He broke off with a frown as I half-choked on my I again. The elf's heavy beard and harsh voice contrasted ridiculously with his name and I was caught trying to swallow and laugh at the same time. Caro's gaze began to turn to concern again and I composed myself.

"Ahem," I said. "Sorry about that. Please go on."

He snorted but continued. "I've come as a representative of the NPWEA to ask for your investigative help, Ms. Sheridan. There's an issue—"

"Sorry," I said again. "A representative of what?"

"The North Pole Workshop Elves Association," he clarified. "We've become aware of an issue with the subordinate clauses that we think is cause for great alarm."

I frowned. "You're having a...grammatical problem?"

"I'm going to need details on this one later," Caro said decisively around a bite of I. "Hearing only one side of the conversation is not cutting it for me."

McJingles sighed. "No. The Subordinate Clauses are another group of North Pole employees. They are the lesser Santas—those who move among 303iftie and gather undercover intel to help the Real Santa fulfill his global obligations on Christmas Eve."

I heard the capital letters this time and the phrase made more sense. "Okay, issues with other Santas, cause for concern, got it. Go on."

He placed pudgy hands on the edge of the table and drummed his fingers. "We believe the Subs—or some of them—are hatching a plot against Santa. The Real Santa."

"What kind of plot?"

I should note here that I had not encountered Santa, North Pole elves, or any other putative winter holiday supernaturals in the course of my business before this. You might think I was handling this interaction with a remarkable level of aplomb, but really, when you deal regularly with ghosts, vampires, demons, witches and other beings from myth and legend...well, you learn to take it in stride. I assumed that the members of the NPWEA were planning to pay me for my work, and that's my basic requirement in a client.

Let's not forget that I was also fortified with hot coffee and an I. And had all my holiday shopping done. I was feeling pretty cocky.

However, it threw me when the elf said gravely, "Holly and Ivy are missing, and we believe someone is planning to kill Santa."

Half an hour after that startling announcement, McJingles and I were seated in my office. I couldn't, in all good conscience, continue our conversation in a coffee shop if such serious matters as kidnapping and conspiracy to commit murder were, so to speak, on the table. So I gulped down the rest of my I, made my apologies to Caro, and gave McJingles the office address. Of course he already had it. I texted Oliver to expect us.

New client on the way. BTW he's an elf.

Oliver, unflappable as usual, responded with a brief:

Stripey socks elf or bow and arrow elf?

Which seemed unnecessarily limiting, but he was right about the stripey socks.

Just don't laugh at his name, I told him, and pointed my somewhat decrepit hatchback in the direction of the office.

By the time I arrived, McJingles had been joined by three other elves, and Oliver had fortified all four with steaming mugs of hot chocolate topped with tiny marshmallows. I didn't even know he stocked such things in the office's tiny kitchen corner, but Oliver often surprised me. We showed the elves into my office and held their mugs while they climbed into the two large blue armchairs facing my desk, two to a chair.

Oliver gave me a look that said, *Don't even suggest that I leave this office*, and I didn't. I sat behind my desk and nodded politely as McJingles introduced the other elves: Candy, a female with fascinatingly candycane-striped braids; Twink, a bespectacled elf considerably younger than McJingles; and Misty—short for Mistletoe—a slender elf of indeterminate gender.

"All right," I began once everyone was settled, "first of all, who are Holly and Ivy? You said they were missing."

McJingles nodded. "Holly is Santa's top Navigator," he said, "and Ivy is Logistics Coordinator. They've been gone three days, and no-one has seen them or heard from them."

"They're responsible for planning and executing Santa's Christmas Eve route," Misty said. "Between them, they know where Santa will be every nanosecond of his journey."

"I'm Holly's second," Candy piped up. "We can make the run without them, because this close to Christmas, it's planned out and locked in. But that's not the real problem."

"If what we suspect is true, and someone has kidnapped them," Twink said with a gravity that belied his apparent years, "then that someone was probably after the route information."

"Would Holly and Ivy give it up?"

McJingles glanced at Candy. Her eyes welled with tears.

"Not willingly," she said, a catch in her voice. "But we don't know what the kidnappers might be capable of."

I nodded. "So if someone is plotting an action against Santa that night, knowing his route and timing would be important."

"Exactly," McJingles confirmed. "And it's too late to plan a new route. That takes months, and we don't have that kind of time before Christmas Eve."

"And you think someone is going to try to take Santa out?" I asked. "Wouldn't that put the Subordinate Clauses out of a job?"

"Oh, no," Misty said. "We suspect one of them actually wants to take Santa's place. The position of Santa will continue, no matter who carries the persona."

"Okaaay," I said slowly, not really understanding.

"It's like this," McJingles said, "Santa Claus is the embodiment of an idea, a feeling—"

"An amalgam of a whole bunch of ideas, really," Twink broke in eagerly. "Spirits, beliefs, religious figures, archetypes from different cultures. It's not just one guy. It's never been just one guy."

"No," McJingles said, directing a quelling glare at the younger elf as he took back control of the narrative.

"There have been a succession of Santas—individuals who took on the job and the persona—donned the avatar, you might say. None of them have been immortal, although some of them do attain a great age. But the succession has never before been accomplished through violence."

"The current Santa has held the position for almost fifty years," Misty added.

"All right," I said. "So what do you want me to do? Protect Santa? Ride shotgun?" I had a sudden thrilling vision of myself, bundled in furs, sailing through the sparkling night sky next to the jolly legend as eight reindeer toiled magically to draw the sleigh.

Although most of McJingles' face was obscured by that formidable beard, I could still read the shock on his face at my suggestion. "No! Er, no," he said.

Apparently the idea of a mere human riding on the legendary sleigh was taboo. Too bad. That would have been pretty cool.

"What, then? Figure out which Subordinate Clauses are in on the conspiracy? How many of them are there altogether?"

Twink and Misty glanced at each other. Misty said, "Roughly twenty thousand worldwide."

I felt my eyes go wide. "Twenty...thousand?"

Oliver whistled low. "That's a lot of intel."

Twink nodded. "Think about it. Most mall Santas work ten-hour days during the season, and listen to the wishes, hopes, and dreams of 30,000 children every year. Multiply that out and you have a decent sample size for figuring out what kids want."

Candy held up a calming hand. "But you don't have to worry about all of them," she said cheerfully. "We've intercepted back channel communications and followed other clues, and tracked the nexus to this city. And there are only three Subs here. So it has to be one of them."

"But you can't figure it out on your own? Which one of them it is?"

McJingles clamped his lips together and they disappeared into the thick white forest of his beard. He shook his head. "We haven't been able to. We can't get very close without them knowing we're here, because although the Subs are human, we're all imbued with the same North Pole magic. They'll spot us as soon as we spot them."

"But," Twink said, holding up a finger, "*you* could get close. And from what we hear, you can pick up on the magic, so you can identify them."

Oliver caught my eye and raised his eyebrows. I nodded. It sounded simple enough. Follow these guys, maybe stakeout their addresses. Figure out who had the missing elves, and we'd have our would-be Santa-assassin.

"There's one minor detail you should know," Misty said.

"Of course there is," I said with a sigh, my dreams of

a simple job melting like snowflakes on a reindeer's nose.

"The Subordinate Clauses will probably appear to you as magical or supernatural while they're wearing their Santa suits," Misty continued. "But without them, they're just normal humans. The magic is in the suits. We can't even identify them without the suits."

"One could walk right past us in the middle of a Christmas tree lot and we wouldn't know it was a Sub," Twink agreed. "And we only know their first names, and not their current work assignments. We couldn't get full access to the Sub database."

I sighed. "Okay. You might as well give me the first names, anyway. We'll have to winnow them out of the fake Santa herd ourselves."

Misty pulled a scrap of paper out of a pocket and wordlessly handed it to me. In fancy curlicued letters were three names.

Harold

Kelly

Bob

I stared at the list. "This is not much to go on," I said.

"Good elves died to get that list," Twink said.

I looked up at the young elf in horror. "Died?" The North Pole was beginning to sound decidedly less jolly than I'd grown up believing.

"Not really," Twink admitted. "I've just always wanted to say that. But an elf named Cardamom sustained a pretty nasty paper cut."

"And don't forget the suits," Misty said encouragingly. "With the suits on, they'll probably stand out to you like Christmas lights on a dark street."

"All right," I said. "Find the Subordinate Clauses, figure out which one has Holly and Ivy—"

"Rescue them," McJingles interjected.

"Rescue the elves, and stop the hostile takeover of the Santa persona," I agreed. "Does that sound about right?"

"And do it before Christmas Eve, of course," Candy added.

I nodded. "Before Christmas Eve."

Good thing I had my shopping done early.

When I arrived at the office the next morning, Oliver was wearing an elegant Christmas-green sweater with a rolled collar and leather elbow patches, dark pants, and a smug grin.

"Why do you look so happy?" I asked with suspicion.

"Because I know I'm coming with you on this case," he answered. "Here, I already made our coffees and we can take them with us." He offered me a festive red travel mug I hadn't seen before and retained its twin for himself.

Whether or not Oliver comes along with me on field work is always a bit of a tug-of-war for us. I maintain I hired him to look after the office while I'm out; he argues he's more of a partner than an assistant, and should get out of the office more.

"What makes you so sure I want you along on this one?"

His grin widened. "Because you hate to go near malls alone during the holiday season."

Well, he had me there. "Get your coat," I told him, taking the coffee. "I want to figure out what we're up against first."

A light dusting of snow had begun to fall as we climbed into my car. Oliver pulled out his phone and read from a list. "The two malls both have Santas; they go on duty at ten a.m. today. Some of the charity kettles around the city will have volunteers in Santa suits ringing the bells but I couldn't get an exact number; two grocery stores have in-house Santas; there's a Santa at the food bank; four photography studios are doing Santa pics; and fourteen staff parties have Santas booked for tonight."

I looked at him and raised my eyebrows. The smug grin was back. Oliver knew how good he was at compiling relevant data. "Why didn't you tell me you had all this information?"

Oliver shrugged. "I wanted to be sure I was coming with you first." He switched on the radio and the tinny tinkle of "Santa Claus is Coming to Town" filled the car.

"Appropriate," I muttered, and pointed the car toward the nearest mall to get started. Traffic was already heavy between commuter and holiday shoppers, so it was stop and go. "So we have at least thirty Santas to check out before we can even begin to find Holly and Ivy?"

"We got one possible break," Oliver said, sipping his coffee. "Of the fourteen staff parties, none of the people booked to play Santa are named Harold, Kelly, or Bob. So unless they're operating under an alias, we don't have to worry about those."

I nodded. "Okay, we'll run down the other leads first and only consider the private functions if we have to. I wasn't looking forward to crashing fourteen staff parties."

"Think of all the free food and drinks," Oliver said. He pursed his lips. "On second thought, you're probably right."

At the Riverside Mall we got lucky. As "The Twelve Days of Christmas" played in the background, I spoke to the mall manager, a thin, worried-looking man named Edgar Bates. He wore a Christmas-themed bowtie but didn't seem full of the holiday spirit. He confirmed that they had a Santa coming on duty that morning, and that his name was Bob Hatcher.

"He's been our Santa for seven years," Bates said, the creases in his forehead deepening. "I hope there's no trouble with him."

I hastened to assure him that I only wanted to talk to Bob about working a Christmas party. Bates looked at me askance.

"You'll never get him on that short notice," he said.

"Bob's here until seven every night, and then he does private parties—but they're booked months in advance. Bob's a very popular Santa. You'd have had to contact him in July for a booking."

I shrugged. "No problem," I told him, "and thanks for your time." His desk phone rang then and Oliver and I made our escape from his office with a wave and a nod.

"You shouldn't tell lies," Oliver told me, unwrapping a candy cane he'd nabbed from a dish on Bates' desk. "You'll end up on the naughty list."

"We'll come back at lunchtime and check out Bob," I said, ignoring Oliver's dig. "If he's been doing the Subordinate Claus gig for seven years, maybe he's getting antsy to do the real thing. Sounds like the life of a fake Santa is pretty demanding."

"And they have to do it all with a smile," Oliver said, dodging a man so laden with parcels he almost staggered. "Friend of mine worked as a mall Santa a couple of times. In two seasons he was scratched, bitten, screamed at, yelled at by parents, kicked in the shins, punched in the groin, and peed on four times."

"Sheesh. I guess I can understand someone wanting to move up from that. Around the world in one night sounds like cake compared to that."

"The pay's pretty good, though," Oliver said. I thought that might be a dig about his salary, so I ignored it.

One of the grocery stores on our list was across the

street from the mall, so we walked over through the thickening snow. Santa wasn't due in until after lunch, but one of the cashiers told me his name was Amir. He'd only arrived in Canada eight months ago and this was his first Santa gig. That didn't sound likely to be our guy. I bought a box of doughnuts at the bakery counter, because it was shaping up to be a long day.

We drove around the city, listening to holiday music on the radio and sharing the doughnuts. It wasn't as festive as it sounds. The snow continued to fall, making the roads unpredictable. The traffic was relentless. None of the charity Santas we passed on the sidewalks gave off any kind of supernatural vibe. We hit two photography studios, the other grocery store, and the food bank without any luck. I was about to suggest going back to talk to Bob, but we found Kelly at the third photo place.

This photographer offered a kids' half-hour special visit with Santa. While the photographer snapped dozens of pictures, the kids talked, sang, chatted and read books with Santa. Sounded like a goldmine for gathering vital Santa intel, especially since the receptionist told us parents also checked in before the visit to offer "inside" information for Santa to use in his interactions with the kids—what activities and hobbies they liked, pet names, favourite toys and tv shows. We peeked through a one-way viewing window into the studio to watch a shoot in action, and sure enough, Santa—or at least his suit— glowed for me and Oliver like the star on top of a tree.

"How late does Santa work?" I asked the receptionist. "I don't want to bother him during a shoot, but I might have another job for him."

She laughed, a tinkling sound like icicles falling from a roof gutter. "This Santa's busy from 9 to 9 these days, and Kelly doesn't take private gigs," she said, eyes twinkling. "If you want to talk, you'd have to be here either before or after those times." She looked like she was trying not to giggle again, and it annoyed me. I felt like she wanted me to ask what was so funny, so I was damned if I'd do so. Instead I thanked her, and Oliver and I got out of there.

"Well, that's a definite Sub," I said as we climbed into the car. "Put a star by Kelly's name. And what was up with that receptionist?"

Oliver fished out the note Misty had given us and dutifully marked an asterisk with a pencil. "Bob's still a question mark—want to go back to the mall now and find out for sure? And I don't know about the girl. She was having some kind of laugh at our expense. But I didn't think we did anything strange."

I shrugged and filed it away, turning the car back toward the mall. Despite the doughnuts, I was ready for lunch, and the mall's food court boasted a local vendor whose French fries could make one weep.

The mall bustled with shoppers and folks on their lunch breaks heading to the food court. I spotted a long line of kids and parents in various stages of excitement, boredom, trepidation, and determination that this year, by all that was holy, there'd be a decent Santa photo. We skirted the lineup and Oliver said, "One Subordinate Claus, dead ahead." The crowd parted and I saw Santa Bob seated on a gilded throne, a squirming toddler balanced on each knee. Even under the photographer's flash and the festive brilliance of the mall, the Santa suit glowed in my sight.

As I watched, Santa Bob somehow managed to get both kids to face the camera, look pleasant, and hold still for the fraction of second it took for the shutter to click. The doting mother and a helpful "elf" assistant in classic North Pole attire cleared away the toddlers to make room for the next child in line. If Santa Bob was sweating—and I imagined he was, in the heavy, probably-padded suit under these lights—he didn't show it, but smiled at the small boy approaching the painted plywood throne.

We passed by, walking purposefully to the food court, and got in line to order fries. The aroma made my mouth water. Oliver took out the note and changed the question mark next to Bob's name to an asterisk. "Two down, one to go. Then we can start figuring out which one goes on *our* naughty list."

"One or more," I said. "Could be one of them wants the big red suit and the others will be content with other perks."

"True," Oliver said, frowning. "I hadn't thought of that. That'll make things trickier."

"Well, we won't worry about it until we're sure. I wonder where number three is? We're running out of possibilities."

"Maybe Harold's not working today," Oliver suggested.

I shook my head. "It's less than two weeks until Christmas. Every Santa in the city's wearing the beard today."

"Not if he's torturing elves for Santa's route information," Oliver said, and suddenly the fries didn't smell so wonderful any more.

Later that afternoon, we found Santa Harold at the other mall. The setup was much the same as at the first one, and the magic in Harold's suit limned him in a soft, golden light. We watched for a few minutes as children took their turns on his lap, laughing, crying, whispering secrets and tugging the big white beard to see if it was real. Harold took it all with aplomb and good humour.

"Well, we know who they are now," I said, turning away.

"Not going to be easy, is it?" Oliver said, keeping stride with me as we wove among hurrying, distracted shoppers.

"None of them exactly screams, 'villain' when you look at them."

"But if the elves are right, one of them must be," Oliver mused.

I stopped short, and Oliver had to pull me out of the way of a woman weighed down with parcels, who almost walked into me.

"What is it?"

"You said, 'if the elves are right,'" I said. "What if they're not? What if they're mixed up about something?"

Oliver narrowed his eyes. "You think we need to check their story? Why would they lie?"

I shook my head. "I'm not saying they're lying. But there could be something else going on."

"So how do we find out?"

"I think," I said slowly, "we go to the source. I think we need to talk to the real Santa."

"And how do you propose we do that?" Oliver asked. "I don't think your car's up to a trip to the North Pole. I think you might be having some kind of sugar reaction from all those doughnuts."

"Nah, it's simple," I told him. "We get McJingles to take us."

McJingles had left me a tiny silver bell, which he'd said would summon him if need be. Elves apparently didn't have cell phones or texting plans, at least none that could be accessed via normal human networks. We went back to the office and I tinkled the bell.

It took about thirty seconds, during which I'd just begun to think the bell wasn't going to work, but then McJingles appeared in my office in a shimmer of snow.

His eyes were wide. "You've got him already?"

I held up a hand to quell his enthusiasm as the flakes began to melt into my carpet. "No, no. We have identified the three Subordinate Clauses, though." Honestly, I thought that was pretty decent progress for one day, considering the slim information they'd given us to start.

The gruff little elf frowned. "Good start, but what do you need me for? I've got a squad of trainee elves making farm playsets, and half of them don't seem to know a horse's head from its—"

"We'd like to speak with Santa," I interrupted.

McJingles stared at me. "You want to bother Santa this close to Christmas? Have you lost your wits?" His stare deepened into a frown. "And I don't want him bothered and worrying over this business, anyway."

"If we can't figure this out in time—and I'm not saying we can't, but just in case—Santa needs to know what's going on. So he can be careful," I said. "Surely you've taken your concerns to him already?"

McJingles glanced away, no longer meeting my eyes. Finally he said, "I did. He...dismissed them. You have to understand Santa. He doesn't like to think badly of anyone."

"Ah. So he wouldn't consider the possibility that he might be in danger."

The elf sighed. "He gave me leave to look into it, but he was only humouring me."

"Even when Holly and Ivy disappeared?"

"We didn't...I haven't told him about that, yet," McJingles confessed. He looked suddenly torn. "I want to! I hate keeping secrets from Santa! But if he starts worrying about them, it'll put him clear off his game. He won't be fit to ride on Christmas Eve, and then where will we all be? Holly and Ivy wouldn't want that. So I've left them out of it."

I pursed my lips. The elf crossed his arms and glared at me defiantly.

"You're in a pickle," I told him. "But how about this: take us to have a chat with Santa, and I won't mention the missing elves. Yet," I added. "If we can't find them before Christmas Eve, he'll have to be told."

"Agreed," the elf said glumly. "It's really hard for me to keep this from him anyway. All right, put these on."

From somewhere he produced a handful of fabric dotted with candy canes, holly, and snowmen. They turned out to be blindfolds. Oliver shot me a look that said maybe he wasn't enjoying this so much any more, but hey, he'd wanted in on this one. I wasn't about to let him off the hook now. We donned the blindfolds.

"Now just relax. This won't hurt a bit," McJingles said.

I was about to say I hadn't expected it to hurt. But then everything exploded in a flash of wild snowflakes and cold, and I closed my eyes and mouth against the onslaught.

McJingles lied.

The transition to the North Pole was not precisely painless—the cold was searing and felt like it penetrated all the way to my bones. Fortunately, it didn't last—it was like opening the door to a blast of intense winter and then closing it again against the wind.

"We're here," McJingles said, and we took off the blindfolds.

We stood in the classic winter wonderland surroundings associated with the North Pole. A snow-coated clearing lay surrounded by deep green forest, branches frosted with a storybook-perfect dusting of white flakes.The snow on the ground held that bright sparkle that glistened like crushed diamonds in the pale sunlight. A fairytale house stood next to a huge, red painted barn-like edifice that must be the workshop. The house's wraparound porch welcomed visitors, its roof supported by candycane-striped pillars. Beyond the two main buildings, rows of neat duplex and triplex cottages provided cozy housing for the elves. Off to one side was a low-roofed stable for the reindeer.

From the workshop, the busy sounds of production filled the air. Apart from the chime of hammers and the buzz of saws, machinery whirred and electronic chirps added to the general cacophony. Scents of sawdust, cinnamon, and melting plastic mingled, faint and not unpleasant, in the air.

McJingles interrupted our wide-eyed and slack-jawed survey of Santa's demesne. "Santa's in the stable," he said, and stomped away in that direction. We were obviously expected to follow. I felt a little pang at not seeing the inside of the workshop, but took Oliver's arm and propelled him after the departing elf.

"This is amazing," Oliver whispered to me. "I never really thought—"

"Me neither," I said. "But let's try to focus on the job."

The door of the stable opened to a dim, muzzy warmth, and we stepped inside. It was much like a regular horse stable, with scents of hay and oats and animal, but when the first reindeer poked his head of out a stall to survey us, all ideas of normalcy fled. His head was topped by an enormous set of branching, velvety antlers, and he regarded us with soft brown eyes as his cow-like muzzle delicately sniffed the air. Down the line of stalls, more antlered heads poked out inquisitively to see who had invaded their space.

My heart thumped in my chest as if I'd been running.

"Ho, visitors!" boomed a deep voice from the end of the stable. I looked into the shadows to see a tall, round form limned with a hazy, sparkling white glow. As he moved toward us, the glow resolved into the classic figure of Santa Claus, although he wore red stable overalls and an open red and black plaid lumberjack shirt instead of his "working" suit. His blue eyes, however, twinkled with just the right amount of humour and good will. His luxuriant beard had been corralled into a thick braid, presumably to cut down on the bits of hay, straw, and reindeer fur that might embed themselves in it.

McJingles hurried forward to meet him. "These are the private investigators I told you about," he said hurriedly. "Acacia Sheridan and Oliver Wolfe. They wanted to ask you a few questions."

"Of course!" Santa boomed. He strode forward and shook hands with us, his eyes twinkling. His grasp was warm and firm and exactly the right pressure and length. "I remember Acacia and Oliver very well."

I swallowed a squawk of surprise and remembered who we were talking to. "We just wanted to check in with you about McJingles' concerns," I managed.

"Indeed." He turned to the elf and said, "Check on the novices in the workshop for me, would you, Cuthbert? I'll be along shortly."

Casting one warning glance at me, McJingles nodded and left us. Santa watched him go, then shook his head slightly. "A good elf, one of the best," he said, "but a bit too fond of his conspiracy theories."

"You think his worries are unfounded?" I asked. Oliver had sidled over to stroke the soft nose of one of the reindeer.

"Cuthbert McJingles is a great friend, a champion toymaker, and a devoted worrier," Santa said kindly, a chuckle bubbling under his words. "Mountains out of molehills, all the time."

"So you don't believe there's any sort of plot brewing?"

"Oh, my dear, whether you work with elves or humans, there's always some sort of plot brewing," he said, leaning slightly forward to tip me a wink. "But I don't think I'm in any danger."

I really wanted to bring up the matter of the missing elves, but I'd promised my client I wouldn't. "You haven't noticed anything out of the ordinary yourself? McJingles and a few other elves seem to think there's unrest among the Subordinate Clauses."

From his pocket, Santa produced a handful of apple slices and handed one to Oliver, who fed it to the reindeer.

"The Subs have a very important job—they're vital to the North Pole team," he said. "I believe they all know that, and how much I depend on them. I'd be very surprised—shocked, really—if Cuthbert's suspicions were true. But," he sighed, "I gave him leave to look into it if that would put his own mind at ease."

"Will you take any extra precautions on Christmas Eve—even if only for the same reason?" I asked. Santa offered me an apple slice and I fed it to the reindeer across the stable walkway from Oliver's.

Santa smiled and patted me gently on the shoulder. "Acacia, I'll be fine. Thank you for working to make McJingles feel better, and please do whatever it takes to satisfy him. But you needn't worry about me."

I smiled back. "That's a tall order. There's a lot riding on you every year."

He nodded. "But Santa's run will always happen, whether it's me or another bearer of the name. It's the idea of Santa—of giving and caring, of recognizing the good—that's important, Acacia. And I believe that will stay alive regardless of what happens."

I didn't know what to say to that. In his resonant, genial voice, he said, "Now, since you're both here, come and meet all the reindeer before Cuthbert takes you back. These ladies are the real stars of Christmas Eve, you know."

"Ladies?" Oliver said, his eyebrows raised.

"Of course," Santa chuckled. "Basic biology, despite the unconventional nomenclature. Male reindeer—what you'd call caribou—lose their antlers in the fall, while the females hang onto theirs until late winter or early spring." He reached up to scratch one of the animals on top of its head, between the branching growths. The reindeer leaned into Santa's hand, closing its dark brown eyes in delight. "Isn't that right, Dasher?"

Santa hadn't entirely convinced me that he was in no danger, but Oliver and I followed him through the warm, musty stable, meeting reindeer, stroking their silky necks and feeding them apple slices. When the job offers you a perk like that, you learn to take it.

When he'd returned us to the office and collected our

holiday-themed blindfolds, McJingles said curtly, "I suppose Santa told you he's in no danger at all, and this is all in my head."

I shrugged. "Something like that," I said cautiously. "But he didn't ask us to stop investigating."

McJingles sighed. "I'm not crazy, or paranoid. Misty and Twink and Candy are worried, too. And there's Holly and Ivy to consider."

"I know. Tomorrow we're going to stakeout Bob, Harold, and Kelly to find out more. We just wanted to get Santa's take on the whole thing."

"And now you have it," McJingles said. "But I don't see that we're any further ahead."

"Who's the investigator here, me or you?" I challenged the elf. I know he was my client, but I was getting a little tired of his grumpy attitude. In contrast to Santa, McJingles could come across as an unpleasant little crank in festive attire.

"Humph," McJingles said, pocketing the blindfolds. "Just let me know if you make any progress." And he vanished in a swirl of snowflakes, leaving the office decidedly chilly.

The next day, despite my aversion to malls during the height of the shopping season, Oliver and I split up. I stopped by the Riverside to make sure Santa Bob had reported for work, which he had. There was already a lineup of kids waiting to tell him their wishes. I confirmed that he'd be on the job, with only half an hour each for lunch and supper, and two fifteen-minute breaks, until seven that evening. No sense hanging around the mall all day then. I managed to get his last name, Parnaby, from the mall manager.

Oliver texted me to let me know the other mall Santa, Harold, was also at work and on a similar schedule for the day. He'd talked to one of the mall's maintenance men, a good friend of Harold's who'd actually gotten him the Santa gig in the first place. And come away with Harold's last name, Bernstein, and an address.

I made a mental note that maybe Oliver had field skills I'd been under-utilizing, and filed it away for further consideration.

My next stop was at the photography studio, where I found that the photographer was on an all-day wedding shoot, and Santa Kelly had the day off. The receptionist, still oddly amused about my queries, provided a last name, Laurier, and a cell phone number. I didn't bother asking for an address because I felt quite certain she wouldn't give it to me, and I was getting annoyed with her barely-smothered chuckles. Maybe this would be enough information for Oliver to track the Santa down— I thought it was within his information-gathering skillset.

It was. Twenty minutes after I'd texted him the information, he got back to me with an address and *I'll meet you there in fifteen. You owe me a coffee.*

I stopped at a takeout and bought him a "holiday

special"—I mocha with whipped cream and red and green sprinkles. He hadn't said what kind of coffee.

Santa Kelly Laurier lived in an apartment building on the other side of the river, not far from Oliver's place. It was a sixties-vintage complex built in a U-shape, with a common parking area and small garden in the centre. All the units opened out onto long shared balconies overlooking the parking lot. However, the grounds were groomed and the lot clean of litter, and the siding on the building looked new.

We found Kelly's apartment on the second level and knocked. No-one came to the door. I slid a couple of feet to the side and peered in through a large window with curtains only partly drawn. Beyond the glass I could make out the dim outlines of living-room furniture, and the glow of the Santa suit. It lay neatly draped over the back of a chair and emanated a very bright North Pole magic aura in the dim room.

"Looks like he's out, and not wearing the suit," I reported to Oliver. I cupped my hands around the sides of my eyes to block the outside light, hoping they'd adjust to let me see more details in the room. Gradually I made out a couple of wrapped presents on the large central table, along with a jumble of green and red paper, scissors, and other crafty-looking supplies. It looked like Kelly was making decorations for a holiday party. Not very sinister.

"I don't think this is our guy," I told Oliver. "Looks

like he's getting ready for a party, not a diabolical takeover bid."

"But with the other two out of commission for the entire day, how can they be looking after hostages?" Oliver asked.

"I guess if those hostages are tied up and quiet, they don't need much looking after."

"What about food?"

I shrugged. "Maybe he feeds them in the evening. Or he has an accomplice."

Oliver shook his head. "All right, we're wasting our time here. Should we take one mall Santa each and watch what they do on their breaks?"

"And then tail them when they get off work," I said. "Are you—do you think you can do that?"

Oliver gave me a withering look. "I may not get out into the field much—which is not my fault—but I think I can follow a guy in a glowing Santa suit."

"They might take the suits off to go home," I said, "but point taken. All right. You take Harold, I'll take Bob. Keep in touch via text."

I dropped Oliver at the Central Mall and headed back to Riverside. Santa Bob was hard at work, and I was faced with the dilemma of how to surveil a Santa for hours on end without looking creepy. I casually browsed every store surrounding the Santa court three times and ended up buying a couple of things I didn't need just to throw off suspicion.

When lunchtime came, I discreetly followed Bob to an employee lounge, where he stayed for the entire half hour and then dutifully headed back to his throne. A text from Oliver told me his day was following the same script, although he'd managed to get some actual Christmas shopping done. I almost teased him because mine was all done, but then I realized his day was actually turning out to be more productive than mine.

I texted Oliver that he could take a break until suppertime, since there was little chance either of our Santas would even leave the mall during their fifteen-minute breaks. I drove past Santa Kelly's apartment again, and was just in time to see a tall woman letting herself into Kelly's apartment. I slowed the car and turned into the parking lot. Wife? Girlfriend? Maybe she was the one planning a party, leaving Kelly himself free to hatch diabolical plots against Santa. Maybe she fancied herself the next Mrs. Claus.

It struck me suddenly that the Santa suit in Kelly's apartment had glowed with a rather intense magic—brighter than the suit Santa Harold wore, even taking the contrasting lighting conditions into account. Why would that be? I drummed my fingers on the steering wheel.

Unless there was more than one magic source in that area of the room. The missing elves? What if they'd been behind the suit, adding their glow to its light?

How fast can you get to Santa Kelly's apartment? I texted Oliver.

What? Why? Are you there now?

I might have figured it out, I told him, *but I need backup.*

I can be there in ten. I'll get a cab outside. Did you call the elves?

I stared at my phone. I hadn't thought about summoning McJingles, but maybe it wouldn't be a bad idea. Neither Oliver nor I routinely carried weapons—that's not my investigative style—so maybe strength in numbers would be good, especially if Kelly was in the apartment as well as the woman I'd seen. And if we found the missing Holly and Ivy inside, having the other elves there to tend to them might be helpful.

I will, I texted Oliver. *I don't know if Kelly's here right now, but his wife or girlfriend just went inside. I think there was too much magic in there to be just the suit.*

On my way.

I pulled out the little silver bell from McJingles and rang it softly. The elf took even longer to appear this time, and when he did it was in a shower of snow that unfortunately happened inside my car. He was standing on the passenger seat and bumped his head on the roof. "Ouch!"

"Sit down," I hissed, brushing snow off myself and the seats. "I think I might have something."

McJingles slid to sitting and regarded me intently. "Tell me," he demanded.

I shared my suspicions and the reasons, and he nodded. "Are we going to confront him?"

"I'm not sure if he's in there, but we're hoping Holly and Ivy are. If so, we'll rescue them and then see about Santa Kelly. I did see a woman go inside, probably his wife or something."

McJingles nodded. "Think I'll summon the others," he said.

I laid a hand on his arm. "Let's get out of the car first." I'd rather not have to shovel out the back seat.

We climbed out and I went around to join him on the side away from Kelly's apartment. The elf, at least, was completely hidden from view. He pulled out a cell phone in a sparkly case with a cartoon reindeer on the back, and sent a text. So they did have such things, I guess on their own North Pole network. After a moment of staring at the screen and a few jingle-bell notification sounds, he pocketed the phone.

"Twink, Misty, and Candy are on their way," he said. "Where's your little helper?"

I smothered a giggle as a cab pulled up on the street and Oliver got out, gathering parcels and bags from the back seat. He hurried over. "Can I put these in your trunk for now?"

As we stowed the gifts, the other elves arrived and McJingles brought them up to speed. I pointed out the apartment and they turned their little faces up toward it resolutely.

"Okay," I said, "Let's go save Christmas."

I figured the biggest obstacle would be getting the would-be Mrs. Claus or whoever she was to open the door. We worked up a plan to pretend to be carolers if necessary, but it didn't come to that. I had the elves stand off to one side, out of view below the level of the window, and I knocked at the door. I strained to hear movement inside, but the door muffled all sound.

Then it opened and the tall woman stood on the threshold. She was almost six feet tall, with a graying pixie cut and bright blue, intelligent eyes. She wore jeans, fuzzy slippers, and a t-shirt that read, *Christmas puns sleigh me*. I put her in her late 333ifties or slightly older.

"Yes?" she asked, smiling a bit warily.

I tried to nonchalantly peer past her for a telltale magic glow. "We're looking for Kelly Laurier," I said, stalling for time. I wondered if Oliver, standing just behind my right shoulder, had a better view into the apartment.

"I'm Kelly," the woman said, and as my brain tried to process that startling statement, the elves blew our cover like a storm in a snow globe.

With McJingles in the lead and the other three close behind, they darted past me and past the woman, into the apartment.

"Fan out!" McJingles barked. "Search the place!"

"Hey!" the putative Kelly said, and turned away from

the door to follow the elves. "What is this?"

"Crazy elves," I muttered, but I figured we were in it now. I entered the apartment, too, pulling Oliver behind me. Maybe inside, with the door shut, we could sort this out.

"Where are they?" McJingles demanded, pointing a trembling finger at Kelly. "Where are Holly and Ivy?"

Kelly folded her arms, radiating anger. "You must be McJingles," she snorted. "Never had the dubious pleasure before this."

"Give it up, Sub. We know what you're up to," Twink said, sounding like someone in an old hard-boiled detective movie. "You'll never work as a Santa again after this."

"Leave her alone!" spat a new voice from a doorway across the room. "McJingles, you big nosy excuse for an elf."

The voice came from a female elf with green hair cut in a short bob. A clip in the shape of a holly leaf held her hair back on one side. She wore the now-expected tunic and striped stockings, and she stood with her hands fisted on her hips. Beside her, another female elf clutching a pair of scissors in one hand and a sheet of red construction paper in the other surveyed McJingles and company with lips pressed together in a thin, disapproving line.

"Is that elf armed with scissors?" Oliver whispered in my ear, but I shook my head.

"I don't think they're meant as a weapon."

I took a step forward. "Holly and Ivy, I presume?"

They glared at me. "Who are you? And why can you see us?"

In the interest of defusing the situation as quickly as possible, I ignored the queries and turned to Santa Kelly. "Let's clarify one thing first. You're actually not plotting the overthrow of the current Santa, are you?"

Kelly's eyes widened. "Of course not! Why would you ask such a thing?"

I sighed and took a guess, turning back to the not-at-all-kidnapped pair of elves. "You're actually planning something like...a party for him?"

"Yes, a surprise party," Holly said. "He's been the current Santa for fifty years this year. Who are you two?"

Misty, Twink, and Candy stared wide-eyed at Holly and Ivy. "A surprise party?" McJingles exploded. "Why didn't you tell me?"

Holly tapped one foot impatiently on the floor, making the curled toe of her shoe bob. A sliver bell on the toe tinkled angrily. "Because you can't keep a secret," she said in a withering tone. "Not from Santa, of all people. And then it wouldn't be a surprise."

"But what were we supposed to think? You went off without a word!"

Holly and Ivy glanced at each other and Ivy shook her head. "Our jobs are finished, everything's ready for Christmas Eve," she said. "You know that, Candy."

335

Candy's striped braids drooped as she hung her head. "I'm sorry, Ivy. I guess I didn't think."

Ivy shook her head and continued. "We didn't think anyone would really notice if we slipped away here for a couple of days to get things ready. We knew we'd never be able to keep it a secret at the North Pole, especially when *some people* are *so nosy*. So Kelly agreed to help us."

"And someone blew it all up out of proportion," Misty said, turning a steely elf eye on McJingles. "And got others all wound up, too."

"So, I didn't realize there are female Santas," I said to Kelly Laurier in an attempt to break the tension.

"Ho, ho, ho!" she said in a surprisingly deep and booming voice. "There are female Santas, Jewish Santas, Santas of colour...you'd be surprised how diverse we are," she added in her normal tone.

McJingles seemed to make one last attempt to bristle, but he couldn't manage it and sagged like a snowman on a sunny day. "Santa Kelly, I'm sorry," he said. "I shouldn't have accused you of plotting against Santa."

She shrugged. "No harm done."

"As long as you keep this secret until the party," Holly said severely.

"All of you," Ivy added, and she might have made a little motion with the scissors for emphasis.

"Well, I guess we're done here," I said, backing

toward the door. "You folks are all busy, so we'll get out of your hair."

McJingles held out his hand. "My bell?"

I grinned at him. "I'll just hang onto it for now, so I can send you my bill," I told him. "After all, we did find the Subordinate Claus and Holly and Ivy for you."

McJingles gave a very un-jolly groan, but he nodded.

"Merry Christmas to you all," I said, and Oliver and I left. As I closed the door I heard Santa Kelly say, "Who was that?"

I took pity on poor Cuthbert McJingles and gave him a twenty percent break on my bill...after all, we'd met Santa and his reindeer, which just about made the whole caper worth it anyway.

Just before lunchtime on Christmas Eve, Oliver and I had celebratory hot chocolate, complete with tiny marshmallows, before we closed the office for the holiday.

Oliver took a sip from his mug. "You know," he said reflectively, "I think Santa knew about the party all along."

I opened my mouth to answer when, with a *whoosh* and a swirl of snowflakes, an enormous box of red-and-white striped candy canes materialized in one corner of the room. There must have been two hundred pieces of candy in the box.

"He did not just pay me in—" I started, but then in

another sputter of snowflakes, a small stack of cash popped into existence on top of my desk.

I grinned and got up to stow the cash safely in the wall safe before the melting snow made it soggy. "I think you're right about Santa," I said. "He didn't want to say it so many words, but I think that's what he was telling us."

"He sees you when you're sleeping," Oliver said. "He knows when you're awake. Pretty hard to put anything over on that guy."

"But I'm sure he'll act surprised," I said, and peeled off a couple of bills before I put the stack in the safe. I handed them to Oliver. "Here you go, Oliver, a little Christmas bonus."

"I already bought your gift," he said, raising one eyebrow. "It's not going to get any better."

I smiled and spun the lock on the safe, then toasted him with my mug. "Can't blame a girl for trying," I said. "Merry Christmas!"

"Merry Christmas," Oliver said with a grin, counting the bills. "Maybe I could drop by the mall one more time."

"Not necessary," I told him. "Get yourself an extra treat or give it to a charity. I think I'm good."

Outside, a light snow began to fall, and I didn't need any special abilities to see the glow of Christmas magic in the air.

THE END

aboUT thE aUThor

Sherry D. Ramsey is a speculative fiction writer, editor, publisher, creativity addict and self-confessed internet geek. When she's not writing, she reads, gardens, makes stuff, hones her creative procrastination skills on social media, and consumes far more coffee and chocolate than is likely good for her.

Sherry writes for both adults and younger readers. Her books include four books in the Nearspace series, *One's Aspect to the Sun, Dark Beneath the Moon, Beyond the Sentinel Stars* and *A Veiled and Distant Sky;* the urban fantasy *The Murder Prophet;* two books for middle-grade readers, *The Seventh Crow* and *Planet Fleep*; and three collections of short stories. *Toil and Trouble* is the fourth Olympia Investigations tale, and a fifth is in the works.

With her partners at Third Person Press (http://www.thirdpersonpress.com) she has co-edited six anthologies of regional short fiction. Every November she disappears into the strange realm of National Novel Writing Month and emerges gasping at the end, clutching something resembling a novel.

A member of the Writer's Federation of Nova Scotia Writer's Council, Sherry is also a past Vice- President, Secretary-Treasurer, and Web Admin for SF Canada, Canada's national association for Speculative Fiction Professionals.

You can visit Sherry online at her website, www.sherrydramsey.com, to find free stories and more, check Facebook for Sherry D. Ramsey Author, and follow her on Twitter, Instagram and Mastodon @sdramsey. She also pins some fun things (including a series of visual writing prompts) on Pinterest – just look for Sherry D. Ramsey.

Sign up for her monthly newsletter at www.sherrydramsey.com to receive a free book, and get all the latest news on releases, giveaways, contests, and more.

Watch for *The Shifter Plague,* the fifth Olympia Investigations story, coming soon!